# A SILVER LINING

Anne Douglas

This first world edition published 2014
in Great Britain and the USA by
SEVERN HOUSE PUBLISHERS LTD of
19 Cedar Road, Sutton, Surrey, England, SM2 5DA

Trade paperback edition first published 2018
In Great Britain and the USA by
SEVERN HOUSE PUBLISHERS LTD
Eardley House, 4 Uxbridge Street, London W8 7SY



British Library Cataloguing in Publication Data
*A CIP catalogue record for this title is available from the British Library.*

ISBN-13: 978-0-7278-8403-9 (cased)
ISBN-13: 978-1-84751-902-3 (trade paper)
ISBN-13: 978-1-78010-554-3 (e-book)

# Part One

# One

There it went, dead on time, the One o'clock Gun from the castle sounding over Edinburgh, sending people's eyes to clocks and watches, making tourists jump and locals smile. Not that there were many tourists around on that November day in 1937, only city shoppers diving into Princes Street stores to escape from the 'haar' – the cold, wet mist that had been hanging about since morning.

Glad I'm not out in it, thought twenty-one-year-old Jinny Hendrie, sitting at her desk in the warmth of the accounts office of Comrie's Bakeries where she was working on staff wages. Maybe it would clear by going home time, which wouldn't be till half past five, ages away. Why, even tea break at three o'clock was far enough off.

Not that Jinny minded. She enjoyed her work, which was mainly with figures, assisting Mr MacBain who was the accountant in charge, though it had all been much more complicated than she'd ever imagined. Who'd have thought there'd be so much to worry about behind all the lovely bread and cakes sold by Comrie's, and the superior morning coffees and afternoon teas served in their cafés?

Not caring to make herself hungry thinking of delicious cakes, Jinny bent her dark eyes over the spread of wage packets she was preparing for delivery to the workforce the next day. All would receive cash, herself included, the only exceptions being Mr Whyte, the bakery manager, and Mr MacBain – Ross, as she was allowed to call him – who were paid by cheque. Her job was to make sure that everyone received the correct amount and that their wage slips tallied; the last thing she wanted was for one of the bakers to come round claiming she hadn't included his overtime.

Oh, my, better check everything again! But she was confident she'd made no mistakes and knew that the bakers and café staff trusted her – even if they did think she was too pretty to know how to count!

There was no doubt that she was pretty, with her dark eyes, her pointed chin and high cheekbones. She wore her dark hair rather longer than was fashionable – but what had looks to do with arithmetic?

She'd always been good at maths at school, and had gone on to more detailed study at a technical college, just like her attractive sister, Vi, two years her senior, who now ran the office of a clothing factory and grew touchy if anyone commented on her looks. But May, at twenty-four the eldest of the three Hendrie girls and a good-looking blonde, liked to say with a laugh that folk thought her just right to work in a West End hat shop. Maybe her sisters should change jobs? What an idea! They were happy where they were and in 1937, unemployment being what it was, if you had a job you hung on to it.

Accounts, where Jinny worked, was a large, airy room on the first floor of the double-fronted Comrie building at the east end of Princes Street. Next to it was the office of John Comrie, the owner of the business, while below on the ground floor was the largest of the cafés, with an attached kitchen and staffroom, and a bread and cake shop.

The bakery that provided Comrie's bread, cakes and scones was some way away in the Broughton area, but Arthur Whyte and Ross MacBain liaised regularly to discuss expenditure and the progress of various lines. Heavens, how they worked to keep tabs on everything! And Mrs Arrow, manageress of the Princes Street shop and café had to be careful, too, to keep an eye on sales.

Only Ross, however, was in charge of the complicated costing system that made sure customers got value for money and the bakery made a profit, though he said one day he would see that Jinny had knowledge of it too, which she was pleased about. In the meantime, of course, she had to work on the wages and be sure she got them right.

She rose and stretched, looked out of the window and saw that the haar was still masking the street, then turned her head as the door to Mr Comrie's office door clicked and Mabel Hyslop came through. In her late thirties, she was thin and narrow-faced, her brown hair rather sparse, and always keen to hear bakery gossip. She was efficient enough, though, working partly as Mr Comrie's secretary and partly as the office typist.

'Ross not back yet, Jinny?' she asked now. 'Mr Comrie's going to lunch with someone at two today but he says he'd like a word with you and Ross before that.'

'Me as well as Ross?' asked Jinny with interest.

'Yes. It's nothing to worry about, just to do with his nephew. Oh, here's Ross now! I'd better tell Mr Comrie.'

With a quick smile at Ross MacBain as he walked into Accounts,

Mabel hurried away while Ross shook drops of moisture from his hat and overcoat and looked across at Jinny.

'Haar's no better – I feel I've been wrapped in a great damp blanket. What was Mabel after?'

'Just came to tell us that Mr Comrie wants a word.'

'A word? Sounds ominous.' Ross ran his hands through his damp, copper-coloured hair and sat down at his desk. 'Wonder what that's about, then?'

'Just his nephew, Mabel says.'

'His nephew? He's not even here. Ah, well, all will be revealed.'

Such a cheerful face, thought Jinny, as she always did when looking at Ross – just the sort of face of a man who would never be taken aback by anything life had to throw at him. Or so you might think. In fact, it wasn't true. As she'd been told by others when she'd first arrived to work with him two years before, Ross had been taken aback – and deeply grieved – by the death of his fiancée from appendicitis shortly before their wedding. And though he never showed it, keeping his cheerful manner at all times, some people believed he was grieving still. Usually Jinny tried not to think about his sorrow, for that was his business entirely, but just occasionally found herself sensing something about him that made her think she was one of the few people who could see beyond his mask. Or maybe she just imagined it.

'I've done the wages,' she was beginning when Mr Comrie's door clicked again and the owner of the bakery – short, portly and in his fifties – came through and accepted the chair Ross leaped up to set for him.

'Ah, there you are, Ross, Jinny. I'm just off to lunch with my bank manager. Send up the usual prayers, eh?' Mr Comrie laughed, his narrow blue eyes crinkling in his heavy face. 'Just want to tell you that we'll be having a new man here from Monday next – my nephew, Viktor Linden, my sister's boy from Vienna.'

Vienna? Jinny's dark eyes widened. She vaguely remembered hearing that Mr Comrie's sister had married an Austrian and moved from Edinburgh years before, and that there was a nephew. But why should he be coming as a new man here? Did Mr Comrie mean he was coming to work?

It was Ross who put the question. 'Mr Comrie, that's very interesting news. Will Mr Linden actually be working here, then?'

'Of course, of course. He's only twenty-five but he's a very experienced confectioner. His father owns a splendid Viennese cake shop – what they call a *Konditorei* – and my sister tells me that Viktor's quite the star.'

'And he's coming here?'

'To visit Edinburgh again – he hasn't been here since he was a boy – and to see how we operate and get some experience of other systems. I also want him to make us some of his wonderful cakes. *Torten*, as they call them.' Again, Mr Comrie laughed. 'But of course he won't be staying long – a few months at most.'

'We'll make him very welcome,' Ross declared. 'I'm sure all the staff will be very interested to meet him. We've all heard about Austrian cakes.'

'Indeed. Well, I'll leave it to you to inform the staff, and I'll introduce him on Monday morning. No need to worry about his English – he's bilingual. My sister, Clara, has seen to that. Now, I must hurry. Can't keep the bank manager waiting!'

When their boss had rushed out, Ross and Jinny exchanged looks.

'Well, that's something new,' Ross commented, sitting down again at his desk. 'It will be good to see some of those amazing Austrian cakes being produced here.'

'Why are they so wonderful? We make lovely cakes ourselves – aren't we famous for them?'

'Of course, but these are different.' Ross was laughing. 'I must sound like a greedy schoolboy, but I went for a walking tour once in Austria and I've never forgotten trying their pastries and cakes when we finished up in Vienna. Chocolate, marzipan, nuts, layers of cream, raspberries—'

'Oh, stop, you're making me hungry!' cried Jinny, joining in his laughter. 'Think I'll put the kettle on.'

What an interesting bit of news, she thought as she set out cups and gave Mabel a call. Just fancy, a chap from Vienna working at Comrie's! All she knew about the Viennese was that they danced Strauss waltzes and made delicious things to eat, but now she would find out much more. Depending on what the new fellow was like, of course, and whether he was friendly or not. Anyway, he'd be something to tell her sisters at home about. They always liked to talk over their news at teatime.

# Two

The Hendrie girls and their father, Joshua, lived over a watchmaker's shop in Fingal Street, off the Lothian Road. Josh, as he was usually called, worked as a scene-shifter at the nearby Duchess Theatre – a job he loved, having always had an interest in the theatre but 'not cut out', as he would say with a grin, to be an actor. Working with the sets, breathing in the atmosphere of the stage and mixing with the cast was the next best thing, and in the years following his dear Etty's death his work had helped him to get over the bad times.

Not as much as his girls had helped, of course. Sometimes he almost came out in a cold sweat when thinking what his life would be without them, for now that Etty'd gone they were everything to him. Such lovely girls, all of them, whose only thought was to make him happy, to make up as best they could for their mother's death. If they were ever to leave him, what would he do? But there was no sign of that at present, thank God.

There was only one thing he wished might be different about them: that they would feel as he did about the stage. They had the looks and the intelligence – they could have been stars, he was sure of it – but no, they wouldn't even give it a try. What a shame, eh?

'Honestly, Dad, can you see us dressing up and spouting all those lines!' Vi had cried, and May had shaken her lovely fair head while Jinny had laughed. When he'd said their mother would have liked it for them, their faces had changed and sadness appeared. Ma would have wanted them to be happy doing what they thought best for themselves, they told him, and with that he could say no more. Seemingly they were as happy as they could be, in the circumstances.

Coming home that evening through the last remnants of the haar, Jinny was herself thinking her family was a happy one. Even though Ma was no longer with them and they missed her still, the girls had all tried to keep their home as she had made it, and felt, especially when they came back after work, that they'd succeeded. All right, nobody claimed there weren't arguments, especially with Vi around, but they never lasted long. The girls soon made up and were content.

'Evening, Jinny,' called Allan Forth, the watchmaker, who was also the Hendries' landlord, as Jinny approached the side door that led up to the flat. 'Not been too bright today, has it?'

He was just locking up for the night, having closed the shutters on his windows full of clocks, watches, tankards, toast racks, lockets and necklaces, for in addition to his watch-making and mending business, he sold a variety of merchandise suitable for presents. Though Jinny often wondered how much of it he sold in these difficult times.

Still, he seemed to keep the shop going and to look after the bungalow in the suburbs that had been his parents' after they'd left the flat the Hendries now occupied. And Allan had never put up the rent of that flat, which was very reasonable – maybe because originally it was his father who'd been the landlord and he'd been a pal of Josh's at the bowling club. Now he was dead, his wife too, and it was tall, grey-eyed Allan who was their landlord. No changes had been made, though, even if he was not a particular friend of Josh's as his father had been. More likely he was a friend of May's, thought Jinny with a smile – or wished he were.

'You're the last in,' he told Jinny, checking the lights on the bicycle he used to ride home to Blackhall. 'Your dad and Vi have just gone up and May was first. Said she had to do the cooking tonight.'

'It's her turn,' Jinny told him, noting that he must have left his shop to talk to May. By the light of the streetlight she studied his good-looking face with its sensitive mouth, always ready to smile. He'd be right for May, she thought, and added: 'We girls take it in turn to cook.'

'Oh, yes, I know, May told me. Said she'd already made a hotpot for you.'

'Did it last evening. Very efficient, May.'

'I'm sure,' he said fervently before finally beginning to wheel his bike towards the Lothian Road, from where a hum of traffic could be heard. ''Bye then, Jinny. Have a nice evening.'

'You must come and have tea with us sometime!' she called after him. 'You haven't been for ages.'

With colour rising to his face, he did not stop but called back that he'd like that very much, and Jinny, smiling again, watched him pedal away.

The flat that had been Allan's home before it was her family's was of good size, with a living room, a separate little kitchen, two bedrooms – one double, one single – a boxroom and a bathroom. It was Josh who nobly slept in the boxroom, having given up the double room he'd shared with Etty to Jinny and Vi, while May had the single room.

How well placed they were in Fingal Street compared to the cramped tenement flat where they'd lived before, Jinny still thought whenever she came home. Ma had always hated that, having to share a WC on the landing with other families and fill up a tin tub to take a bath. She'd been so glad when Mr Forth had offered them his old flat at a rent they could afford, but used to shake her head and say that how things went for you in life was all down to luck. And so it was, thought Jinny, though there were some who said you made your own luck. Whatever the truth of that, one thing was for sure – good luck had run out for Ma, through no fault of her own, when she had been taken by the pneumonia that killed her.

Everyone was in the living room when she came in. May was setting the table while the hotpot she'd prepared for them all cooked in the oven, and Vi and Josh were sitting by the open fire, reading separate pages of the evening newspaper. Everything seemed warm and comfortable.

'Och, that's grand!' Jinny cried when she'd taken off her coat and moved towards the fire. 'Let me in, I'm frozen! Makes a difference, eh, having a fire like this instead of a kitchen range?'

'A range is more useful,' said Vi, looking up from her paper, her face so like Jinny's yet somehow subtly different, perhaps only because her thoughts were different and reflected her dissatisfaction with the world. While Jinny took things as they were Vi was all for reform, her dark eyes regularly flashing over some injustice, making Jinny feel guilty that her dark eyes weren't flashing too.

'You can cook on a range,' Vi added now, 'and get hot water and warmth. Can't say the same about a fire.'

'Why, there's a back boiler for the hot water!' Jinny fast retorted. 'Trust you to look on the dark side, Vi!'

'Only facing facts,' her sister replied with a sudden grin. 'I'll admit the fire's nice to sit beside.'

'Aye, come and thaw out, lassie,' said Josh, rubbing Jinny's cold hands. 'That haar's enough to chill your bones, eh?'

'It's just moving away now.'

'Thank the Lord for that, seeing as I've to get back to the theatre after tea.'

A handsome man in his late forties, with the dark eyes and hair his younger daughters had inherited, Josh looked across at May, who was bringing in her dish from the adjoining kitchen.

'That ready, May?'

'Quite ready, Dad. Come to the table and I'll dish up.'

# Three

May's hotpot was excellent, with beef, potatoes and carrots, and as they all ate heartily Jinny said it was just the thing for a cold night and worth all her sister's trouble the evening before.

'Only thing is it's my turn tomorrow and I'm only doing sausages, so don't expect anything like this!'

'Can't expect beef every night,' Vi remarked. 'We're lucky to have it at all.'

'It was only brisket – pretty cheap,' said May.

'Aye, well, think of the folk in the tenements living on bread and dripping – if there's any dripping.'

'Come on, now, Vi,' Josh said easily. 'Don't spoil our pleasure in May's grand meal, eh?'

'I'm not, Dad, it's lovely – I'm only reminding you how it is for others.'

'And I don't need reminding, seeing as I was one o' the others, as you call 'em, when I was a lad.'

Vi lowered her eyes. 'Sorry,' she said after a moment. 'I know times were hard for you then.'

After another pause Jinny, to lighten matters, said cheerfully, 'Saw your admirer tonight, May!'

'What admirer?' asked Josh, instantly diverted and frowning, while May was already beginning to turn pink.

'Exactly – what admirer?' she responded quickly. 'Who on earth are you talking about, Jinny?'

'Why, Allan, of course! He'd just locked up when I got home, said he'd seen you, May, and you'd told him what you'd been cooking.'

'And how does a few polite words in passing make him my admirer?'

'He must have been watching out for you because you were so early back, and – you know – it's just the way he looks when he says your name. He's always been sweet on you, May – isn't that right, Vi?'

'Don't ask me, I've no time for all that romantic stuff,' replied Vi, shrugging, and Josh nodded in agreement.

'Nor me. Allan's a nice lad but he's never shown any romantic interest in you lassies that I've ever noticed.'

That you'd decided *not* to notice, thought Jinny, who knew her father couldn't yet bring himself to see that his girls might one day marry and 'leave the nest'. Aloud, to calm things down, she changed the subject again to her own exciting news from Comrie's.

'Guess what? We've a new chap starting next week and he's from Vienna! Mr Comrie's nephew, no less, and a qualified confectioner. He makes gorgeous Austrian cakes, so Ross says. I can't wait to meet him!'

'What makes him so exciting?' asked Vi. 'Because he's from Vienna, or because he makes gorgeous cakes?'

'I don't know if he's exciting or not – he'll be different, that's all.'

'There's nothing different at Madame Annabel's Hats,' sighed May. 'Except I did make a new hat today. A winter felt, dark red, with a curved brim – all set for Christmas.'

'And I had a new row with the foreman over starting hours,' put in Vi. 'I mean, it's ridiculous that women clock in at eight o'clock when they've everything to do at home before they come to work! Of course, Bob Stone said it wasn't up to him, I'd have to take it up with the union – as though I haven't done that already!'

'Uphill work there, Vi,' commented Josh, his eyes on what was left in May's dish. 'Any chance of me finishing that off, May? Don't want to waste it, eh?'

'Sure, we'll let you finish it, Dad, before you go back to work. What shall we do, girls? There's a Ronald Colman picture on at the Princes cinema – anybody keen?'

'I am!' cried Jinny, and even Vi said she wouldn't mind.

'All workers need escapism, eh?'

'Right, then,' said May. 'When we've done the washing up, we'll go – right?'

'Right!' they echoed, and while their father was on duty at the theatre they were far away in the country of Shangri-la, watching *Lost Horizon* in the cinema, caught up wonderfully in the escapism Vi said all workers should have, all their slight frictions forgotten.

# Four

Monday morning came at last, a grey cold day but without the haar, and Jinny, early to work, hurried into Accounts even before Ross, who usually beat her to it. For some moments she stood irresolutely, wondering if the man from Vienna had arrived yet, before realizing that of course he'd be coming in with his uncle. He didn't usually arrive till getting on for nine.

'You're nice and early!' came Ross's voice and she swung round to find him smiling at her, knowing, of course, why she'd made her special effort.

'Not here yet?' he asked lightly.

'Who?'

'Oh, come on! *Herr* Linden, of course. Or, should I say *Der Leutnant*? That means lieutenant.'

'Whatever are you talking about, Ross?'

'I'm just guessing that he's done service in the army. Don't all Germans and Austrians do army service?'

'As though I'd know. Anyway, there's no need to make fun.'

Jinny moved to her desk and began to bang open drawers and look as though she was starting work, but Ross only laughed, and then of course she laughed too, for she could never be cross with him for long.

'Suppose I am being a bit nosy about wanting to meet him. It's just like I said to my sister – he's different, that's all. Maybe we won't see him at all today. Mr Comrie will want to take him to the bakery.'

But it wasn't long before they did see the man from Vienna, for Mr Comrie, arriving earlier than usual, brought with him a tall, straight-backed young man in a long dark overcoat and a trilby hat, which he swept off to reveal fair hair cut very short.

'Ross – Jinny – this is my nephew, Viktor Linden,' Mr Comrie announced. 'Viktor, may I introduce Mr MacBain, my accountant, and Miss Hendrie, his assistant.'

The young man, smiling gravely, gave a bow, then shook hands, first with Ross and then with Jinny, his hand cold and firm, his light blue eyes meeting theirs very keen, very direct. Was it Jinny's imagination or did his gaze linger a little longer on her than Ross? Her imagination, undoubtedly, she told herself at once, feeling foolish.

'I'm so glad to meet you,' he said now, his tone formal, his Austrian accent only slight. 'I'm so looking forward to working here at the bakery.'

'Everyone is looking forward to working with you,' Ross assured him cheerfully. 'We hope you'll be very happy here.'

'Very happy,' Jinny added quickly, not wanting to be seen studying the newcomer more than was polite but making no effort to look away from his face. It did not appear to her to be particularly foreign, just very good looking, the nose high bridged, the brow quite noble, the mouth finely shaped. That stubbly short haircut, though, did seem different and the way the young man held himself, so straight, so erect – wasn't that a bit like a soldier's style? Ross had joked about him, calling him '*Der Leutnant*', but perhaps he'd been right, after all?

Glancing at Ross, Jinny saw that he was looking slightly amused – as though he'd been thinking what she'd been thinking. But why be amused? If the young man had had to do military service, he couldn't be blamed for having the air of a soldier – and didn't the look suit him, anyway?

'I have two right-hand men in my business, Viktor,' Mr Comrie was saying. 'One is Mr Whyte, my bakery manager – you'll meet him soon – and the other is Mr MacBain here, who knows everything there is to know about costings, prices, wages, estimates, insurance and business in general. What I'd do without him I do not know, but I'm hoping I never have to find out! Right, Ross?'

'If you say so, Mr Comrie,' Ross answered, smiling. 'But don't forget, Miss Hendrie here is knowledgeable too. We'll both do our best to help you, Mr Linden, if there's anything you need to know.'

'Thank you, Mr MacBain, I appreciate that.' Viktor gave another little bow and turned to Jinny, who now lowered her eyes. 'Miss Hendrie.'

'Oh, I hope I'm not late!' cried a voice at the door and Mabel Hyslop came hurrying in, wrapped in a checked coat and woollen scarf, a beret over her thinning hair. 'My tram was full, I'd to wait for another, Mr Comrie, and I did want to be on time today—'

'Don't worry, you're not late,' he told her genially, 'we're early. Let me introduce my nephew, Viktor Linden. Viktor, meet Miss Hyslop, my secretary – another expert on all things to do with Comrie's.'

Mabel blushed, and there was the shaking of hands and more polite words again, until Mr Comrie ushered his nephew into his office, telling him to hang up his overcoat, exclaiming over his fine grey suit: 'My word, Viktor, you won't want to be wearing that in the bakery, will you? Is that what you wear in your Viennese place?'

'Not at all, Uncle, I wear a white overall and hat – see, I have them here in this bag.' Viktor smiled. 'I think I know the effect flour has on good suits!'

'Ha, ha, of course, you do!' Mr Comrie gave one of his ready laughs. 'But now, before we go to the bakery, let me take you down to meet the manageress, Mrs Arrow, and the staff of the shop and the teashop. Why, we might even have a coffee down there! They won't be open yet, but they'll open for us, eh? Miss Hyslop, I'll be with you later. Meantime, there are couple of letters on my desk to type.'

'Certainly, Mr Comrie.'

As soon as the uncle and nephew had departed, Mabel rushed into Ross's office, her eyes gleaming. 'Oh, my, what a handsome young man, eh? He'll have all the girls after him here, mark my words. Did you ever see such blue eyes? So keen – like sailor's eyes, I'd say!'

'As I think he seems like a soldier, we only need someone to say he looks like a pilot and we'll have him in all three services,' Ross said coolly. 'And I rather think the girls downstairs won't get very far.'

'Why not?' Jinny asked at once. 'There are some very pretty girls in the shop and the café.'

'Why, he's sure to have a *fraulein* of his own back home,' Ross said carelessly. 'Shall we get to work, then?'

'I'm sure I'm ready to do my work, Ross!' Mabel cried, her face puckering. 'No need to tell me, I promise you!'

'Nor me,' said Jinny, seating herself at her own desk as Mabel, sniffing, returned to Mr Comrie's office. 'Why so snappy, Ross?'

'I'm not being snappy. When am I ever snappy?'

'Not often,' she agreed, and gave him a long, level look. 'You don't like him, do you? You don't like Mr Viktor Linden?'

'I've only just met him.'

'Don't always need time to know what you think of someone.'

Ross shrugged. 'I expect he's all right. What did you think of him, then?'

'He's very good looking,' she replied obliquely, and began to study the wages book, while Ross, after giving her a return stare, suddenly laughed.

'I've just thought – if Mrs Arrow gives him a coffee downstairs he'll be in for a shock. Probably won't know what he's drinking.'

'Something wrong with our coffee?'

'No, no, it's just that in Vienna drinking coffee is almost a religion. There are so many kinds – maybe as many as fifteen – and all so delicious that you're absolutely spoiled for choice. Our one brand will seem strange to anyone used to Viennese ways.'

'Well, he's come here to learn about our ways, hasn't he?' Jinny asked quickly. 'And I'm sure he'll be very polite, whatever he thinks.'

'Of course,' Ross agreed. 'Of course he will.'

And no more was said.

# Five

After the exciting morning, things seemed flat for Jinny. Viktor Linden had returned only once to his uncle's office – to collect his overcoat before going to the bakery, and though he had very definitely smiled at Jinny as he walked through Accounts, he didn't linger to speak. Ross was out at the time, which meant that if she and the Viennese had exchanged a few words she wouldn't have been inhibited by Ross's presence, but there it was – Viktor Linden hadn't stopped. He probably wasn't interested. Why should he be, when this was his first day and he had so much to see and learn and so many people to meet?

As she worked, totalling up figures and costs of ingredients used the previous week, she put the new man firmly out of her mind, deciding that Ross was probably right, he no doubt had a girlfriend back home, and anyway, why should she be so interested? She'd never been interested in the young men she had occasionally been out with – why should this chap from abroad be any different? Oh, because he was. Different.

When her lunchtime break came and Ross was back she went down to the shop, as she usually did, to buy at staff discount a couple of filled rolls to eat in the back room which adjoined the kitchen, and found the assistants agog with chat about Mr Comrie's nephew.

In between expertly wrapping up bread and cakes for customers, Kirsten, Polly and Rhoda were fizzing with excitement. Had Jinny met him, then? Was he no' a charmer? Such blue eyes and so tall! And such wonderful English! Why, they hadn't expected to understand a word he said, but he was so nice, so interested!

It was the same in the tea shop when Jinny went to pick up her cup of tea, with the waitresses – Audrey, Joan and Fiona – as full of admiration for Mr Linden as the shop girls, and even Mrs Arrow, the thin, sharp manageress, was keen to talk about him.

'Asked me if the customers liked to sit outside in the summer, and when I told him we never put out tables he said that folk in Vienna love to sit outside. And outside or in they stay for hours, just chatting away over a single coffee sometimes, and I said we'd never hold with that – why, we need the space!'

'Of course you do,' said Jinny at the door, cup in hand. 'But things are very different there.'

'So it seems. But I gave him a cup of our coffee and he seemed to like it. At least, he didn't say he didn't. And he said our cakes looked excellent.' Mrs Arrow suddenly frowned. 'Just hope he doesn't go making too many of his own, though. Mr Comrie muttered something about trying out his sort in the shop and in here too. I'm no' sure how they'll go.'

'Have to see what Mr Whyte thinks.'

'That's right. Arthur will sort it out. I mean, there's a slump on at the moment. Who's going to pay for elaborate cakes at a time like this?'

'I would!' cried Audrey, a redhead with a mind of her own. 'If Mr Linden was making 'em, eh?'

'Now, now, Audrey, let's no' hear too much of your opinions, eh?' snapped Mrs Arrow. 'I see a customer at table four looking round for service.'

'I'll go for my lunch,' said Jinny, escaping to the little room at the back and thinking ruefully that Mabel had been right – the girls at Comrie's would certainly be 'after' Viktor Linden. She'd not be joining in, then. No, indeed. And opening a copy of *The Scotsman* someone had left on the table, Jinny carefully studied the news, which wasn't too good, as it happened. There was no let-up in the depression yet. Japanese troops in their war against China had captured Shanghai. Someone in an article forecast war with Germany the following year.

Oh, dear. She put the paper aside. As soon as she'd finished her lunch she'd go round the shops and do a bit of Christmas shopping. That would cheer her up.

After a very routine afternoon she was glad to be going home. There was no doubt that, whatever she'd decided about putting the young Viennese man from her mind, she'd been disappointed not to have seen him again on his first day. It seemed like he'd been caught up at the bakery meeting the men who made the loaves and rolls and the two girls, Norah and Trixie, who decorated the 'fancies' and iced the Christmas and wedding cakes. Of course, the bakery would be where he'd be spending most of his time, especially if he was going to be making his own cakes; over here in Accounts she probably wouldn't see him at all. But then, there was a bit of a question mark over his making cakes, wasn't there?

'I suppose Mr Whyte will have to OK any baking from Mr Linden, won't he?' she asked Ross as she put on her coat. 'Mrs Arrow's worried that we can't afford his sort of elaborate cakes.'

'Old groaner, Mrs Arrow,' Ross answered with a grin. 'She's one for doing what we've always done. Madeira, Ginger, Sultana, Seed Cake, Swiss Roll – those are our staples. Anything a bit different doesn't get a look in.'

'Yes, but what will Mr Whyte say?'

'You mean, what will Mr Comrie say? He's all for letting his nephew show what he can do, and he has the last word. No need to worry about Viktor Linden's baking, Jinny.'

'I'm not worrying!' she cried, at which he smiled.

'Of course not. Why should you?'

'Goodnight,' she called. 'I'm away for my tram. Are you coming?'

'Got some things I want to clear up. Goodnight, Jinny. See you tomorrow.'

It's Vi's turn to cook tonight, thought Jinny, turning into Fingal Street, which meant they'd be having fish. They usually did when Vi cooked – easiest and quickest to do, she always said, and she was always short of time. There was her studying to fit in – she'd joined an evening class on politics – or she had to go to a Labour meeting, or do some canvassing if there was a local election coming. That trip out to the cinema the other evening with Jinny and May had been unusual for her, though she'd certainly enjoyed it.

Thinking of May, there she was, standing in the lamplight, talking to Allan Forth. At once, Jinny halted. They were standing so close together, so obviously enjoying their meeting that it seemed a shame to interrupt them.

'I was wondering, May,' Allan was saying, his eyes never leaving her face, 'if you'd care to come to the pictures with me one night this week? There's a good film on, *Lost Horizon* with Ronald Colman.'

'Oh, Allan, that would be lovely!' May hesitated. 'The thing is—'

'What?' he asked quickly.

'Well – no, it's all right, I'd like to go, Allan. What night were you thinking of?'

'Any night, May. Any that would suit you.'

'Wednesday?'

'Perfect. I'll come round for you at about half past six, shall I?'

'Half past six would be grand. Oh, here comes Jinny!' May's keen eyes had spotted her sister now approaching slowly up the street, and at once had stepped back from Allan at the same time as he moved away from her.

'Hello, Jinny!' Allan cried. 'Had a good day?'

'Oh, yes, you had the new man starting today, didn't you?' asked May, talking a little fast. 'What's he like, then?'

'All right. Speaks good English.' To Allan, Jinny added, 'He's Viennese.'

'Really? I've heard those Austrians make nice cakes.' Allan was pushing his bike away. 'Goodnight, then. May, I'll see you Wednesday, if not before.'

'Lovely. Goodnight, Allan.'

Not looking at Jinny, May hurried along to the side door to the flat, but Jinny was close behind.

'Wednesday?' she repeated.

'We're going to the pictures,' said May, and went up the inner steps so quickly Jinny couldn't catch her.

# Six

'The pictures?' cried Jinny at the door of the living room. 'You and Allan?'

May swung round, shaking her head. 'Ssh! Dad'll be home and I don't want to tell him yet.'

'You'll have to tell him sometime, May. Best get it over with.'

'He'll be in a mood right through tea.'

'Yes, but then he'll accept it – what else can he do?' Jinny smiled. 'You're over twenty-one, eh?'

May sighed. 'All right, I'll tell him now.'

At the sisters' entrance Josh looked up from his evening paper, his face brightening.

'Hello, you two, you're back! Had a good day?'

'Same as usual,' May answered, moving towards the kitchen. 'Is that fish I smell?'

'Spot on,' cried Vi, appearing red-faced, a fish slice in her hands. 'Frying tonight – how did you guess?'

'Just genius,' said Jinny. 'And the fact that you usually do fish for us when it's your turn to cook.'

'Aye, but this time I've done chips as well. And they're all ready, so you'd better sit down. Dad, did you hear that?'

'We'll just wash our hands,' said May, sending a look of apprehension to Jinny, who mouthed, *Go on, tell him!*

But when they sat down to Vi's speciality, which was perfectly cooked, for if she only did one thing she at least did it well, it was clear that May was biding her time to speak to her father, and talk centred on the new man at Comrie's.

'So, Jinny, what's the German like, then?' Vi asked as she buttered some bread. 'Wasn't he starting today?'

'Yes, he started today, but he's Austrian, not German.'

'Same difference.'

'No, Austrians are not like Germans.'

'If we go to war with 'em, they'll be the same, all right.'

'Who says we're going to war?'

'Why the papers are full of this chap Hitler wanting to start a war with everybody. *And* he was born in Austria, too, so there you are.'

'I'll never believe that we'll go to war with Germany again!' Josh cried. 'We'd enough o' that last time. Was it all for nothing, then?'

'Don't worry, Dad,' May said quickly. 'The government won't let it happen. It's all just talk. Jinny, tell us about this new chap. Do you like him?'

'He's all right,' Jinny answered cagily. 'Very polite.'

'And nice looking?'

'Well, yes, fair, you know, and tall. But we didn't see much of him in Accounts – he was away to the bakery.'

'He's going to make some Austrian cakes?' asked Vi. 'A bit different to Comrie's Seed Cake and Madeira, eh?'

'I expect so.' Jinny, to hide her unwillingness to talk, leaped up to clear away their plates and, when they'd all had the remains of yesterday's apple tart, looked meaningfully across to May, who said she'd make the tea.

'Think she seems bit strange tonight?' asked Josh, moving to his fireside chair as May went into the kitchen 'As though she's got something on her mind?'

Jinny, looking down, said nothing.

'Seems just as usual to me,' Vi answered. 'May doesn't usually have things on her mind.'

'My imagination, then,' said Josh.

'Must be.'

No one said anything more until May, rather flushed, brought in the tea.

'Everything all right, pet?' asked Josh, taking his cup. 'I was saying you seemed a bit – what's the word? Preoccupied.'

'Me?' May's gaze on him was limpid. 'No, I wouldn't say so.

Though I have got a bit o' news. Allan Forth's asked me to go to the pictures with him. On Wednesday.'

A silence fell, enfolding Josh and his girls in a curtain so thick only Vi was brave enough to speak through it.

'What are you going to see?' she asked May lightly, though her dark gaze was on her father.

'*Lost Horizon*,' answered May.

'Why, you've seen that!'

'So? I suppose I can see it again. It's very good.'

'Very good,' agreed Jinny.

'Wait a minute, wait a minute!' cried Josh, setting down his cup with a crash. 'What's all this about you seeing Allan Forth, May? He's our landlord, for God's sake, and years older than you!'

'Five,' she said quietly.

'But what's he got to do with you? We don't know him like we knew his father.'

'He's had tea with us, Dad,' Jinny put in quickly. 'He's a friend, he isn't just our landlord, and we all know he's been sweet on May for ages – don't know why he's taken so long to ask her out.'

'Sweet on May?' Josh rose from his chair. 'I don't want him to be sweet on May! He's the wrong type for her, there's nothing to him, canna say boo to a goose – she deserves better than that!'

'What do you mean – I deserve better?' cried May with sudden passion. 'We're going to the pictures together that's all. And didn't you say the other evening that he was a nice lad? Has he stopped being nice because he's asked me out?'

'I want you to know I don't approve of you seeing him,' Josh said, pushing aside his chair and snatching his jacket from the back of the door. 'If you want to see him, I canna stop you – you're over twenty-one—'

'Certainly am!' said May.

'But I'm never going to say I'm happy about it – I never will be, and that's that. Now, I'm going back to work.'

Slamming the door behind him he went out, leaving the girls to sigh deeply and exchange hopeless looks.

'I suppose he doesn't want to think you might leave him, May,' Jinny said at last.

'It's only because he's lost Ma,' May declared. 'He's come to rely on us to fill her place.'

'He got very upset when I went out with Iain Baxter, that one I went to school with.'

'Gets upset about anyone,' said Vi. 'You're just going to have to take a firm hand with him, May. Now, I'd better get off to my politics class or I'll be late.'

'So we do the washing up?' asked Jinny. 'Och, nae bother, we don't mind, do we, May?'

'As long as Vi does it on Wednesday. Thing is, though, I'd just like to say that none of us is thinking of getting married, so Dad can stop going off like a rocket, eh?'

'Try telling him that,' Jinny laughed as they began to pile up the dishes, 'when you go out with Allan.'

'One trip to the cinema doesn't mean much.'

'It's a start.'

# Seven

Wednesday, the day May and Allan were to go out, was when Jinny met the Viennese man again, though afterwards she rather wished she hadn't. Not because of anything he'd said or done – quite the reverse. It came about when Arthur Whyte, the bakery manager, brought Viktor across to Ross's office to sit in on one of the regular meetings on costings and sales. Seemed that Mr Comrie had expressed a wish for his nephew to get some idea of how expenditure and profit were monitored in a Scottish bakery, so that he could compare the system with the one at home, and Viktor, arriving with Mr Whyte, was interested. He still found time, before greeting Ross, to give Jinny a smile which she hastily, if a little shyly, returned.

'All going well, Mr Linden?' asked Ross, offering Viktor a chair. 'You getting to know the bakery?'

The Viennese inclined his head. 'Please, call me Viktor. Yes, thank you, I am enjoying my time there. Everyone is being so kind.'

'He is already planning to begin some baking of his own,' remarked Arthur Whyte, a chunky figure in his late forties, grey-haired and pleasant enough but best known for his keenness to save money. His smile now was cautious. 'Have to see how that goes, eh?'

'Indeed,' Viktor returned politely. 'But I believe my uncle would like me to make some of our *Torten*, as we call cakes, out of interest, perhaps?'

'Oh, yes, certainly, we'll be very interested,' Ross said agreeably.

'I know something of Austrian baking, Viktor, and I am a great fan. Jinny, will you pass me the stock book? Then we'll make a start.'

It was not usual for Jinny to sit in on the costings meetings, although Ross had instructed her on what was involved, and she now took her place at her own desk, her eyes on her work – until they just managed to light on Viktor sitting at a distance.

Yes, there was no doubt about it, she decided, observing him at her leisure. He was very attractive. She saw the way his blond hair seemed to fit his finely shaped head, and how he held himself so elegantly, his shoulders flat, his slim neck showing his youth. Maybe, after all, it was his looks and not just being Viennese that made him seem so different from the few young men she'd gone out with in the past? She was pleasantly dwelling on this question when, to her horror, he suddenly turned his head and their eyes met. He had caught her watching him.

A great rush of colour flooded her face from her pointed chin to the top of her brow, but she could not seem to detach her gaze from his and kept on looking as he returned her look and then gently smiled. Oh, God, what must he be thinking? She couldn't smile back, couldn't pretend she wasn't embarrassed, and even when she'd dragged her gaze away and was bending her head over her work, all she felt was the embarrassment and the painful flush staining her face that Viktor must have seen.

Even though she was staring down at a column of figures, she was aware that he had turned his attention back to the meeting where Mr Whyte was going on about . . . something to do with Swiss Rolls not selling well that week and should they cut down on numbers for a while? Better than losing money having to sell them off at reduced prices, eh?

How many Swiss Rolls did they need? Mr Comrie was asking, and Jinny sighed. Heavens, who cared? Usually she was interested in snippets of information she heard from the meetings, but just then she felt she'd rather be elsewhere. Anywhere, in fact.

Of course, she had to face Viktor when the meeting was over. Smile politely, as though she'd never been caught staring at him; wish him all the best with his cake making while he bowed and thanked her, giving no sign that there was anything between them. Well, there wasn't, except that she'd been caught gazing at him and could have kicked herself for being such a fool.

When Mr Whyte called from the door that they'd better be getting back to the bakery, Viktor buttoned on his overcoat, turned to thank

Ross for allowing him to sit in on the meeting and, with a last look at Jinny, left Accounts without another word. Was that all then? Her heart weighing her down, Jinny returned to her desk, feeling so crushed she didn't even remember it was her lunch hour until Ross reminded her.

'Hey, shouldn't you be gone?' he asked easily. 'Not so carried away by the sight of our *leutnant* that you've forgotten to eat, I hope?'

'Oh, what a piece of nonsense!' she flared, then lowered her eyes and muttered an apology.

'Sorry, Ross – shouldn't have spoken to you like that.'

'Not at all, I shouldn't have teased you, it never goes down well. All right now?'

'Of course. I'll get off to lunch, then.'

But still she lingered a moment. 'Meeting go well, Ross? Did Mr Linden enjoy it?'

'Seemed to. Asked some intelligent questions – maybe you heard?'

'No, I didn't hear.'

'Well, he certainly seems a bright lad. And, by the way, he's asked us to call him Viktor. Anxious to mix in, I suppose.'

'Yes, I suppose so.' Jinny glanced at the clock. 'I'd better run, then.'

'Take your time. I don't mind when I go to lunch.'

'I'll be back at one.'

Not caring to read Ross's expression, for it seemed to her that he knew she was upset, Jinny quickly left Accounts and made her way to the bakery shop downstairs, took her usual rolls and added a cup of tea from the tea shop. After the familiar chat with the girls she was glad to find herself alone in the back room, where she could desolately eat her rolls and think about how silly she'd been.

Gradually, though, she began to feel better. So he'd caught her studying him. What of it? She sipped her tea. A cat could look at a king, the saying went, and he needn't have found her gaze anything remarkable. He was new; he would expect to be a focus of interest. No need to worry, then.

But she had no sooner cheered herself up than she remembered Viktor's intense blue eyes.

'Did you ever see such blue eyes?' Mabel had asked. 'Like sailor's eyes, I'd say . . .'

Long-sighted sailor's eyes, then, that could have seen even from a distance that Jinny was looking at him because she was attracted to him. As, of course, she was. Attracted. She hadn't really admitted it to herself till then. More than attracted? Maybe. She'd heard about people falling in love at first sight. Was this what it meant? To have this line drawn between yourself and someone you'd just met? To want that person to feel the same?

Oh, it was all so crazy! Viktor Linden wasn't someone who was going to stay in her life, even if they did get to know each other. He came from another country and he'd be going back to it. There was no future to her feelings and the best thing she could do was to stamp them out – to let them die as a plant dies without light or water, not let them blossom.

Which meant that tomorrow, when she took the wages over to the bakery, she would just be very polite but cool if she saw Viktor, and let him see she wasn't especially interested in him. And she wouldn't be staying long at the bakery, in any case, as she had wages to take to the other shops. There, that was her little plan of campaign, and having worked it out Jinny felt better – so much so that she felt quite hungry and went back to the shop to buy a vanilla slice which she enjoyed with another cup of tea.

Wonder how May and Allan will get on this evening? she thought idly. And guessed very well, once they'd overcome their first feelings of strangeness at being together.

But first, of course, for May, there'd be the ordeal of tea with Dad to get through. Oh, heavens, and she, Jinny was cooking! Help! She'd better get home early and make sure everything was ready so that May could leave by half past six, hoping, of course, that Dad didn't make difficulties. Oh, why did folk want to do that?

As she ran back to Accounts at exactly one o'clock – there was the gun sounding off again – her only consolation in worrying about her father making difficulties was that, for a little while, she'd stopped thinking about Viktor Linden.

# Eight

Ordeal by Tea. Yes, you could call it that, with Josh sitting at the table with a face of stone, Vi sighing with exasperation, and even cool May seeming to be on edge, fiddling with her knife and fork and looking at the clock.

At least her cooking had been all right, thought Jinny, serving

Josh and Vi second helpings of ham shank and split peas, but then May rose and said she must get ready and a dark red colour rushed to Josh's brow.

'Still going out, then?' he asked shortly.

'Yes, I am.'

'Even though I'm not happy about you seeing Allan Forth?'

'Dad, you know you're never happy when we go out with anyone.'

Josh frowned. 'When did I ever complain about you lassies going out?'

'Oh, Dad, how can you say that?' Jinny asked. 'You know the awful fuss you made when I went out with Iain Baxter.'

'That laddie you knew from school? He wasn't right for you, Jinny. Just like the fellows May was seeing weren't suitable for her. I wasn't complaining, just pointing out what was true.'

'And now you're saying the same thing about Allan?' May asked. 'Well, that certainly isn't true. There's nothing at all wrong with Allan, as you know very well. You've always been very friendly with him up till now.'

'Aye, well that was before I knew he was playing up to you behind my back.'

With a sigh of exasperation, May shook her head. 'Dad, I don't know what you expect! I'm a grown-up and can say what I want to do; there's no need for Allan to ask your permission.'

'Get going, May,' advised Vi. 'Don't argue any more. Dad's only holding you up.'

'Vi, I'll thank you to stay out of this!' Josh jumped angrily to his feet. 'It's between May and me and no one else!'

'Well, I'm going to get ready,' May told him calmly. 'So you should just sit down and finish your tea. Jinny's taken a lot of trouble with it, remember.'

'Och, I'm no' hungry.' Josh glanced at Jinny. 'Sorry, pet. I think I'll away back to work.'

But as he made no move, May caught at his hand and held it. 'Oh, please, don't be like this again,' she said softly. 'I'm only going to the pictures. I know you're upset but you needn't be. Even if we make other friends, we're still your girls, isn't that right – Vi? Jinny?'

'Sure,' said Vi.

'Oh, yes,' Jinny agreed. 'You have to remember that, Dad.'

Slowly he let go of May's hand and rested his sombre gaze on her face. 'Still my girl, May? I don't think so. These friends you talk about – you just mean Allan Forth. And who says he wants to be a friend?'

'He's a friend already!' she answered swiftly. 'A friend to this family. It's unfair for you to be so much against him.'

For some moments Josh was silent. Finally, he said heavily, 'Listen, May, since your ma died we've all made the best o' things, eh? Maybe we haven't been like we were before, but still as happy as we could manage. We never needed so-called friends wanting to come between us, spoiling what we had.'

'Are you saying we shouldn't have friends at all, then?' asked Vi, her tone blunt, her eyes hostile.

'Of course not! All I say is that you should have real friends, not fellows pretending to be what they're not.'

'You're hinting Allan is like that?' cried May. 'Dad, you couldn't be more wrong! He's sincere and honest in every way!'

'And causing trouble!' Josh, breathing fast, strode across the room and snatched his coat from a peg on the door. 'You go out with him if you want, May, but I'm telling you, he'll never be welcomed here by me! Now, I'm away.'

After he'd slammed the door behind him, just as before, and they'd heard his feet thundering down the stairs, the sisters sat in silence for some moments.

Finally, Vi spoke. 'He's like a five-year-old, eh? Throwing a tantrum if folk won't do what he wants. May, you'll just have to ignore him.'

'He's really upset,' she answered in a low voice. 'I hate to see him like that. Shows how deep his feelings are.'

'Never mind his feelings – he's no right to 'em.' Vi began to clear the table. 'Off you go, get yourself ready and go down to meet Allan.'

'Will you tell him – about Dad?' Jinny asked.

'Don't know yet. Look, I'm sorry to leave the clearing up—'

'Och, just go!' cried Vi. And May finally went.

But how pretty she looked, her sisters thought, when she was finally ready. Worries about her father or not, in her blue coat with matching hat of her own making and a blue scarf that brought out the colour of her eyes, she appeared only to be looking forward to her night out – her first with Allan Forth. Once again, Vi and Jinny marvelled at how she could set aside her feelings and present such a serene face to the world, and wished they could have shared her gift. No point in that, they were different and must make the best of it, but all they wanted now was for May and Allan – two lovely people – to enjoy their evening together.

'Thank the Lord she's not going to let Dad spoil things,' said Vi, crashing dishes into a bowl after May had run lightly down to meet Allan and walked away with him to the tram. 'There's a lot to be said for being calm as a cucumber, eh?'

'Think something might come of this going out?' asked Jinny, reaching for a towel.

'Don't ask me. You were the one who said Allan was sweet on May.'

'Depends if she's sweet on him, though.'

'I think she might be. Look at the way she defended him to Dad. That's what's got him worried.'

'Poor Dad. He makes himself so unhappy.'

'I've no patience with him. Face facts is what he should do. You and May will be sure to get married one day and leave the nest, and I'll depart to live my own life, eh? He'll have to get used to it.'

Jinny laughed a little. 'The way you talk, Vi! You're not really as hard as you make out, you know. And why shouldn't you get married one day anyway?'

'Because I'll have better things to do.'

'Maybe I will too, then. I'm in no hurry to get married – I like my job.'

'Especially when you can meet interesting guys from foreign parts, eh?'

Glancing away from Vi's amused gaze, Jinny made no reply.

# Nine

Meanwhile, across the city, May and Allan, in the darkness of the cinema, their eyes on the screen, were conscious only of each other yet still not drawing close. Only as the film progressed did it seem natural that Allan should reach to take May's hand, that her eyes should turn to meet his, and that both should smile.

'That was a wonderful picture,' Allan whispered as the credits rolled at the end and they were blinking at each other in the returned lights. 'I suppose everyone would like to live in a place like Shangri-la where you'd never grow old and always be happy.' He looked down at May's hand in his. 'You wish there was somewhere like that in real life, May?'

'I don't know. I think, maybe, I'd rather have life as it is. I mean, where you'd know what you had was true.'

'Yes, I suppose I agree. And people can be happy in the real world, eh?' His gaze on her was steady. 'For instance, I'm happy now, just being with you.'

'It's the same for me, Allan.' But May was quietly withdrawing her hand from his. 'There's something I should tell you, though.'

'Oh?' He was trying to smile. 'Nothing bad, is it?'

'Well, it's just that – look, I don't want to make too much of it but my dad isn't keen for me to go out with you.'

Allan's effort at a smile disappeared. His eyes on May were wide, their look bewildered.

'What are you saying? I don't understand – your dad doesn't like me? But he does! We get on well. How can it be true that he's not keen for you to go out with me?'

'He does like you, really,' she said earnestly. 'It's hard to explain, but since Ma died, he's, well, he likes to think that we only need him.'

'You and your sisters? All three of you?'

'Yes. Well, Vi isn't interested in going out with anyone – it's Jinny and me that Dad gets worried about – I mean, if we . . . see people.'

'See young men, you mean,' Allan said quietly. He put his hand to his brow and shook his head. 'But this is just crazy, May. He can't keep you as little girls for ever, you have to grow up, have lives of your own—'

'I know, and I think he knows that too, deep down, but he can't accept it, that's all, so we have these . . . arguments.' May sighed heavily, then suddenly reached forward and took Allan's hand. 'The thing is I'm not going to take any notice of him. If I want to go out with someone I will, and as he says himself, there's nothing he can do about it.'

'Go out with someone,' Allan repeated, his eyes intent on hers. 'Would that be me? Do you mean you'd like to go out with me again?'

'Yes, I would,' she said softly.

'Even if it means upsetting your father? I don't like that, May. I don't want to cause trouble between you and your dad.'

'You'd rather we didn't see each other?'

'Oh, God, no!'

As the lights began to dim for the second feature, Allan pulled May to her feet.

'Come on, let's go,' he said urgently. 'We don't need to see the B-picture, do we? Let's just get out of here.'

They'd meant to walk home but the night air was so cold and the pavements so slippery with frost that they took the tram and sat together on the jolting bench seat, holding hands and closely studying each other's faces.

'This has been a blow,' Allan said quietly. 'And so unexpected.'

'I know,' May replied. 'It was for me, too, because you're different from other fellows. I mean, I knew Dad liked you, so I thought he might not mind so much if I went out with you.'

'If he sees all men as a threat there wasn't much hope of that.'

'No, but he's so obstinate – he won't listen to anything anybody says.'

Allan, his eyes brightening, squeezed May's hand in his. 'Did you defend me?' he asked softly. 'Against what, I don't know, but I suppose there must be something.'

'Only that you're older, which is a piece of nonsense as you're not that much older than me, and Dad was older than Ma, anyway. Don't worry about what he says, Allan. We've agreed, haven't we, to see each other?'

'Nothing will stop me from being with you, if it's what you want, May.'

'I've told you it is.'

'Just makes things a bit awkward, that's all. I mean, what do I say when I see your dad?'

'Be as you always are. If he wants to quarrel with you, say there's no point.'

'You make it sound so easy,' he was beginning, when she knocked his arm and began to rise from her seat.

'Our stop, Allan.'

'I wouldn't have minded travelling on,' he said with a laugh.

They made the walk up Fingal Street last as long as possible, keeping close together, their arms entwined, enduring the cold until they reached the Hendries' door, where they stopped and gazed at each other in the lamplight.

'I wish I didn't feel your dad was looking out,' Allan whispered. 'Think he might come down if he sees us?'

'No, he'll probably not be back from the theatre yet. He's one of the last to leave.'

'In that case . . .' Allan was drawing her into his arms when she stiffened and took a step back.

'He's here?' he asked, turning quickly to look down the street, but May shook her head.

'It's Vi. She must have been to one of her meetings – oh, Lord, why does she have to come back now?'

'Why indeed?' groaned Allan.

They stood still, facing Vi, who was jauntily approaching.

'Had a good time?' she cried brightly. 'Enjoy the picture?'

'Very much,' Allan answered politely. 'Certainly takes you into another world, eh?'

'Shangri-la? Yes, it's grand – as long as you remember it's not real.'

'Only have to come out into the cold here to know that,' May said, rubbing her arms. 'Suppose we'd better go in.'

'Och, don't let me interrupt things.' Vi hurried past them to the door of the flat. 'I'll go in and you two can say goodnight.'

'Goodnight to you, then,' called Allan, and when she'd gone and closed the door he turned eagerly again to May.

'Sorry about that,' she said, looking embarrassed. 'Vi came just at the wrong time.'

'She seemed pretty understanding, though.' Allan was slowly drawing May into his arms and bending his face to hers. 'Didn't linger.'

No further words were spoken as they stood very still, their eyes searching each other's faces, then let their mouths meet in their first kiss, a kiss that promised so much more, and finally drew apart, breathing hard.

'When can I see you again?' Allan asked urgently. 'I must see you, May. Will you come into my shop one evening?'

'Yes, I will, I promise. It's for the best, to meet like that.'

'You mean to keep out of your father's way?'

'He'll settle down, he'll be all right – don't worry.'

'I can't believe he doesn't like me, May. I mean, there's never been any hint—'

She put her finger to his lips. 'I told you, he'll be all right. We'll just have to give him time to get used to things. Now, I'd better go.'

'You won't forget? To come into my shop?'

'As though I would!'

He made to take a step towards her but she blew him a kiss and opened her door.

'Goodnight, Allan!'

'Goodnight, dear May.'

He watched as the door closed behind her, standing there for several minutes before walking away.

# Ten

'Dad not back yet?' asked May, taking off her coat in the living room of the flat.

'Too early,' Jinny answered, studying her sister with interest. 'But have you had a good time?'

'Yes, did you enjoy seeing the picture all over again?' Vi put in with a laugh. 'Did you let on you'd seen it already?

'No, I didn't,' May told her coolly. 'Why should I? Anyway, I enjoyed it just as much the second time.'

'You certainly look happy," Jinny observed. 'You'll be seeing Allan again, eh?'

'Ssh!' cried Vi. 'There's the door! Dad's back!'

The sisters looked at one another, Jinny with apprehension, Vi with a frown and May with her usual calmness. When their father came in, his face cold and set, it was she who stepped forward to greet him.

'Hello, Dad, want some tea?'

He stared. 'You're back then?'

'Of course I'm back!' She smiled. 'It wasn't such a long picture.'

Josh took off his coat and hung it on its peg. He moved towards the fire and held out his hands to the blaze.

'I don't want to hear about it,' he said over his shoulder. 'You know my views, May. If you don't tell me what you're doing, the better we'll get on.'

'Oh, Dad, don't be so ridiculous!' cried Vi as Jinny hurriedly set about making tea. 'You can't ask May not to talk about Allan! She's every right!'

'Do you mind not speaking to me like that?' Josh's face was mottled red. 'If May does as I say we can all get on as we were. I don't think I'm being unreasonable to want that.'

'Not unreasonable!' Vi gave a short laugh but May shook her head at her, and as Jinny poured the tea and handed round the cups an uneasy peace descended. Finally Josh stood up and said he was weary, he'd be away to his bed. Goodnights were said, with Josh looking at no one, and then he was gone and the girls sighed and relaxed.

'Oh, it's a shame Dad's being so difficult,' said Jinny. 'I mean, we usually get on so well.'

'Aye, it's especially hard for you, May,' Vi commented. 'Your first time out with Allan and he goes and spoils it all, eh?'

As her sisters' eyes rested on her, May's own gaze seemed far away and her mouth curved slowly into a small, secret smile.

'Not all,' she replied softly. 'I wouldn't say "all", Vi.' With that she rose and put the guard over the fire. 'Shall we call it a day?' she asked. 'Things will look better in the morning.'

'I shouldn't bank on it,' said Vi shortly. 'Dad shows no sign of coming round to things.'

'We'll just have to be patient. The good thing is that he does like Allan really and, remember, Allan is our landlord. Dad won't want to fall out with him.' May began to gather up the teacups. 'Look, I must get to bed – I'll just take these away. Goodnight, girls.'

'Poor May,' said Vi, standing up and yawning. 'She's putting a good face on it but she knows there'll be trouble if she and Allan get serious. Thank the Lord I've nothing like that to worry about.'

'Nor me,' said Jinny promptly, at which Vi gave her another of her amused looks.

'Aren't you forgetting *Herr* Whats-his-name? Don't look so embarrassed – I can tell you're interested.'

'I don't know what you're talking about!' Jinny flared, jumping up and making for the door. 'You just like to tease, eh? I don't know why.'

'Sorry,' said Vi. 'Honestly, I don't mean to upset you. I won't say another word.'

'Thank you!'

'Friends again?'

'Of course. As long as you forget about Mr Linden.'

'Wiped clean from my mind! cried Vi, as they put the light out and left the living room.

But not from mine, thought Jinny with a sigh as she made her way into the bathroom. Only Vi needn't know that.

# Eleven

Friday. Wages day. For Jinny it was a day to enjoy, when she could make her rounds of the Comrie shops and the Princes Street café, as well as the bakery at Broughton Street, bringing the staff what they wanted and being welcomed on all sides.

'Here she is, then, good old Jinny! What have you got for us this week, then?' the bakers would cry. 'Our overtime gone up, has it? No' taken too much off, have you?'

'Everything's just as it should be,' she would always answer, smiling, and feel a wonderfully warm feeling inside at the sight of all the cheerful faces.

Actually, not all the bakers would be there. Those on the first shift who started work at four a.m., would have already gone off duty after sending their new loaves and rolls for early delivery in the van driven by cheerful, ginger-haired Terry Brown. But there would still be plenty of activity going on in the delicious-smelling bakery, as Jinny always liked to see. Men kneading, slapping and rolling out dough, or preparing cakes in the electric mixing machine; women icing and decorating fancies and large fruit cakes.

On that Friday morning in cold November, when Jinny arrived at the bakery, all her intentions of being cool with Viktor intact, she found Terry Brown back from his first deliveries, smoking a cigarette outside the door.

'Hallo, Jinny!' He gave her his usual grin. 'Want your lift over town?'

'Oh, yes, please! I'll just find Mr Whyte and give him the wages and then I'll be with you.'

'No' forgetting mine, eh?'

'Have it right here.'

Hurrying on into the bakery, Jinny returned the usual greetings with Alf, Ronnie and Bob loading up the big ovens set into the wall, and waved to Trixie and Norah, both attractive forty-year-olds who'd worked for Mr Comrie since leaving school, though Senga, the young trainee, didn't seem to be in sight. And nor was Viktor Linden.

'Mr Whyte around?' Jinny called, wondering where Viktor might be. Wasn't he supposed to be baking his own wonderful cakes?

'Right here, Jinny!' called Arthur Whyte, appearing from his small office. 'Good to see you. All present and correct?'

'Yes, except that I haven't got anything for Mr Linden. He's not been put on my list.'

'Oh, no, he wouldn't have been.' Mr Whyte spoke in a stage whisper. 'Mr Comrie's making special arrangements for him.'

'I see,' said Jinny, her eyes still checking round the bakery. 'I can't see him, anyway. Is he in today?'

'Why, of course. He's over at the small oven with Senga – don't you see him?'

Oh, yes, there he was, standing next to young Senga, a snub-nosed girl with a mass of thick brown hair stuffed into a cap, who was animatedly talking to him. Rather pushy, Jinny always thought her, and with a very good opinion of herself, but Viktor, dressed in a chef's white top and trousers with his hair also covered by a cap, appeared to be listening to her with great interest. Was she explaining how to work the oven? As though he wouldn't know!

Removing her gaze from Viktor – who hadn't seen her – Jinny followed Mr Whyte into his office, where they checked off her list and sorted the wage envelopes ready for distribution.

'Got time for some tea?' asked Mr Whyte when Jinny rose to leave, but she shook her head.

'Thanks, but Terry's giving me a lift to the Morningside shop – I don't want to keep him waiting.'

'All he'd do is light another cigarette.' Mr Whyte shrugged. 'And how he and other fellows can afford to smoke these days is a mystery to me. I mean, elevenpence ha'penny for twenty, eh? It's a lot. Take care not to get the habit, Jinny.'

'I'm far too sensible for that,' she said with a laugh.

But when she'd left him to open his office door, her laughter died. Seemed she'd be leaving the bakery with no chance to speak to Viktor Linden when she'd hoped she might somehow make it clear that she wasn't interested in him. If he hadn't been so busy chatting to Senga, or, at least, listening to her, she might have spoken to him then, but now it was too late. Better to forget her plan – maybe it wouldn't have worked, anyway – and just find Terry and head off for Morningside. So she was deciding when she saw Viktor making his way towards her, and then she stood very still.

'Miss Hendrie, how good we meet again!' he said as he snatched off his white cap and made one of his small bows. 'I was not expecting to see you at the bakery.'

'It's Friday, wages day. I always come here on Fridays.'

'You are responsible for the wages?'

'Among other things.'

Her little laugh was nervous. The one thing she'd wanted was to meet Viktor and convey to him that if he'd seen her watching him it was all a mistake, it didn't mean a thing. Yet here he was and she had the feeling that her eyes on him were showing just the sort of interest she was so anxious to deny. How had she ever thought she could do otherwise? Her plan had been ridiculous, would never have worked, and all she could do now was be polite and hope he wouldn't be able to read what her eyes were telling him.

'I didn't think you'd seen me,' she said quietly. 'You were busy at the small ovens.'

'Yes, with the young lady called Senga. Now that is a strange name – she told me it was another name backwards.'

'Agnes,' said Jinny shortly. 'It is used in Scotland.'

'Well, she has been very helpful.' Victor's smile was radiant. 'Today, I am to begin my baking and she was showing me the ovens which are a little different from those I know. But I still saw you, Miss Hendrie.'

Senga was Senga, but Jinny was Miss Hendrie?

'I wish you'd call me Jinny,' she told him.

'If you will call me Viktor.'

'I'd like to. It's a name we have too, but spelled differently.'

'And "Jinny" – that is a name short for another?'

'Virginia, maybe, but I don't know any Virginias. My real name is Jean – which is shorter, in fact, than "Jinny".'

They both laughed at that and Jinny would have relaxed, for she felt suddenly at ease with the young man looking at her with such interest, except that she was aware of another kind of interest coming their way. Not only from the bakers, but also from Trixie, Norah and, most obviously, Senga, who was gazing so intently at Viktor! Clearly she was another of the girls Mabel had said would be 'after' him. Only to be expected, wasn't it? But Jinny couldn't avoid an inward little stab at the thought.

'I must go,' she told Viktor. 'Terry's giving me a lift to one of the other shops – you've met Terry, our van driver?'

'Sure he has,' said Terry, suddenly joining them and speaking in a very loud voice, as though Viktor wouldn't otherwise understand him. 'Is that no' right, Mr Linden? Everything OK with you? Finding your way around?'

'Yes, indeed, thank you,' Viktor replied politely. 'Everyone is being very kind.'

'That's the ticket, folk are very friendly here. Jinny, you coming?'

As though I wouldn't be, she thought, but only smiled.

'Goodbye, Viktor, it was nice to meet again. Good luck with your cake making.'

'Thank you, Jinny.' He inclined his head. 'But I think you will soon be seeing what I have made. On Monday, I am bringing my cakes to the café.'

'The café? On Monday? Oh, I'll look forward to that – I really want to see your Austrian cakes!'

'Jinny!' Terry said warningly and as she hastily followed him out, looking back once, Viktor replaced his white cap and watched her go.

'Bit stiff, our Jerry friend, eh?' asked Terry, driving them easily and efficiently across town. 'All those wee bows and suchlike.'

'Viktor?' Jinny frowned. 'I don't think he's stiff – he's always smiling. And you needn't call him Jerry. He's not German, he's Austrian.'

'Reckon they're the same. Fought together in the war when my dad died.'

'My dad fought in the war as well, and it was horrible, but Viktor had nothing to do with it any more than we had.'

'All I'm saying is that Austrians and Germans have the same ideas. This chap Hitler even thinks the Austrians should be part of Germany, and I bet they do too.'

'I don't think you can say that. Anyway, Viktor's not to blame for what other people might do.'

'Viktor?' Terry gave Jinny a quick glance and grinned. 'Soon got to know him, eh?'

'Ross says he wants everyone to call him by his first name.'

'Never asked me,' Terry supplied.

'Look, let's talk about something else. He's not even really part of Comrie's.'

'Only the boss's nephew! And makes fancy cakes, they say. I can understand fellows making bread, but fancy cakes – best left to women, I'd say.'

Jinny, sighing, refused to be drawn into an argument, and no more was said until they arrived at Comrie's in Morningside, where they unloaded trays of small buns and doughnuts and Jinny thanked Terry for her lift.

'Always grateful, Terry.'

'Nae bother, you ken that.' He hesitated. 'Look, sorry if I spoke out of turn about Mr Linden, if he's a friend o' yours, I mean.'

'He's not specially a friend of mine, Terry. We've only just met.'

'Oh, well, I daresay he's a nice enough guy – just no' a Scot, eh?'

'Can't all be lucky!' She smiled. 'See you next week, then.'

'Sorry I can't take you on to Stockbridge, but I've to get Glasgow – need a part for the van.'

'That's all right. Plenty of trams.'

Taking the wages into the shop, Jinny found Terry's words echoing in her mind.

'If he's a friend o' yours, I mean . . .'

Were other people thinking that, too? Look how the bakery folk had stood, openly watching, as she and Viktor talked together! Her feelings must have been too obvious, then. To Viktor, as well? A little while ago she would not have wanted to think that, but since he had come to speak to her, since she had read something in his eyes, in his manner towards her, she no longer minded. Was it possible that they both felt the same?

As she greeted Phyl and Sal in the shop and met their usual teasing – had she brought them a rise that week, if not, why not, et cetera – she only laughed and accepted a cup of tea and one of the new doughnuts. It was amazing how much better she felt than when she'd set out that morning, especially thinking that on Monday she would be seeing Viktor again.

# Twelve

Even if Jinny had not been looking forward to seeing Viktor again, she would have wanted Monday to come, for the weekend had been depressing in the extreme. Josh had shown no signs of 'coming round', as the girls had hoped, and as he was at home on Sunday and had seen May go out, obviously to meet Allan, his misery was like a great cloud hanging over Vi and Jinny, who had to go out themselves to be free of it. Not that they felt much better when they returned, for their father was the same as when they'd left him and refused to listen to any arguments they wanted to make on why he should let May see Allan and be happy about it.

'You're only making things worse for yourself,' Vi told him. 'I mean, you might have to accept Allan one day, mightn't you?'

Josh raised his shadowed eyes. 'What are you talking about?'

'Well . . .' Vi glanced at Jinny. 'May and Allan might want to get married, mightn't they?'

'Married?' cried Josh. 'She'd never want to marry Allan! I'm no' denying that she might want to marry – don't accuse me of standing in her way – but she'd never want to marry him!'

'Why ever not? asked Jinny. 'He's got his own business, he's got his own house, but the main thing is he's nice, he's kind – he'd be just right for May!'

'He's a milksop!' cried Josh, rising. 'He's got no personality! He's like a long drink o' water! I'd never want to see my May married to him.'

As his daughters stared, their hearts sinking at the way their father was inventing a character that didn't exist to suit his own ends, it seemed clear that there was no point in saying any more. When he threw on his coat and cap and said he was going out for some fresh air, all the girls could feel was relief, which lasted until he returned some time later. May also returned, and the dark cloud stayed with them until they thankfully went to bed.

Roll on Monday! was Jinny's last thought before drifting into sleep, which only came after she'd spent some time wondering how things would be when she saw Viktor and his cakes the next morning – and, of course, had decided what to wear.

Her new raspberry jumper she'd been saving to wear at Christmas was in the end her choice, though when Monday morning actually came and she arrived in Accounts wearing it, she felt a bit of a fool to be making such a fuss about how she should look to see Viktor Linden.

It was true, she did feel attracted to him, and had felt a definite interest in herself flowing from him, but where was the point in trying to take it further? Viktor didn't live in Scotland and would never live in Scotland. Within a few short months would be returning home to Vienna. To picture herself there – well, even her vivid imagination couldn't take her as far as that! Why on earth hadn't she just put on her old blue twinset?

'You're looking very smart,' Ross observed when he joined her in the office. 'Have I seen that jumper before?'

'No, I haven't had it long.' Jinny played with the papers on her desk. 'Thought I'd give it an airing.'

'The colour suits you.'

Exactly her own view. She flushed a little and gave her papers another shuffle.

'Have you seen Mr Comrie yet? He's coming in with Viktor this morning.'

'Bit early for him.'

'Yes, but Viktor's bringing in some of his cakes – they're going to try them out at the shop.'

Ross raised his eyebrows. 'You're very well informed. No one's told me about this.'

'Viktor told me when I took the wages to the bakery on Friday. I think it had only just been decided. He'll have been working over the weekend, I expect, to get the baking done.'

'And they're going to be sold at so much a slice, I suppose? What price has been set?'

'Oh, I don't know. I don't suppose Viktor had even thought about it.'

'Probably not,' Ross said coldly. He reached for the telephone. 'I'll give Arthur a ring.'

'You're not cross, are you?' Jinny asked quickly. 'It was always what Mr Comrie wanted, to try out the Viennese cakes here.'

'I just like to know what's going on, that's all.' Ross began speaking to someone on the line then put his phone down. 'Seems Arthur's on his way here. I'll discuss this when I see him.'

'I'm sure no one wanted to keep you in the dark, Ross. It's all happened so quickly.'

'I know. I'm sorry.' Ross gave a quick smile. 'Must be that Monday morning feeling, eh? Let's go downstairs and see if anything's happening.'

But Mabel was already coming in the door, her cheeks rather red, her look excited.

'Oh, Ross – Jinny – Mr Comrie's just arrived at the shop with Mr Whyte and Mr Linden. They've got the cakes – just the six – the poor boy's been working all weekend on them but they're beautiful! Oh, you must see them.'

'We're on our way,' Ross said shortly. 'Jinny here can't wait.'

'Nor can you!' she answered spiritedly, rather wondering at his manner. Usually so easy-going, he seemed to still be in a bad temper in spite of his apology. 'Aren't you the one who was praising up Viennese cakes to me?'

'Looks like I'll be praising up Viktor's, too. Come on, let's get to the shop and join the admirers.'

And admirers there were, standing around in the shop that was not yet open, for not only was Mr Comrie looking down at the large trays containing Viktor's cakes with the proud expression of a new father, but Mr Whyte had something of the same look and Mrs Arrow appeared astonished and her girls thrilled. As for Viktor himself, and Jinny's eyes went to him at once, he was standing to one side, wearing his jacket and flannels instead of his baker's whites, and looking suitably self-deprecatory at all the excitement his cakes were causing. At the sight of Jinny and Ross his smile changed, broadened, and he took a step towards them.

'Miss Hendrie! Mr MacBain! Look, see my cakes – I have them ready!'

'*Wunderlich!*' Ross commented with a grin, bending to see the cakes, while Jinny, flushing, joined him, her eyes widening at the works of art, as she judged the cakes on the trays to be.

There were six, as Mabel had reported. Two large chocolate cakes, covered in the smoothest icing ever seen and carrying the magic name of Sacher written in darker chocolate. Then two towering layer cakes iced with a toffee-coloured glaze and decorated with triangular sponge slices. And finally, two white iced cakes, on which were beautifully made flowers of sugar paste and lines and shapes in marzipan. Only six, yes, but with the general effect of so much more, like a display for a grand buffet, perhaps, in some elegant house or special hotel, something quite out of the ordinary. Certainly, nothing like them had been seen before in Comrie's Bakery.

For a few moments no one spoke, then Mrs Arrow, clearing her throat, looked across at Viktor.

'Tell me, Mr Linden, how did you make cakes like these in just a weekend?'

'It is my job, Mrs Arrow.' He shrugged a little. 'On Friday and Saturday, there was the baking. On Sunday, the icing. It was no trouble to me.'

'Of course, I'd already organized the ingredients you wanted,' Mr Comrie put in. 'But you did a grand job, Viktor – I think we'll all agree on that?'

After an immediate chorus of approval Viktor spoke again, saying that he would like to tell everyone a little about the cakes. That the *Sachertorte* had been invented by a famous chef named Sacher back in 1832 for Chancellor Metternich, and was the favourite cake of Vienna. That the cake with the triangles was the *Dobertorte* from the Hungarian border, and the white-iced cake an almond sponge his own creation. He always liked to – what was the word – improvise from time to time, but never with the most famous cakes, of course. He would never presume to do that.

After he'd finished speaking another silence fell until Mr Whyte, exchanging looks with Mr Comrie, said that now, of course, there were decisions to be made.

'True,' Mrs Arrow agreed. 'And I've a shop to open and the café to be made ready.' She clapped her hands. 'Girls, away you go, then!'

'Meantime, what's happening to these splendid cakes, then?' asked Ross. 'If they're to be sold here by the slice, what charge is to be made?'

'That's to be discussed,' Mr Comrie said firmly. 'Viktor, will you and Mr Whyte put the trays into the room at the back and we'll adjourn there. Mrs Arrow, we'll need you as well. Get the girls to open up this morning, eh?'

'Certainly, Mr Comrie.'

As the girls hurried to their tasks everyone else moved to the back room, Viktor and Arthur Whyte carefully bearing away the trays of precious cakes so they were out of sight of any arriving customers for the time being.

# Thirteen

Their eyes moving from those cakes to Mr Comrie standing before them, everyone waited for him to speak. Viktor, close to his uncle, seemed unworried, but Jinny – who wasn't even sure she should be there – could tell that Mr Whyte and Mrs Arrow were on pins wondering what would be decided and probably already working out what they would say if they disagreed with Mr Comrie.

'Well, now,' he began, smiling round at the watchers, 'time to fix a price for Viktor's delectable cakes. I think we've decided, haven't we, to have slices from three in the café and three in the shop here?'

'That's what we decided,' Arthur Whyte agreed.

'Without me, actually,' Ross put in, smiling as though he wasn't annoyed, which he was. 'Of course I'm quite happy about it, provided the price is right.'

'That goes without saying, Ross,' said Mr Comrie smoothly, 'and I think we have discussed this in general terms already, haven't we?'

Ross shrugged. 'Perhaps so. What are the views on prices then?

We'll have to remember that the ingredients for these cakes are a good deal more expensive than for our usual cakes.'

'Exactly so.' Mr Comrie looked round again at his staff. 'That's why I'm suggesting a price of sixpence per slice in the shop and ninepence in the café.'

Silence fell. While Arthur Whyte and Mrs Arrow exchanged looks, Ross stared straight ahead, Jinny gazed at Viktor and Viktor gazed at his uncle.

'Sixpence and ninepence?' Arthur repeated at last.

'That's my suggestion.' Mr Comrie's smile was pleasant but his eyes were cold. 'You think they're too high?'

Arthur hesitated. 'They might be thought so,' he said at last.

'Compared with our usual prices,' added Mrs Arrow.

'As Ross has just said, the ingredients will be more expensive and we'll have to take account of that.' Mr Comrie's smile was fading. 'We haven't done any costings yet but I think the prices I've suggested will have to be charged anyway. Slices are not usually sold in the shop but are in the café. How much are we charging for a slice of cake there, Mrs Arrow?'

'Threepence!' she cried, as if to say, *You see my point?*

'Yes, well, that may be so, but I am certain that customers will see the difference between the Viennese cakes and our usual Madeira and so on. They will expect to pay more and, don't forget, there are still people with money about who come into Comrie's.'

Mr Comrie's face was rather red and his eyes were still cold.

'That being the case, perhaps you'd care to tell me, Arthur, what price you would like to see put on my nephew's cake slices?'

'Off the top of my head, Mr Comrie, no disrespect, you understand, but I'd say fourpence in the shop and fivepence in the café. If this doesn't take into account the difference in ingredients, I'd suggest that if the cakes become popular we'll sell enough to cover the difference.'

'Fourpence in the shop, fivepence in the café?' Mr Comrie's eyes were now flashing disapproval. 'Well, I don't know what you make of those prices, Ross, but I say they do not reflect my nephew's artistry and I'm not going to accept them. Mrs Arrow, please begin selling the cakes at the prices I've recommended and report back to me this afternoon. Ross and Arthur, I'll see you in my office, right?'

'Certainly, Mr Comrie,' they both chimed, while Mrs Arrow hurried away, saying, with an anxious face, that she'd send her girls to fetch the cakes, while Viktor and Jinny stood together uncertainly.

'Uncle, what about me?' asked Viktor. 'Shall I return to the bakery?'

'Take the rest of the day off,' his uncle ordered, wiping his brow. 'We owe you time, don't we? You worked the entire weekend.'

'That's kind of you, Uncle.'

As everyone else went, he and Jinny were left staring at each other, he looking so lost that her heart went out to him. Suddenly it seemed that everything had changed for him. One minute he was being praised to the skies, the next people in this strange country were squabbling over how much his beautiful cakes should cost. Probably that would never have happened in Vienna, and it had made him aware that he was far from home. Though he might have his uncle to turn to, being with him in Edinburgh was obviously not the same as being with his family and all that he knew.

Impulsively, she pressed his hand.

'Try not to worry about it, Viktor – the pricing, I mean. Everyone loves your cakes and they're sure to be very popular. This will all be forgotten in a day or two, you'll see.'

At her words, his face lit up and he pressed the hand she had put in his with so much warmth she could hardly pull it away. But of course, she had to go. Shouldn't be still downstairs, anyway.

'Jinny, thank you,' he murmured as she moved away from him 'You are so kind. I appreciate it very much.'

'I have to go back to Accounts, Viktor. And you must have a lovely day off.'

'No – wait – could not you be free too? Spend time with me?'

Oh, heavens, what was he saying? She felt as if she was almost physically spinning with joy, but there was no way she could take an afternoon off, just like that. No way at all.

'It's not possible. I'd love to but I can't. I'm so sorry!'

'Lunch, then?' His blue eyes were shining. 'We could have lunch? *Mittagessen?* I could meet you outside the shop?'

Lunch? She was still spinning. 'You could, yes, that would be grand. Thank you.'

'What time?'

'Twelve o'clock? That's when I go to lunch.'

'Till twelve o'clock,' he said solemnly, and their eyes met, holding them as though by physical bonds. 'I will meet you then.'

At last, as he formally bowed, she managed to leave him, hurrying from the back room through the café to the stairs, then upwards to Accounts where there was no Ross and no Mabel. Thank God for that. Long may they stay out of the office, or at least until twelve o'clock. For no one must see her looking as she did – so happy.

# Fourteen

Of course, they did see her. First, Mabel, returning from the post office where she'd been buying stamps for the office. Next, Ross and Arthur Whyte, released from Mr Comrie's office, though Mr Whyte, his face grim, gave just the briefest nod as he passed by, and Mabel was only interested in getting back to her typewriter now that the meeting was over. Only Ross actually looked at Jinny before he sat down at his desk, but then he only laughed and held up his hands.

'Sixpence it is, for the shop, Jinny! And ninepence for the café. All that time waffling and we might just as well have said yes in the first place.'

'Did you say yes at all?'

He shrugged. 'For the try out, I did, but we're going to work out how much we'll lose on making the new cakes, and if they don't sell well . . .' He shook his head. 'It'll be sorry, Viktor. Thank you and goodbye.'

'Goodbye? He's going to be working here anyway.'

'Oh, yes, of course.' Ross gave Jinny a thoughtful look, but made no further comment, and both worked quietly until Jinny rose and said she'd be going for her lunch.

'Couldn't just find me our flour account before you go, could you? I'm planning to compare it with one from that new firm, Rowley's.'

'Do you need it now? I'm meeting . . . my sister. I have to go.'

'Your sister? The one in the hat shop?'

'Yes, May. Could I get the account for you later?'

'No, no, I'm just being lazy.' Ross smiled. 'Have a nice lunch, then. Take a bit longer if you like – you don't often meet May.'

For a long moment Jinny stared ahead, not looking at him. Then she met his eyes. 'All right, Ross, you win. I'm not meeting May, I'm meeting Viktor. I don't know why I had to lie about it.'

'Didn't want to be teased, perhaps?' Ross was looking rueful. 'And now I've teased you, anyway. I'm sorry, Jinny. Away to see Viktor, then, and cheer him up, but not too much.'

'What do you mean?'

'Well, he's not here for ever, that's all.'

'Think I don't know that?'

'All I'm saying is remember it.'

'I'll see you at one o'clock, as usual.'

'Fine.'

As she turned, to speed down to the street, Jinny's eyes were stormy and her colour high, but by the time she'd found Viktor waiting on the pavement a little way from the shop, Ross's words had already faded from her mind.

'Viktor!'

He had been looking down Princes Street over the gardens towards the castle, his shoulders back, his head erect, every inch '*Der Leutnant*', as Ross had called him. As soon as he heard Jinny's call, however, he spun round and went to her, taking her hands and looking down into her face, his own face brightening as he said her name.

'Jinny!'

'I hope I'm not late?'

'No, no.' He pushed back his hat from his fair hair and smiled a little. 'So good to see you, after my morning that was so . . . I must say *schrecklich*. No word in English will do.'

'*Schrecklich?* Does it mean awful? Terrible?' Jinny searched his face. 'Viktor, it wasn't so bad. I told you, everyone liked your cakes, it was only the price they couldn't agree on.'

'My cakes are not worth your six pennies a slice?' He grasped her hand. 'Come, let us forget it. Where may I take you for lunch?'

Careful of cost and not knowing how Viktor was placed for money, Jinny took him to a small café in the West End where they could have something light that would not be expensive. Of course, it was crowded, but they were lucky, able to spot a table as two city workers rose to leave, and settled themselves down at once, ready to talk.

# Fifteen

'Such a beautiful colour,' Viktor remarked as Jinny removed her winter coat, revealing her raspberry-coloured jumper. 'May I say it suits you?'

'I'm glad you like it.'

She was surprised to find herself feeling quite at ease. Perhaps because Viktor had shown a vulnerable side she hadn't thought he had, or perhaps because she might indeed be the one to cheer him, as Ross had suggested. 'Not too much,' he had added, but she dismissed those words from her mind.

The waitress brought a menu and they chose mushroom soup, followed by sausages and mash for Viktor and a toasted sandwich for Jinny.

'What are sausages in German?' she asked. 'I'm sorry to say I never did German at school, but maybe the Austrian language is different anyway, is it?'

'It's a version of standard German, one that Germans understand, as we understand theirs. Just as you understand American and English English.'

'But did you know that Scots itself is a proper language?' Jinny smiled. 'I just speak with a Scottish accent. You do understand me, don't you?'

'Of course! Don't forget, I'm used to my mother's.'

'But now she'll speak fluent German. I don't speak one word.'

'And your first word will be the German for sausages?'

They laughed, all traces of stress vanishing from Viktor's face, making him look suddenly so young, Jinny felt she could visualize him now, not so much as a lieutenant, but a schoolboy. Handsome, of course, he must always have been handsome.

'*Wurst*,' he whispered, leaning across the table. 'That is your first word, but if you would like me to, I can teach you others.'

'I'd like it very much, Viktor. But first you must tell me about your Vienna. I know it's lovely.'

Viktor looked away. 'Not only lovely, it's splendid. Though maybe not quite as splendid as it was.'

'Why's that?'

He shrugged. 'Well, because of what we've lost. We had an empire, we were an imperial capital. Our emperor, Franz Josef, looked as if he would last for ever. But he died during the war and the empire died with him. Our country was defeated, and Vienna was defeated, too.'

'But it's still lovely? Still splendid?'

'Yes, well, it rebuilt itself and became beautiful again. Still had its palaces and boulevards, you know, and of course restaurants and coffee houses. But – I do not know how to put it – the people know things have changed.' Viktor sighed. 'Enough of that – here comes our soup!'

Over the soup, which Jinny was relieved to find was very good, he seemed to relax, grow lyrical almost, as he began to talk of the coffee houses back home, describing them simply as the best in the world.

'Jinny, I cannot tell you all that they mean to us in Vienna. For they are not just cafés, you understand, but places to gather and meet friends, to read the paper or talk all day, if you like – and never be asked to move on.'

'And they have wonderful cakes like yours?'

'Of course!' Viktor's eyes glowed. 'From the shops like my father's, where I learned my baking. How I wish I could show them to you!'

Their looks met and lingered, but the moment passed as the waitress removed their soup bowls and served their next course.

'*Wurst!* My favourite!' Viktor exclaimed when she had left them. 'You know, we have as many varieties of sausage at home as we have coffee.'

'Oh, dear! Do hope our sausages will be all right for you, then.'

'They are excellent, I assure you.'

'And what about our coffee?'

He gave a wary smile. 'Well, there I must confess, I am missing home.'

'I did wonder if you might be homesick.'

'Because of how I was today?' He shook his head. 'That was only because of what was said about the price of my cakes.'

'Viktor, I explained—'

'I know, I know, but let's not discuss it. Let us just enjoy being here, together.'

Lulled for a moment by the beauty of the idea, Jinny dreamily finished her cheese roll and was about to let Viktor order some of the local coffee he evidently didn't enjoy when some inner warning made her look at the café clock.

'Oh, no, look at the time! I have to be back by one and it's nearly that now!'

'Surely you can take a little longer?'

'Ross said I could, but I told him I'd be back as usual, I don't know why. Maybe I didn't want him to think I was using you to take extra time.'

'Would he have thought that?'

'Probably not. I suppose I was just cross with him and didn't want any favours.' Putting on her coat with Viktor's polite help, Jinny shook her head. 'Come on, let's go.'

The coffee cancelled, the bill paid, they left the café and hurried back towards Comrie's, but before they reached it Viktor slowed down and touched Jinny's arm.

'I am sure, you know, you need not worry,' he said gently. 'Ross will not be cross if you are late when he told you to take more time.'

'Oh, I know, it's just that – like I said – he upset me, so I wanted to make sure he'd no reason to complain.' Jinny laughed apologetically. 'I'm sure I'm not making sense to you – sorry.'

'Jinny, I'm sure you will always make sense.' Viktor's tone was light but his eyes were serious. 'And I'm sure, too, that you and Ross usually get on very well. Am I right?'

'Yes, it's true. In fact, I'm feeling sorry now that I've made such a fuss.' She put her hand on his. 'Viktor, I'm so sorry I have to go. It's been so lovely.'

'Lovely for me, too.' He held the hand she had given him. 'It has made me feel better – to be with you.'

'So, what are you going to do now, with your free afternoon?'

'I don't know. Sightseeing, maybe, though the weather is not good.'

'You must be so tired after all you did yesterday – why don't you just have a rest?

'Rest? I never rest.' He laughed. 'But I almost had help yesterday, you know.'

'Help? With your baking?'

'With the decoration. Senga asked if I'd like her to come in.'

'Senga!' Jinny's dark eyes flashed. 'What was she thinking of?'

'Well, she said she'd a lot to learn, and if she could work with me it would be a great help to her.'

'I'll bet! Viktor, you didn't let her come, did you?'

'No, no, I never want anyone around when I have work to do. Especially not someone who needs training.'

'So, you said no. Quite right, too.'

Watching her face with its obvious look of relief, Viktor made no comment, but as he released her hand he fixed her with an intense gaze.

'Jinny, we are wasting time. Tell me when I may see you again, before you vanish for the afternoon.'

'You mean, see me . . . not at work?'

'Of course. Not at work. When will it be?'

'Depends what would be best.' Her heart was beating fast. 'What about Sunday?'

'Sunday? That's too far away. Why not one evening? We could go to the theatre. I read in the paper that there is an Agatha Christie play on at the Duchess theatre.' Viktor's face was animated. 'It's called *Black Coffee*. They said it was very good.'

The Duchess Theatre, where her father worked? Oh, no, she'd have to tell him she wanted to go to the theatre with Viktor, and what in heaven's name would he say? What would Viktor say if she told him she couldn't risk it? But of course, she must risk it. If she wanted to see Viktor regularly she would have to tell her father soon anyway.

'I know the Duchess,' she said levelly. 'My dad works there – he manages the scenery and effects.'

'Why, that is wonderful!' Viktor cried. 'You will know all there is to know about the theatre! Shall we say we'll go, then?'

'Yes, why not? I'll book the tickets. No, don't say anything, it will be easier for me. Shall we try for Thursday? We can arrange when to meet later.'

'Fine. Excellent. I'll leave it to you, then, but I wish to pay.'

She put her finger over his lips and shook her head. For a long moment they gazed into each other's eyes, until finally she broke away and ran for Comrie's, looking back once to wave and to catch Viktor smile.

She couldn't have put it clearly into words how she felt when she reached Accounts and met Ross's interested gaze. Happy? Over the moon? Oh, yes, but also apprehensive, now that she'd realized what it would be like telling her father about Viktor. If he had thought Allan unsuitable what would he think of a foreigner, one whose nation had been his enemy?

'Had a good lunch?' she heard Ross ask, and from somewhere produced a radiant smile.

'Lovely. Sorry I'm late, though. And that I was – you know – a wee bit snappy.'

'No need to apologise. I was to blame.' Ross was putting on his coat and smiling. 'But there's good news for Viktor – did they tell you as you came through the shop?'

'No, I didn't stop. What good news?'

'All his slices have sold like hot cakes – pardon the pun – and several orders have been taken for the full-size versions. No need to worry about the price now – we're on to a winner.'

# Sixteen

When their father had returned to his work at the theatre that evening, Jinny told her sisters of her fears. Of how she'd had lunch with Viktor and enjoyed being with him. Of how they wanted to see each other again and Viktor had suggested the theatre. Of how they'd agreed on the Duchess, though it was the last place Jinny would have chosen, and were planning to go on Thursday. But how was she going to tell Dad?

'Oh, for heaven's sake, you're not going to let Dad throw another tantrum, are you?' cried Vi. 'It's been bad enough with May here, still not allowed to mention Allan's name – such a piece of nonsense!'

'You tell me how to stop him throwing a tantrum then! If May couldn't do it, what chance have I?'

'You must be firm. We must all be firm. Tell him straight out that we're grown up now, not children any more, and we've a right to our own lives.'

'The thing is, we live here,' said May. 'It's Dad who pays the rent; he could just show us the door.'

'We pay our way!' Vi retorted. 'We don't live here for nothing, so it's our home as well as his. He wouldn't want us to go, anyway.'

'So, I tell him about Viktor and wait for the explosion?' asked Jinny. 'It's a shame, because Viktor seemed quite interested that Dad worked at the Duchess. I think he likes the theatre, he really wants to go with me, and if Dad had been OK about it he might have given us complimentary tickets.'

'I shouldn't ask him for any tickets if I were you,' said Vi with a mock shudder. 'That'd be adding insult to injury in his eyes. Giving free tickets to a man taking his daughter out – a foreigner at that!'

'Oh, don't!' Jinny wailed. 'I know exactly what'll happen. He'll say Viktor's from an enemy country, there's no future in it and that I'll be sure to get hurt. You wait, see if I'm right.'

'Suppose you might get hurt, but that's not the point, you should be free to do that. Just like May should be able to see Allan and talk about him if she likes.'

'True,' May agreed. 'But Allan has decided to have it out with Dad, anyway. He says we can't go on the way we are, and that's that.'

'That's good, but what will you do if Dad won't climb down?'

'We'll cross that bridge when we come to it. But Jinny, I think you should speak to Dad tonight as soon as he comes back. Tell him he needn't worry about you and Viktor, because you know the situation and you can cope with it.'

'Glad you've said all that,' said Vi. 'Because I think I hear Dad now, coming up the stair.'

'Oh, no, is it that time already?' cried Jinny, rising and looking as if ready to run. Even if she'd had any such thought, however, it would have been too late, for Josh, rosy with the cold, was already on his way in.

'Hello, girls!' he called, taking off his cap and coat and rubbing his hands. 'Got the fire made up? It's enough to freeze your hair off outside!'

In a good mood, wasn't he? That was because May hadn't been out for a day or two. The sisters all knew, without needing to put it into words, that their father's moods were a barometer registering May's evenings out, for when she was with Allan gloomy weather could be forecast, and when she stayed at home there was sunshine. As she was clearly at home that evening Josh, as he approached the fire, was the mellow, good-natured father his family loved, which didn't make it any easier for Jinny to know that she must soon bring this pleasant situation to an end.

'Like some tea, Dad?' asked Vi, leaping up from her chair.

'Aye, when have you known me to say no to tea? Won't have anything to eat, though, as I've had sandwiches with the lads. Might manage a biscuit.'

'The digestives are in the coronation tin,' May said, rising to join Vi, not only to help with the tea but to look meaningfully at Jinny, who was too concerned with gazing at her father to take their unspoken hint.

'How d'you like the play this week, Dad?' she asked with an attempt at casualness. '*Black Coffee* by Agatha Christie. I've heard it's good.'

'Aye, she can turn a fine plot.'

'As a matter of fact, I'm thinking of going to see it.'

'You are?' Josh sat up in his chair. 'Jinny, that's grand. You lassies haven't been to the theatre since I don't know when. It's all the pictures with you, eh?'

'I like a play sometimes, especially if it's a thriller.'

'What night are you going? I can get you some tickets.'

Instantly, Jinny's face flamed.

'Thursday's the night, but the thing is, Dad, I'm going with someone from work. He's – well, he's the new chap from Austria. I think I told you about him. He's Mr Comrie's nephew, just here for a short time, but he said he'd like to go to the theatre and we settled on *Black Coffee*. It's not new but it's had good reviews – should be worth seeing.'

All the time she'd been rattling on she'd seen her father's face change as he took in what she was saying, and the register of his barometer dropped from 'Set Fair' to 'Storm'. Now, as her sisters stood, watching, he held up his hand.

'Jinny, that'll do. I want to get it straight, what you're saying.'

'Don't be cross, Dad. There's nothing to be upset about.'

'When you're telling me you want to go out with a foreigner? Don't be cross, you say. It's what you girls always say, but I'm never cross, just worried, that's all. Worried you're storing up trouble for yourself. How can I stand by and let you go out with a fellow who's only a ship passing in the night? A German, or as good as, from a country that caused a war where millions died—'

'He isn't a German, Dad, and he'd nothing to do with the war, it's not fair to say that!' Jinny's eyes were shining with feeling, her colour still high, yet she was trying to appear reasonable, trying to make her case. 'He's just a cake maker, here for a few months, and he's nice, he's friendly – why shouldn't we go to the theatre together? You talk as if he's my young man!'

'That's how things start,' Josh said doggedly. 'You go out with a fellow, he wants to see you again, and before you know it you're in love and all set to get your heart broken. I don't want that for you, Jinny!'

'But you don't want May to see Allan either,' Vi pointed out, as she brought across a tray of tea things. 'She's not going to get her heart broken with him, but you still don't want her to see him.'

'We're talking about Jinny,' Josh snapped. 'What she wants to do is risky and she knows it. Girls don't go out with men when they know there's no future in it, and there's no future in this except heartache. Why should I say I'm happy about it when I'm not?'

'I'm just going to the theatre with Viktor,' Jinny said in a low voice. 'That may be the end of it.' But she knew her heart didn't believe her, and neither did Josh.

'The thing is you don't want it to be,' Josh said, fixing her with his dark eyes so like her own. 'Look me in the face and tell me that's no' true.'

A silence fell as her family waited, and Jinny, lowering her own gaze, knew what she should say, knew what she wanted to say, opened her mouth to say it – and then closed it again. She couldn't say it.

'There you are,' Josh said with grim satisfaction. 'Pour the tea, Vi. I think I've made my point.'

'I'm still going to the theatre with Viktor,' Jinny said, clearing her throat. 'He wants to pay for us, anyway, so you needn't worry about complimentary tickets.'

'I wasn't going to.' Josh reached forward and took a biscuit from the plate May had set down. 'Let's consider this subject closed. For the time being.'

Later, at bedtime, Jinny's sisters tried to console her, but she said she didn't need consoling. She'd just go her own way as May had done and let Dad say what he liked. She knew the situation, knew what it would mean if she and Viktor did become close and he had to leave her, and would be prepared. It was her heart that was involved, after all – no one else need worry.

'Oh, Jinny,' May sighed. 'Maybe Dad's right. It might be wiser not to see him, eh?'

'Who wants to be wise? Anyway Viktor might not want to see me again after this next time, anyway.'

Somehow, no one thought that likely.

# Seventeen

The clash with her father had certainly spoiled Jenny's pleasure in looking forward to her theatre visit with Viktor. Perhaps she'd had her misgivings as soon as he'd suggested the Duchess, for it meant she'd had to mention it to her father, and the thought of Josh's likely views on her meeting with Viktor had been enough to cast a cloud over her excitement. The reality of hearing his actual views, however, had been even worse than she'd expected, and though she'd put on a good act when Viktor came over from the bakery to check their arrangements, she wasn't sure she could keep it going when they met for the play.

'All well?' Viktor had asked, grateful for finding her alone in the office. 'You have the tickets?'

'Oh, yes, I was lucky. I got a couple of stalls – all they had left.'

At least, as he stood close, she could take pleasure in remarking again on his fine features, his vivid blue eyes, his attention that was all on her, and feel that Dad couldn't spoil any of this, at least. Or, could he? He'd reminded her, as if she needed it, that these looks, this attention, would not always be close, for one day Viktor would have to go away.

'Now, you know the arrangement,' Viktor was saying softly. 'I'm going to pay for the tickets. Perhaps you could let me have them?'

'I'd like it to be my treat, Viktor. No arguments.'

'Jinny, it is not possible that you should treat me. I have an allowance from home and I have a salary here – it is best that I should pay. Come on, now!'

'This time, I'd like to pay.'

'There will be another time?' he asked quickly.

'If you'd like it.'

He smiled. 'I think you know the answer to that. Very well, then. I give in, for this time only. What time shall we meet on Thursday?'

'At seven o'clock? The play begins at half past.'

'Excellent.' He glanced at his watch. 'I'd better go before Ross finds me. I'm not supposed to be here.' His blue gaze held hers and he seemed to want to say more, but finally turned to the door.

'Till Thursday, then?'

'Till Thursday.'

For some time after he'd left, she sat at her desk staring into space. Only when Ross came in noisily, bringing with him a rush of cold air and wearing a heavy coat and hat brushed with rain, did she smile and put down her pen, as though she'd just been interrupted from hard work. She was acting a part again, of course; it seemed to be becoming a habit.

When she saw Viktor waiting for her outside the theatre, however, there was no need to act any part, for the great rush of feeling that consumed her then was genuine and natural, and though she hadn't experienced it before she knew it for what it was. As she stood looking at him before he looked at her, studying his straight shoulders, his height, his elegance in his dark coat and his hat set at an angle over his blond hair, all thoughts of her father's disapproval melted from her mind and she was filled with elation that this man was really waiting for her, that he really wanted to be with her. He might in fact return what she now recognized in herself for him, though she still didn't put that into words.

'Viktor?'

At the sound of his name, he turned, his face lighting up, and at once he was with her, making a pathway like an arrow through the crowd around him, smiling down at her as he touched his hat and took her arm.

'Jinny, you're here! Wonderful!'

'As though I wouldn't be! I've been looking forward to it all day.' She held up her bag. 'And I've got the tickets – let's go find our seats.'

Everything seemed so magical. Joining others searching for their stalls, looking up at the people in the boxes, the circle and the edge of the 'gods', sensing the atmosphere that went with the anticipation of a live performance that was not found going to a cinema.

Why don't we go to the theatre more often? Jinny found herself wondering. And be interested in it, like Dad? But at the thought of her father working somewhere behind the scenes her mind reared away and she glanced quickly at Viktor as they took off their coats and settled into their seats. Don't let me think of Dad, she pleaded wordlessly. Don't let him spoil this for me.

'Very good seats,' Viktor commented. 'I think we should enjoy this.'

'I'm sure we will. But do you know about Agatha Christie in Vienna?'

'Know about Agatha Christie? Of course we do! My mother has all her books in English and I've read them, in English and German. Such good plots! But this, of course, is a play. I don't know it at all.'

'No, I don't. But it has Hercule Poirot in it, so it should be like the books.'

'Here is the programme – we must study the characters.' Viktor hesitated a moment, then put a wrapped package into Jinny's hands. 'First, you must have a chocolate.'

'You've brought chocolates? Oh, Viktor, that's so kind!' As she read the name on the box, Jinny's eyes widened. 'And these are very special – the best – but so expensive! You shouldn't have spent so much!'

'They are to celebrate something special, Jinny.' Viktor's smile was radiant. 'Our first evening together. It means so much. And also—' He paused. 'I expect you can guess what else might matter to me.'

She thought, but only for an instant. 'That the customers liked your cakes? Viktor, of course they did! I knew they'd be a success.'

'I could only hope, but now I am so happy.' He lowered his voice. 'For those two things.'

'Shall we open them now, before the play begins?' asked Jinny, feeling almost dazed by his apparent pleasure in being with her. 'I can't wait to taste them.'

They spent a happy few moments deciding which ones to try first before the lights dimmed, the safety curtain rose and there they were, transported into the house of a famous physicist shortly to meet his end by foul play, as Hercule Poirot would discover. The spell Agatha Christie could cast so well was beginning its work.

# Eighteen

Absorbed as they were in following the plot, time passed quickly until suddenly it was the interval, the lights were coming on and people were stampeding for coffee, while Jinny and Viktor were blinking at each other and smiling.

'Enjoying it?' asked Jinny.

'I am; it's just the thing to relax with. But would you care to go for coffee?'

'Oh, it's such a scrum – let's just stay here and have another chocolate.'

They made their choices – caramel for Jinny and marzipan for Viktor. 'Of course, I am Viennese – we love marzipan,' he said, laughing.

'You are half Scottish, too,' Jinny remarked. 'Because of your mother.'

'That's true. Poor Mother.'

'Why do you say that?'

'Well, she will be missing me. I am an only child. "All she has", she sometimes says, though of course she has my father and they are very happy.'

'You're all alone? I've got two older sisters, May and Violet – we call her Vi. But my mother is dead.'

'Ah, I'm so sorry. That must have been a terrible loss for your family and your father.' Viktor's eyes had moved to the curtains drawn across the stage. 'Is he working here tonight? Behind the scenes somewhere? That must be strange for you, to think of him so close, yet not seen.'

Jinny was silent, bending her head away from Viktor, who, quick to sense a change in her, waited for a moment, hoping she would look at him.

When she did not, he took her hand. 'Is everything all right, Jinny?'

She wanted to say 'Oh, yes, of course' but, raising her dark eyes, said nothing.

'I don't want to pry,' he murmured, 'but I feel you are suddenly not happy. Please tell me if there is something troubling you – but only if you want to, that is understood.'

'I suppose I should tell you,' she said slowly. 'If – if we want to see each other again.'

'We do,' he said at once, and she felt his hand around hers – dry, firm and reassuring.

'Well, it's just that after Ma died, my dad came to depend on us – my sisters and me. We made him happy again, he said. But as we got older and, you know, wanted to go out with people, he got upset. He thought we shouldn't think of it, that home, that the four of us, must be enough. You can guess that there has been . . . trouble.'

'I can,' Viktor said strongly. 'I understand completely.

'I don't see how,' she said hopelessly. 'Men are always so free.'

'Jinny, I understand what you are telling me, because – because my mother is the same.'

Jinny's eyes on him had widened. 'Your mother is . . . like my father? I never would have imagined it.'

'Of course you wouldn't have, if you think all men are free. I've never been free since I grew up and wanted a life of my own. It's just because she loves me so much, of course, but whenever I wanted to go out with a girl – and there haven't been so many – my mother could not stand it. My father used to take my side, but she could never accept that there might be others in my life.'

'Yet she let you leave her to come here? That must have been very difficult.'

'It was my father's idea that I should come, and yes, it was difficult, but in the end, Mother gave in.' Viktor smiled. 'So, here I am. With you.'

'Seemingly, we're in the same boat,' Jinny said, trying to speak lightly. 'I can't get over it – that you should have my sort of problem.'

'Not when I'm here, Jinny. Here, I am free to ask you to go out with me.'

'You won't mind if you don't meet my dad? He doesn't want me to see you but I'm not going to give in to him.'

Jinny looked around at people returning to their seats – it was time for the second act of the play.

'But quick, before the bell goes, tell me: these girls you used to see back home . . . were any of them . . . are any of them . . . special to you?'

He laughed, delighted at her little show of jealousy. 'Not one, *liebchen*, not one!'

And then the bell did go; people hurried to take their seats, the lights went down, the curtains opened, and Jinny and Viktor held each other's hands tightly and sat as close as they could while still in two seats. Interested in the stage, of course, but so much more fascinated by each other.

After the play they stood in the frosty night air outside the theatre, buffeted by going home crowds, staying close.

'May I take you home?' Viktor asked. 'Do we catch a tram?'

'No, we can walk down from here to Lothian Road, then turn off for our flat in Fingal Street. You don't mind walking? It's a fine night.'

'I like walking.' Viktor took her arm. 'This cold air will do us good – reminds me a little of home, though it's much colder there, of course.'

'I expect you'll go skiing?'

'For holidays, yes. Many people enjoy skiing and skating.'

'Sometimes, in a hard winter, folk here like to skate, but I don't know anyone who's been skiing. No one can afford to go abroad.'

'I wish you could come with me some time.'

Jinny laughed. Another impossible wish, that was, on a par with visiting Viktor's father's cake shop in Vienna. Best just to think of what was wonderful here and now, which was walking arm in arm with Viktor, feeling him close and knowing he wanted to be with her.

They continued to walk, step for step, down the busy city road lined with people going home from cinemas, the theatre, pubs and late-night cafés, some looking highly respectable, others scuffling and shouting in hoarse voices Viktor couldn't understand.

'Neither can I,' Jinny told him. 'When they get to drinking the laddies aren't too clear – maybe just as well! But here's our turning. It's quiet here.'

Walking slowly, for their time together was running out, they walked past the shuttered shops and lighted upstairs windows of the quiet street, pausing at last outside Allan's shop to look up at the Hendries' flat.

'That's us,' said Jinny. 'As you can see, we're over a watchmaker's. The man who owns it is Allan Forth, our landlord and my sister May's admirer. In fact, I think they are in love.'

'And there has been trouble?' asked Viktor, turning to look down at her.

'Yes, with my dad. Allan's father was a very good friend of Dad's – you'd have thought Allan would be ideal, but no. Dad can't find a good word to say about him. He won't even let May mention his name. It makes us so angry.'

'It is, in fact, very sad. Your father is making himself very unhappy – he's really the one to suffer.'

'Yes, but he brings it on himself. Nothing we say can change him.'

'Just like my mother,' Viktor said heavily. 'This is all so familiar.'

By the light of the street lamp, Jinny studied his face, which had taken on a seriousness that contrasted with his earlier look of happy contentment. And there was, too, something in his eyes which seemed to show that in his thoughts he was far away from Fingal Street. Probably he was thinking of his mother, who had made him so unhappy when he'd wanted to see girls. So what would she make of him now, out with Jinny? Well, thank God she didn't know. As he'd said earlier, in Edinburgh, he was free, even if Jinny wasn't.

With a sudden movement he seemed to bring himself back to his surroundings and, gently taking Jinny's arm, moved her a little way down the street.

'Away from the lamp,' he whispered and kissed her swiftly and sweetly, releasing her so she could look into his face as he smoothed back her hair and then kissed her again. This time the kiss was long and passionate, but afterwards he stepped away, shaking his head.

'Jinny, what will you think of me? Kissing you like that the first time we've been out together? I really do apologise – please forgive me!'

'Viktor, there's nothing to forgive. I wanted you to kiss me. It was lovely.'

'But does your father come this way? How terrible it would be if he were to see us!'

'He won't be along yet, and what's so terrible about one kiss? Don't worry about it.' She drew him back into the lamp light. 'Viktor, I've had a grand evening. Thank you.'

'I should be thanking you – it was your treat.'

'You brought the chocolates!'

'Which reminds me—' He put the box into her hands. 'You must finish them. And now, I must say goodnight.'

'I wish you could have come in to meet my sisters. Maybe another time . . . when my father isn't due back.

'Another time . . . all I can think of is when we can meet again. Jinny, when will it be?'

'Sunday? Sunday afternoon?'

'When? Where?'

'The Scott Monument, two o'clock?'

'Jinny, you are an angel. I'll see you then, if not before. I may be bringing my cakes in on Saturday. But now, I'd better let you go.'

'You know the way to your uncle's? From Princes Street, go to the Queensferry Road, cross over the Dean Bridge and Belgrave Crescent is on your left.'

They hesitated, longing to kiss again, but only waved as they separated, Jinny to go inside the flat, Viktor to walk away fast.

Pray God he doesn't meet my dad, thought Jinny, for Josh would be sure to guess who a tall stranger would be, leaving Fingal Street at this hour. Oh, well, if he saw him, he saw him. They wouldn't speak, that was for sure.

'Had a good time?' asked her sisters.

'Oh, I can't tell you!' Jinny cried. But she told them, all the same. Or, at least, as much as she wanted them to hear.

# Nineteen

While Jinny was getting ready to meet Viktor on Sunday afternoon, and Vi was pulling on heavy shoes to go walking with friends, May was hovering around looking strangely anxious. As she had already told her sisters, today was the day, the time of the decision, when Allan 'had it out' with their father, telling him outright that they couldn't go on the way they were. No, Allan must be accepted, or . . . what? Well, that was the question.

'Supposing Dad just says no?' asked Vi, her head emerging from a heavy sweater. 'What's your bargaining counter?'

May sat down on Jinny's bed, her lovely face so troubled that Jinny gave her a sudden hug, at which May sniffed and looked as if she might cry.

'Allan says I must leave.'

'Leave?' Vi and Jinny cried in unison.

'Leave and go where?' asked Vi.

'Find somewhere to stay – a bedsitter, maybe – and then . . . get married.'

'Married?'

Her sisters stared at May, then at each other, and Vi gave a short laugh.

'Why are we so surprised? I'm sure getting wed is what Allan wants anyway.'

'But I don't,' May answered quickly. 'I mean, not yet. I need time to save up for the wedding – I want that to be paid for by me, not Allan.'

'Well, just keep the idea of leaving home as a threat,' Vi advised. 'You might find it works. Now, I've got to go.'

'Me, too,' said Jinny, putting on her outdoor coat. 'Oh, May, I'll be thinking of you.'

'Even when you're with your Viktor?' May managed a smile. 'Maybe, if Dad listens to Allan, he might be easier on you, Jinny.'

'I'm not counting on it. He's not been speaking much to me lately.'

Vi, who had left them, came back to put her head round the door. 'If you want Dad to listen to anybody you'll have to wake him up first. He's fallen asleep by the fire. Just thought I'd warn you.'

As soon as Jinny had left, hurrying with breathless anticipation to meet Viktor, and Vi was on her way to walk up Calton Hill, Allan, very pale and stern, arrived at the flat's outer door.

'Is he in?' he asked May, who had flown down to let him in.

'He's asleep over the Sunday paper.'

'I'll have to wake him up, then.'

'No, let me.'

Like two conspirators, they were breathing hard as they faced each other, their eyes fearful.

'Come on,' May whispered. 'Let's get it over with.'

A great Sunday silence seemed to hover over the living room as they approached Josh, asleep in his chair, his paper on the floor beside him and no sound coming from him except a slight whistle as he breathed in and out.

'So damned peaceful,' Allan muttered. 'You wouldn't think he could cause so much trouble.'

'Ssh!' said May as she bent to shake her father gently by the arm. 'Dad, wake up! Wake up, there's someone to see you.'

A strangled noise came from his throat and he stirred in his chair. Then his eyes opened. Dark, unknowing eyes stared into May's face, then recognition came.

'May? What's – what's wrong?'

'Dad, it's Allan. He's come to see you.'

With a cry, Josh sat up straight, his colour deepening to an angry red, his gaze going to Allan standing before him as May moved away.

'Allan Forth? What the hell is he doing here? I thought I said he wasn't to enter this house, my home!'

'Don't speak about him like that!' May cried. 'This is my home, too, and I invited him. We want to talk to you and you must listen.'

'I'll be damned if I'll listen to him!'

Rising to his feet, Josh looked down on Allan, who did not have his height but who was standing his ground, not looking away. As Josh stared at him with flashing eyes, Allan reached across and took May's hand.

'Mr Hendrie, do you want to lose your daughter?' he asked quietly.

'What do you mean, lose her? May will never leave me.'

'She will, if you don't accept me. We want to marry – not now, in the future – but if you won't give us your blessing, and continue to stop May even mentioning my name and forbid me in this house, which I actually own, May will leave you and we'll be wed. Do you want that to happen?'

Josh's flush had died away, leaving him looking white and suddenly much older. For a long moment he held Allan's gaze, then turned to May.

'May, this isn't true, is it? You'd never leave me like that? Leave the family? I can't believe it. I won't believe it!'

'Dad, have you ever thought what would have happened if Ma's father had refused to let her marry you? Wouldn't you have wanted her to come to you?' May's usually calm face was showing a passionate feeling that Josh did not recognize, that was surprising even to Allan.

'Wouldn't you?' she cried, moving closer to her father. 'But you were lucky – Granddad liked you, they were happy for you to marry Ma. All we're asking is that you'll do the same for us.'

'Mr Hendrie, you liked my father,' Allan said urgently. 'And I know you liked me – until I fell in love with May. You thought I'd take her away from you, but that's not true. If you'll accept me she'll still be a part of the family, and I'll be a part, too. Isn't that the way the world works? For God's sake, Mr Hendrie, let us be happy. Let yourself be happy. Please, give us a chance!'

A silence fell and deepened. Josh was standing like stone, his eyes on the floor, his hand sweeping his brow as the two young people watched, their hands clasped and hearts beating fast, and waited.

Finally, Josh sank back into his chair. 'I don't know,' he began. 'I don't know . . . if I can.'

'Can be happy?' asked May.

'Can . . . do what you want. It's too much – to lose you, May. I lost your mother, but I thought I had my girls.'

'You have, you have!' May said, her voice trembling. 'It's like Allan says, it's the way of the world. People grow up and marry, but they don't have to go away. The family grows bigger, that's all.'

'I'd have another father,' Allan murmured. 'You'd have a son. I promise I'd be a good one.'

'Oh, God, I don't know . . .' Josh shook his head. 'It's true, I did like your dad, Allan, and I did like you, but to be happy about you and my May . . . I haven't been able to face it. I still don't know if I can.'

'We won't be getting married for at least a year, Dad,' May told him. 'Everything will just go on as usual, till you get used to it.'

'Aye, well, all I can say is we'll have to see how things go. I'm no' promising I'll be happy. Don't ask that.'

'But you'll let Allan come here? You'll let me mention his name?'

Josh, struggling, got the words out. 'If it's what you want.'

May and Allan exchanged looks. There was no doubt that Josh wasn't happy – his tone could only be called grudging – yet it was more than they'd hoped for; it was truly a breakthrough. As Josh sank into his chair and asked if they'd have a cup of tea, it was all they could do not to embrace in front of him, but they were sensible, and knew that what they had was fragile and must be carefully handled. There would be time, later, to celebrate.

It was only when May was handing tea and cutting the sponge cake she often made on Sundays that she ventured, very cautiously, to mention Jinny.

'Dad, do you mind if I say . . . about Jinny—'

'What about her?'

'Well, she says you haven't been talking to her lately. I know you're not happy about the Austrian chap she's seeing, but couldn't you, you know, discuss it with her and try to understand?'

Josh set down his cup and fixed May with a dark, brooding stare. 'Try to understand? I understand, all right. She's just storing up trouble for herself, getting involved with a foreigner who's already said he's no' staying here. Where's the future in that?'

'Maybe she's not thinking of the future,' Allan suggested. 'Maybe she's just enjoying being with someone different. It's not often a girl here meets a guy from Vienna.'

'And when he goes home, she's quite happy then? When he says goodbye, it's been nice knowing you?' Josh gave a hard laugh. 'You've only to look at her, sitting around, all starry-eyed, to know she'll never be able to do that. She's going to be very unhappy, I promise you.'

'Well, maybe we should just try to support her,' May said desperately. 'People can't help falling in love, can they?'

'And maybe this Viennese fellow will want to stay here, anyway,' said Allan. 'Isn't his mother Scottish? She obviously decided to follow her heart and moved to her husband's country.'

'Women often follow their men,' Josh declared. 'Doesn't happen often the other way round. No, he'll away home and Jinny will be left to pick up the pieces. There'll be nothing we can do.'

'Except talk to her,' said May. 'Say you will, Dad.'

'All right, all right, I'll talk to her.' Josh took another slice of cake. 'As though it'll do any good.'

Walking round the battlements of Edinburgh Castle with Viktor, Jinny would have agreed with Josh that talking would not change how she felt. In some ways, being with Viktor had widened her horizons. In other ways, her universe had definitely shrunk to contain just one man and that was Viktor. No amount of talking could ever change that.

# Twenty

There were very few places to have tea on an Edinburgh Sunday, but Jinny and Viktor found a little café in Rose Street that was open and gratefully squeezed in to escape the dark and cold.

'None of your grand cakes here,' Jinny whispered to Viktor, 'but the scones look all right.'

'And Scottish scones are famous,' Viktor answered as a waitress brought a menu. 'Shall I order, then?'

'You could have toasted teacakes if you'd rather. Teacakes are another thing we're good at.'

But they settled for tea and scones and, until they came, took pleasure in studying each other's faces and talking about the castle, the first of the Edinburgh 'sights' on Jinny's list for Viktor to see.

'If only the days weren't so short at this time of year,' she sighed. 'And on Sundays there's nowhere to go in the evening.'

'At least the shop windows look wonderful, dressed for Christmas, even if the shops aren't actually open. Which reminds me . . .' Viktor paused. 'About Christmas – I meant to tell you earlier . . .'

Again, he halted, watching the waitress set down their tea things and a plate of fruit scones, after which they busied themselves spreading the scones with generous amounts of butter.

'Tell me what?' asked Jinny, pouring the tea.

'That I'll be going home for it. Christmas, that is.'

She set down the teapot, her dark eyes wide. 'Going home for Christmas? Why, you've only just come!'

'I know, and I had no plans to go back. It was arranged that my parents would come over and we'd have a Scottish Christmas and New Year – my mother's idea. My father was in a state about leaving his business with his assistants. But now it seems my mother's health has not been good and she doesn't want to make the trip, so I said I'd go home.' Viktor's eyes on Jinny were appealing. 'I'll only be away for the week – it's not long.'

'Oh, well, if your mother's not well of course you'll have to go.' Jinny ate a piece of her scone, keeping her gaze on her plate. 'I expect she'll be missing you anyway, won't she?'

'You're thinking of what I told you about her?'

'Well, you did make out she couldn't do without you, like my dad says about my sisters and me.'

'She agreed to my coming here, though. And it's natural to want family at Christmas. If she'd been fit we'd have all been together at my uncle's.'

'Yes, well, as you say, you'll only be gone a week.'

Viktor caught at Jinny's hand across the table. 'Why did I say it would not be long? It'll be a lifetime, to be away from you.'

She raised her head. 'You mean that?'

'You know I do!'

Happiness was restored and the café seemed filled with sunlight, even though outside the city remained gripped by winter, and as they drank more tea and took a second scone each, Viktor's Christmas departure seemed very far away.

Eventually, of course, they had to leave, and as they met the cold rush of air in the street Jinny, clinging to Viktor's arm, said she supposed she'd better go home.

'Oh, why?' cried Viktor. 'It's not late. You need not go yet.'

'I think maybe I'll go back and sweeten up Dad by not being late.'

'From what you've told me he's not likely to be sweetened unless you stop seeing me.'

'That's not going to happen. But come on, you can walk me home.'

'A little more time together – that's good.'

As they faced the bitter wind and made for the Lothian Road, Jinny looked up into Viktor's face. 'Mind if I ask you something? It's about your uncle.'

'Uncle John? Why has he entered your head?' Viktor laughed. 'What is it?'

'Well, I was wondering – have you told him we've been out together?'

Viktor hesitated for only a moment. 'No, I haven't.'

'But doesn't he wonder what you do? I mean, going to the theatre, for instance. Does he think you went on your own?'

'Well, he's out so much – to Rotary and so on, that he's hardly ever in when I go out, and so far he's never asked exactly what I do.'

'I suppose that's easier.'

'Yes, much easier than someone checking on you all the time.'

'But would he – you know – mind if he thought you were with me?'

'No, why should he?'

'I don't know.' Jinny walked in silence for a few moments. 'He might not think it's a good idea.'

'I don't see why. He's not like your father.'

'But you're only here for a short time; he might not want you to get involved.'

'Is that what you think, Jinny?'

'No! You know I couldn't think that. I don't let myself think of how long you'll be here.'

'Nor do I!'

Viktor stopped and drew her into his arms, holding her close and disregarding passersby. They began to kiss and continued kissing, strongly and passionately, over and over again.

'Don't let us spoil this,' Viktor whispered as they finally drew apart, catching their breath. 'All that matters is that we have found each other and are together now. Who knows what will happen in the future?'

But Jinny was too out of breath to answer, and too enchanted to consider anything but the present.

After a lingering farewell outside the flat in Fingal Street, Jinny was dreamily mounting the stairs only to find Allan Forth appearing above her with a smiling May in the background.

'Allan? What are you doing here?' asked Jinny.

He, too, was smiling. 'There's been a development. I'm allowed to come to the flat now. I'm off, but May will tell you all about it.'

'When I've said goodbye to you, dearest. Wait there, Jinny.'

Standing in wonder at the flat door, Jinny waited for her sister, who eventually came back, looking, Jinny told her, as though she was a cat who'd been drinking the cream.

'You should know – you look the same yourself.'

'Do I?' Jinny blushed. 'Oh, well, never mind, tell me what's been happening.'

'You know I told you what Allan was planning to say to Dad? Well, he said it, and it did the trick. As soon as Dad heard I'd leave and marry Allan straight off if he didn't turn reasonable, he more or less caved in. I asked him how he'd have felt if Granddad had refused to let him court Ma, and that brought it home to him as well – that he had to change. In the end he agreed to let Allan visit here. We're to have a long engagement but get married in the end, and that was that.' May flung her arms round Jinny. 'Oh, I'm so happy, Jinny – so relieved!'

'And I'm happy, too. For you.' But then Jinny drew back a little. 'How about me, then? Is Dad going to speak to me again? Am I allowed to go out with Viktor without thunder in the air?'

May's smile faded. 'I don't think Dad's happy about Viktor yet. He says you'll end up with a broken heart.'

'That's my business, May. He's no need to interfere!'

'I did get him to agree to talk to you, Jinny, so let's see how things go, eh? Vi's back – she's frying up some cold potatoes and bacon. We haven't had any tea yet.'

'Smells good,' Jinny said cheerfully as she and May entered the living room, and Vi, bouncing in from the cooker, grinned, while Josh looked up from a mystery novel he was reading but said nothing.

'Hello, Dad!' Jinny called.

'Dad,' warned May, as he returned to his book again.

'Hello, Jinny,' he replied at last. 'Been out with that German, then?'

'Austrian, Dad. Yes, we went round the castle and had some tea in Rose Street.'

As May began to set the table, Jinny sat down by the fire and held out her hands to the blaze. 'He's going home for Christmas. His mother's not well.'

'Oh, yes?'

Josh turned a page of his book and Jinny, glancing across at her sisters, sighed heavily and asked herself: if this was what Dad called talking, it wasn't exactly a breakthrough, was it? One step forward, how many back? But what did it matter? As she turned her eyes to the fire and watched the leaping flames, all she could see was Viktor's handsome face as he drew her into his arms, and all she could think of were his kisses. No cold treatment from her father could blank those things from her mind.

# Twenty-One

In the December weeks that followed, Jinny and Viktor met outside work as often as they could, though each had decided that they should play down their relationship at the bakery itself.

'Imagine the teasing!' Jinny had exclaimed to Viktor, without adding that she really didn't want folk such as Senga pointing the finger and delighting in thinking Jinny would be left high and dry when Viktor returned to Vienna. As though Senga wouldn't have changed places with her at any time! You only had to see the way her eyes followed Viktor, and to know how disappointed she'd been when Bob and Norah had been chosen to help him with the making and decorating of his cakes that had become so popular.

Jinny's idea, then, was to keep her affair with Viktor secret, hugging it to herself with special elation, while Viktor himself was relieved that his uncle need not know about his feelings for Jinny – at least for the time being. He might not object. On the other hand, he might inform his sister, and the last person Viktor wanted to be told was his mother. He would certainly not be telling her himself when he went home at Christmas, for what she didn't know couldn't hurt her. Whether or not she would have to know sometime was a question he kept at the back of his mind, just as Jinny kept the knowledge that he would one day return to Vienna at the back of hers.

Were they living in a fool's paradise? That was another question not to be asked, though when they were together they might well have considered they were in paradise anyhow. Other considerations could be put aside while they went to see films or plays, visited the sights on Jinny's list – museums, galleries, the Canongate, the Palace of Holyroodhouse – or walked in wintry landscapes outside Edinburgh, while Viktor put German names to the things they saw and Jinny practised her pronunciation.

What her father thought of the continuing relationship was plain enough, but he no longer spoke of it, saying very little at all, in fact, to Jinny. Although grieved by his attitude, she had trained herself to put up with it. Meanwhile, as time flew by, she and Viktor made the most of what they had, dreading farewell even for a short period.

'My uncle says with Christmas coming I must do some overtime.' Viktor sighed. 'Work with Bob and Norah so that they can be sure of supplying orders while I'm away. Seems everyone wants my *Sachertorten* for Christmas cakes here, though at home we usually have the *Stollen*. That's the marzipan fruit bread, you know.'

'Oh, don't let Mr Comrie make you do more hours!' Jinny cried. 'Time is slipping away so fast, soon you'll be away and I'll be on my own!'

'Why, I have been told there is staff party to look forward to. You'll be able to dance with Terry Brown and Ross and I'll be jealous thinking of it.'

'There'll only be an old gramophone for the dancing, and you are the only one I'd want to be dancing with, anyway.'

'Though Terry and Ross are very nice fellows, particularly Ross.'

'Yes, and Ross does know about us, you know, though he'd never tell anyone else.'

'As I say, he is a nice fellow.'

It was true that Ross knew about Jinny and Viktor, not just that they were seeing each other but that Jinny was very deeply into the relationship and unwilling to listen to any advice he would have liked to give her. In fact, he no longer gave her any, only smiled indulgently when he saw her looking particularly excited at the end of the day, when it was obvious she was looking forward to meeting Viktor.

Sometimes, catching that smile, Jinny felt bad that Ross seemed to have so little in his life compared to her. He had friends he played golf with, she knew, and he also did some charity work, raising funds for tenement children, but when he went home to the house he'd inherited from his late father there was no one there to greet him, no girlfriend for him to arrange to meet, have a meal with or take somewhere. At least, she'd never heard that anyone had taken the place in his life of the dead fiancée, and she was sure she would have been told.

Once, she'd asked him what his interests were, and he'd told her he liked working with his hands, as a change from getting the poor old brain to work in Accounts all day. Perhaps what he did would not be interesting to her, but he liked to make things in wood – small furniture, book cases, tables, and such.

'Why, I think that *is* interesting!' Jinny had cried.

But none of it made up for his being so much on his own in her eyes. None of it was to be compared with what she had, which was being with the person she loved and who loved her. For though she and Viktor had never actually declared their love for each other in words, their eyes said it for them. Certainly, only love could cause the pain she felt as she looked at the calendar every day and saw that the day was drawing nearer and nearer when he must leave for home, and she knew from Viktor's face that he was feeling the same.

Maybe they were foolish to feel so tragic about one week's separation, but then a week was a week, and time could stretch and seem like a year, if you were missing somebody.

# Twenty-Two

On the day before he left, which was 22 December, they agreed to have a farewell meal together, for Mr Comrie was to see Viktor off at the station, which meant they could not meet there to say goodbye.

'I didn't want him to come,' Viktor said wretchedly over their dinner, 'but he thought he was doing me a favour, driving me to the station, so what could I say?'

'Never mind. Everybody says it's awful, saying goodbye at the station.'

Jinny took a wrapped parcel from her bag. 'It's better here where I can give you this and you can take it back to put in your luggage.'

'Oh, Jinny, it isn't a present, is it? cried Viktor, turning the parcel in his hands. 'You shouldn't have been spending your money.'

'As though I wouldn't want to give you a present at Christmas!'

He smiled fondly. 'Well, as a matter of fact, I have something for you.'

He fumbled in his pocket as the waitress removed their plates and asked what they'd like next.

'Just coffee, I think,' said Jinny, adding in a low voice to Viktor, 'if you can bear it.'

He gave the order and when the girl had gone, put a very small package into Jinny's hands.

'Oh, Viktor!' Her eyes were dancing. 'May I open it now?'

'Strictly speaking, we should wait for Christmas Eve – that's when we open presents at home. But as we're not going to be together then . . . yes, let's open ours now.'

Viktor was the first to reveal his present, which was a fine history of Edinburgh, complete with illustrations, something he said he truly wanted and had been thinking of getting for himself, but would Jinny write in it for him? Here was his fountain pen – she could write something now.

'What shall I put?' she asked, taking the pen.

'With love to Viktor, from Jinny, Christmas, 1937.'

'With love?'

'With love.'

He leaned forward, his eyes tender, his hand seeking hers, but she was blushing and writing what he'd told her. 'With love to Viktor . . .'

'That's the first time that word has actually been used,' she remarked quietly.

'Though it's always been there, Jinny. That's a fact. Would you like me to say it again?'

'I think I would.'

'*Ich liebe dich*, I'll say, then. And you know what that means?'

'I love you.'

'There, now you've used the word, too.'

He sat back as the waitress appeared with their coffee and began to replace the Christmas wrapping paper around his book. 'Aren't you going to open my present?'

Still flushed, she waited for the waitress to go, then looked down at the small, neat package he had given her. 'I'm too excited.'

'Ah, but I want to know what you think. Please . . . open it.'

Inside the wrapping was a small box and inside the box was a brooch on a velvet pad. A beautiful brooch, showing white, star-shaped flowers, so exquisitely fashioned that Jinny was mesmerized, already thinking it the most wonderful thing she'd ever be given.

'Viktor, what is it?' she whispered. 'What's the flower?'

'Why, the Edelweiss, of course! Our national flower, as well as Switzerland's and maybe Hungary's. It's a mountain flower, anyway.'

'But it's so beautiful, Viktor! Where did you find it – I mean, an Austrian brooch in Edinburgh?'

'You'll never guess where I got it, never. But it was somewhere very well known to you.'

'Well known to me? Where? I can't think! Tell me, Viktor, tell me!'

'What is next door to where you live, Jinny? What sort of shop?'

'You mean . . . Allan's shop?' She was shaking her head in wonder. 'I can't believe that Allan had a brooch like this – it'd be such a coincidence!'

'No, I went there secretly and asked him if he could find one for me, and he said he'd do some asking around, which he did and was successful. A jeweller in Glasgow specializes in continental jewellery and had just what I wanted. That's how I got it.'

As Jinny continued to look astonished, Viktor gently took the brooch from its box and pinned it to her dress. 'I'd better say it's not what you could call valuable,' he said quickly. 'Only costume jewellery, but well made and something to remind you of me.'

'Viktor, I'll treasure it all my life.'

'Just as I'll treasure my book. Now, we'd better drink this coffee before it gets cold.'

When they had left the restaurant and were making their way to Fingal Street, Viktor told Jinny more about the Edelweiss – how the Emperor Franz Josef had ordered it to be the insignia of the Austrian/Hungarian mountain troops, and how young men had once climbed mountains to find the flower for their sweethearts, the higher the mountain the better for their reputation.

'And I only bought it for you from a shop,' Viktor finished, laughing. 'I must climb a mountain or two to find the real thing when I get home.'

'Oh, don't!' Jinny sighed. 'You know how much your brooch will always mean to me, and I can't bear to think of you going home.'

'Think about the New Year – that's what I'm doing. Only a day or two later, I'll be back.'

They stopped to kiss and hold each other close before walking on, finally passing the closed door of Allan's shop next to the flat and pausing again to look in his window, in which he only showed clocks.

'So Allan has met you,' said Jinny. 'He must have liked you – and you must have liked him, mustn't you?'

'A very pleasant man, I thought he was, kind and helpful.'

'He never said a word about you to me.'

'I told him the brooch was to be a surprise and he promised not to tell you.'

'I think I'll keep it a secret until Christmas, then I'll wear it and thank Allan for helping you find it.'

'And I'll keep my book a secret until Christmas Eve, and when I read it I'll think of you.'

But will you say who gave it to you? Jinny wanted to ask, though she didn't put the question into words. There must be nothing to cause worry to either of them on this last evening before their separation, and as she went quietly into Viktor's arms for a long, passionate farewell, she put everything from her mind except their love.

Only her sisters were at home when she finally let herself into the flat, which was a relief – no Dad to face with Viktor's kisses fresh on her lips, only sympathetic looks from May and Vi.

'Poor Jinny,' murmured May. 'Does it seem a long time till New Year?'

'It had better be,' laughed Vi. 'I haven't done my Christmas shopping yet.'

'I suppose it's only a week – I shouldn't be making such a fuss.' Having removed her brooch from her dress and put it into her bag while on the stairs, Jinny now took comfort that it was safely there and asked whether Dad was rather late back.

'Yes, they're preparing for the pantomime. The theatre's closed at the minute – it reopens on Boxing Day.'

'What's the show this year? Are we going?'

'You bet,' Vi answered. 'It's *Aladdin* – my favourite. And Dad's getting us tickets.'

'One for Allan, too,' said May happily. 'Who'd have thought it?'

'I'm so pleased for you,' Jinny murmured, which was true, but already her thoughts had moved from her home to the man who was returning to his home the following day, and she was wondering, just to cheer herself up, if in the future he and she might have a home together. Well, why not? There was no harm in dreaming.

# Twenty-Three

How the time dragged for Jinny after Viktor's departure! It didn't matter that she had plenty to do at work before the holiday, and of course, the staff party to think about, she still felt that the days were empty and her life was just marking time until she saw Viktor again.

The staff party, always held on Christmas Eve in the Princes Street café after its early closing, was not something she expected to enjoy; it was more just a duty to get through, though Ross did try to make it as pleasant as possible. But even he caused a surprise, appearing with an attractive young woman whose burnished copper hair was the same colour as his own, leading to guesses that she was his sister, though nobody had heard that he had one. In fact, she turned out to be his cousin from London, who was staying with her parents at Ross's home for Christmas.

'Meet my cousin, Lorna,' he told Jinny. 'My uncle and aunt are having a quiet evening but Lorna has bravely agreed to accompany me. Lorna, this is Jinny, my valued assistant.'

They shook hands and murmured politely, Jinny still taken aback to see Ross escorting a pretty girl, for this was a first for him, surely? She'd always thought of him on his own, not willing to replace his lost love, and maybe she should be glad to find him getting over his loss at last. If that was the case, for Lorna was his cousin, not a girlfriend. Cousins, though, were not quite the same as sisters.

'It's lovely to meet everyone,' Lorna was saying, her green eyes moving round the crowded café where Comrie's staff members were enjoying drinks, sandwiches and mince pies, or endeavouring to dance to a gramophone in very limited space, while Mr Comrie and Mr Whyte looked on, smiling and at the same time checking that none of the bakers drank too much.

'And to be in Scotland,' Lorna was continuing. 'Because I'm really a Scot myself – it's just my father's business took him to London.'

'Our loss,' said Ross. 'But it's nice you're here now.'

He does seem fond of her, thought Jinny, her feelings strangely mixed on the issue, but then Terry Brown arrived to ask Lorna if she'd like to risk a turn on the floor, and as she accepted and they moved away, Jinny was the focus of Ross's kind gaze again.

'Getting through it?' he asked softly. 'I know how you're feeling.'

'I'm being silly about it. He'll only be gone for a few days.'

'Days, or years?' He laughed a little and, looking at the couples on the makeshift dance floor, seemed about to ask Jinny if they shouldn't join them, when Norah, wonderfully smart in a blue taffeta dress and jacket, appeared at his side.

'Come on, Ross, this won't do. Let's see you on the floor for the quickstep. and no arguing!'

'Who's arguing?' asked Ross, holding up his hands in surrender, and as he was led away Jinny laughed, thinking she would go for another drink and maybe try a mince pie, when she felt a touch on her arm and turned to find Senga at her side.

'Think she's had too much blackcurrant cordial?' she asked, nodding towards Norah.

'She's just in the party spirit,' Jinny replied coolly, noting that Senga, though looking very young, could still seem confident, even arrogant, her dark brown eyes never warm as brown eyes could be, and her mouth a straight, expressionless line.

'No' like you, then, Jinny,' she said now. 'What's the matter? Missing your young man?'

'I don't know what you're talking about!'

'Oh, come on – everybody at Comrie's knows there's something going on with you and Viktor Linden.'

Stunned, Jinny had no answer. What Senga was saying couldn't be true, could it? They'd been so careful. She realized Senga was watching her and wanted to answer her but, before she could think of what to say, Senga had begun to laugh.

'You should see all the chaps knocking each other in the ribs when you come over on wages day and try no' to look at Viktor and he tries no' to look at you! And even Norah and Trixie have to stop themselves from smiling. Why all the secrecy, anyway? What've you got to hide?'

'Nothing,' Jinny answered huskily. 'It's just that . . . we don't want to go broadcasting our feelings to everybody.'

'To Mr Comrie, more like. He's about the only one who doesn't know already.'

'Why should we worry about him?' Jinny cried, trying not to let Senga see she'd hit a nerve.

'Well, there's sure to be trouble when the time comes for Viktor to go home, eh? And he won't want trouble with his nephew.' Senga was silent for a moment as the record playing for the dancing came to an end and couples began to return from the floor. Finally, she gave Jinny a long, hard look.

'You may think I envy you, Jinny, but it isn't true. I wouldn't want to be mixed up with a foreigner, especially one who's a German, or as good as. I mean, what'll you do if there's a war?'

'Why should there be a war, Senga? And Viktor isn't a German – why don't folk believe that?'

'I said as good as.' Senga, seeing Terry approach, was smiling. 'You watch which side he'll be on if we go to war, then you'll know what he is.'

# Twenty-Four

'Hello there, you lovely ladies!' Terry had taken out a handkerchief and mopped his brow. 'Why aren't you dancing?'

'We weren't asked!' Senga replied smartly. 'You were too busy dancing with Mr MacBain's cousin.'

'What a looker, eh? None o' my cousins look like her. But come on, let's all go for another drink – my treat, eh?'

'That's rich, seeing as they're provided by Mr Comrie.' Senga laughed. 'You coming with us, Jinny?'

'No thanks, not yet. Just want to say goodbye to Ross.'

When she'd found Ross, now back with Lorna, Jinny said she had a lot to do back at home and she'd better be going.

'Oh, what a shame!' cried Lorna. 'But I suppose it is Christmas Eve – you'll be busy.'

'I've got the car; may I give you a lift home?' asked Ross. 'Lorna, you stay on and I'll come back for you.'

'No, no, thanks all the same, Ross.' Jinny was very earnest. 'I want to walk for a bit; I've got a headache coming on.'

Shaking hands with Lorna, she wished her and Ross a merry Christmas, said she'd just say thanks to Mr Comrie and make her other goodbyes.

'See you after Boxing Day, Ross!'

'After Boxing Day, Jinny. Have a lovely holiday with the family.'

Well, perhaps she would – she'd always enjoyed Christmas with her family before, and there'd be presents to exchange and the showing of her brooch next morning. Much depended on how Dad was, of course, and that remained to be seen. In the meantime, when she'd made all her goodbyes at the party, it was grand to be out in the fresh night air and to be on her own, seeing only strangers in the streets and not thinking of Senga's words, only of Viktor.

But how pleasant her home looked, she thought as she went into the living room. How Christmassy! Clearly her sisters had been busy while she was out, putting up balloons and paper chains, and with the fire crackling, her mother's old glass decorations and the Woolworth's tinsel glittering on their little tree, all was as cheerful as a Christmas card. May was setting out her mince pies on the table while Josh was lying back in his chair, looking relaxed, and Vi, sorting about in the Christmas box, was seeking the Christmas tree fairy.

'Got her!' she called, standing up with the rather battered little celluloid doll in her fingers. 'You're just in time to put her on the top, Jinny, though I reckon she's about ready to retire. Might get a new one next year.'

'Shame!' cried May. 'We've always had that fairy; she's a tradition.'

'That's right,' agreed Jinny. 'She's not ready for her pension yet.'

'Put her up, then!' Josh ordered, and Jinny obediently fastened the doll to the top of the tree then stepped back with her family to admire the result.

'Looks lovely,' she commented. 'You've done a good job, Vi. In fact, you both have. The whole place is transformed!'

Vi tossed back her dark hair and shrugged. 'Just makes me think how much we have. I mean, when you consider how many bairns across this city will be lucky if they get anything to eat at Christmas, never mind presents and a tree.'

There was a short silence, then Josh said, rising from his chair, 'You're no' the only one remembering them, Vi. A percentage of the Boxing Day takings from the panto is going to a children's charity.'

'We do care,' added May. 'We give what we can.'

I should give more, thought Jinny, and be like Ross, not just think of myself and Viktor.

'We need to change the system,' said Vi. 'It's fine giving to charity; the point is no one should need it.'

'Agreed,' said Josh. 'But for now it's Christmas Eve. Can we have our mince pies and a cup of tea?'

'It's all ready,' said May with some relief. 'Jinny, we never asked you – how was the party? Did you have a good time?'

'It was the same as usual. Yes, I suppose we had a good time but I missed having a mince pie – yours look nice.'

'Help yourself, and merry Christmas, eh? Merry Christmas, Dad, merry Christmas, Vi!'

'Merry Christmas!' they called back and, as May passed the cups, Jinny whispered in her ear, 'And tomorrow you'll have Allan here for Christmas dinner – think of that.'

'Thanks to Dad,' May whispered back happily, and Jinny's eyes moved to meet her father's. Dark eyes looked into dark eyes until, hardly daring to venture it, Jinny smiled – and after a long moment of suspense, Josh smiled back.

Better not spoil things by saying anything, thought Jinny, but it was a start, eh? A hope for reconciliation?

# Twenty-Five

Christmas certainly made a difference to Jinny's spirits, though when alone all her longing for Viktor rushed back to consume her, and the time till his return seemed, as Ross had joked, to be years, not days.

Still, it had been sweet to see Allan arriving on Christmas Day with his bottle of wine and box of chocolates, his eyes only for May, yet making a valiant effort to greet Josh as though there was nothing to worry about. And the good news was that Josh responded pretty well – not exactly with warmth, but then not with coldness, either.

The girls flew about preparing the dinner with May, the expert, in charge of the crackling on the roast pork while Vi and Jinny prepared the vegetables and put on the pudding to steam away, leaving the two men to sit by the fire and chat. Which, of course, annoyed Vi, who declared such a division of labour, always weighted against women, to be ridiculous.

'Oh, don't say anything!' whispered May. 'There's no point.'

'If you keep on saying so there certainly isn't!' cried Vi.

But Jinny wasn't getting involved. She'd taken a break to show Allan she was wearing the brooch he'd found, and ask in a whisper what he'd thought of Viktor.

'Oh, I thought him a very nice young man! A bit foreign in style, you know, but so polite and so good looking!'

'He was really pleased you'd found this brooch for me, Allan. Everyone thinks it's beautiful. Even Dad.'

'You liked it, Mr Hendrie?'

'Liked what?'

'Jinny's Edelweiss brooch?'

'Oh – yes. Very nice.' Josh's tone was non-commital.

Vi called across, 'Come on, Dad, you were impressed! We all were!'

'I said it was nice – what more do you want? Now, how about joining in the carols on the wireless?'

Two steps forward, one step back, that's the progress with Dad, thought Jinny. But at least there had been those steps forward for May and Allan, and there had been that smile for her last night. How would it be if one day she saw Viktor with her family, like Allan today? So much was against their love it was hard to picture him in her home, but why shouldn't it happen? She determined fiercely that it should – especially as, on a day like this, any idea of war seemed very far away.

Boxing Day brought the panto, and how they all enjoyed that! More than enjoyed it, really. Rather, they were grateful for the way they could give themselves up to a world that didn't exist, find a true escape from all their worries while watching larger-than-life characters weaving through an impossible story, singing, dancing and finding bliss in the grand transformation scene that the sisters especially admired. Their father, after all, was working away behind the scenes on that, and if there'd been any justice, would have been brought on for the line-up for the applause at the end. Still, he enjoyed his work and always said that that was his reward.

'You have to admire him,' Allan had remarked when they were all together in the interval. 'He's a very clever and resourceful chap.'

'Nice of you to say that,' said May.

'Well, I mean it. I do admire him and still remember that train he put on for Arnold Ridley's *Ghost Train* play. You said he and the stage director had worked together on that, but it was your dad who had to create the effect.'

So lovely for May that such a nice fellow as Allan would be coming into the family, Jinny was thinking, but couldn't help feeling a stab of envy – until she decided again that one day, yes, she would see Viktor in her home, accepted by her father, and joining in all that her family did, being a part of their lives.

Even going to the panto? Her lips curved in a smile. She couldn't imagine what he'd make of something so peculiar to her own country. Whatever would he think of Widow Twankey in *Aladdin* being played by a man? And of Aladdin himself played by a woman – the principal boy, of course, dressed in the shortest costume ever, to display her splendid legs? And then there'd be the slapstick and the jokes, and the singing with the audience joining in, and then the wonderful ending, when everyone was set to live happily ever after. Why shouldn't he enjoy it all?

One day, she decided, she would take him along to see a pantomime, and it would be just one more strand for him to learn about and enjoy, as she would learn German and all the things he would teach her about Vienna in their future life together.

A happy daze seemed to occupy her then, and she had to concentrate hard to return to her seat for the rest of the performance. Already, in her mind, she was seeing Viktor arriving at the station, stepping off the train and looking for her, and they were meeting at last, holding, touching, their eyes filled with delight – had it not really happened, then?

Not then, but only eight days later, when she'd taken an extra day's holiday, all that she'd dreamed came true. She really was on a Waverley Station platform, seeing Viktor's train come steaming in from London. She really did see his handsome face at one of the doors, his far-sighted blue eyes searching, finding, smiling – and then he opened the door and hurtled out with his cases, dropping them as she ran to him and they were in each other's arms.

'Oh, Jinny, *liebchen*!' he was murmuring against her face. 'It's been so long! So long without you! Wasn't it long for you?'

'Never ending, never ending! But you're back now and I'm so happy!'

At last, their mouths were able to meet in a first ecstatic homecoming kiss that seemed as though it would never end, when a voice sharp as a shot close by made them made them spring apart, their faces stricken.

The voice was Mr Comrie's.

# Twenty-Six

The bakery owner's face was scarlet, his round eyes outraged as his gaze went from Viktor to Jinny and back to Viktor.

'What's the meaning of this?' he asked, oblivious of the flow of passengers from the London train hurrying around the tableau of their three standing figures.

'I come to the station, Viktor, to give you a lift home, and what do I find? My nephew kissing one of my own employees, a young woman whose welfare I'm responsible for, as I am for all who work for me!'

'Uncle, I didn't know you were coming to meet me,' Viktor interrupted. 'I didn't expect you to come.'

'That's obvious! But I knew which train you were likely to get, and I thought I'd do you a favour and take you home quickly as you'd be tired. And all I see is you and Miss Hendrie, behaving in a way that shows me there's been something going on between the two of you behind my back for who knows how long?'

Taking off his hat, Mr Comrie mopped his brow with his hand then, replacing the hat, pointed to Viktor's cases. 'Pick those up, Viktor, and come home with me – you as well, Jinny – I want the truth from both of you about what's been going on and what you've got to say for yourselves. What your mother's going to say, Viktor, is another matter.'

'My mother?' cried Viktor, stricken. 'Uncle, there's no need to bring her into this!'

'We'll discuss that when we're out of this public place, if you don't mind. Come away now, the pair of you – the car's parked nearby.'

Following Mr Comrie's plump figure, Jinny walked by Viktor's side without any conscious feeling of putting one foot in front of the other. To be plunged from delight to the fear of unknown consequences was almost too much to bear, and even Viktor, she felt, could not help her now, though when she looked at him he smiled in encouragement. As though he could make things better! There was too much at stake. At that very moment she might be facing the sack – 'not a suitable person for his workforce', Mr Comrie might say. And as for Viktor, he might be made to go home. She caught her breath, thinking of it, seeing the wonderful feeling they shared as a glistening bubble rising away from them, waiting for Mr Comrie's stick to burst it.

In the car, Viktor was made to sit next his uncle at the front while Jinny sat at the back, and for the drive to Mr Comrie's house, in an elegant terrace off the Dean Bridge, no one spoke, the atmosphere carrying so much tension that the trip for Jinny was an ordeal. At one time, she knew, she would have been fascinated to see where Mr Comrie lived because that was where Viktor lived, but now she felt so numb with apprehension that all she wanted was to learn what was going to happen so she could somehow face it.

Opening his front door, Mr Comrie ushered the young people into a handsome hallway and, as Viktor set down his cases and caught Jinny's hand in a strong squeeze, a middle-aged woman wearing a dark dress and her grey hair in a bun came forward.

'There you are, Mr Comrie!' she cried, though her eyes were on Jinny. 'And Mr Viktor! Did you have a good time in Vienna, then? How was your ma? And your father?'

'Not too bad, thank you, Mrs Orchard, and I had a very good time—' Viktor was beginning, when Mr Comrie interrupted to say she would hear all the news later.

'For now, Mrs Orchard, we'd like some tea in my study, please. I have some things to discuss with Miss Hendrie here from Accounts. Jinny, this is my housekeeper, Mrs Orchard.'

After exchanging polite greetings, Jinny, followed by Viktor, was shown into a large, high-ceilinged room furnished with shelves of books, a mahogany desk and comfortable chairs, at which Mr Comrie pointed. 'Take a seat, please. Tea won't be long. Then we can talk.'

# Twenty-Seven

Silence fell. Jinny, glancing at Viktor for possible comfort, thought he seemed calm as he sat in his armchair, but when he met her gaze she saw in his eyes the same sort of anxiety that he must see in hers. He smiled, and his smile was as encouraging as before, but though she tried she couldn't manage to smile back. For this was no time for smiling.

She'd never before felt so ill at ease, so afraid for the future, which was now so much in the power of another person. Could she really lose her job for kissing a man on a station platform? A man she loved? Circumstances alter cases, it was said, and it seemed to her quite possible that in this case Mr Comrie would consider himself within his rights to give her the sack.

'Tea, Mr Comrie,' Mrs Orchard announced, entering with a loaded tray. 'And I've brought some of my shortbread, Mr Viktor, as I know you like it, eh?'

'I do, Mrs Orchard. Scotch shortbread is not served in Vienna, but when I've learned to make it perhaps it will be.'

'That'd be grand. Shall I leave it to you to pour, Miss Hendrie?'

It was the last thing Jinny wanted to do, but as Mrs Orchard withdrew she poured the tea with a shaking hand and passed the cups. Only Viktor ate some shortbread, which he said he should to please the housekeeper, and after the tea was drunk Mr Comrie put the tray on to a side table and sat down to face his nephew.

'Now, Viktor, you can tell me how long this affair has been going on and who knows about it?'

'It's not an affair, Uncle.'

'Whatever you care to call it, then. I say again, how long has it been going on, and who knows about it?'

Viktor sighed and moved uneasily in his chair. He looked across at Jinny, who was winding her fingers together, and whose dark eyes were fixed on him.

'How long has it been going on?' Viktor shook his head. 'I suppose since we first met.'

'First met?' echoed Mr Comrie. 'You mean, as soon as you saw Jinny you decided to make a play for her?'

'A play?'

'Oh, don't pretend to misunderstand me, Viktor. You know what I'm talking about, and I want to make it plain that I blame you for this whole thing. Jinny would never have thought of getting involved with you if you hadn't swept her off her feet.'

'That's not true, Mr Comrie!' Jinny cried, stung into finding her voice. 'We were both attracted from the beginning and before we knew what was happening, we were in love. Viktor never swept me off my feet. Our love just happened.'

Mr Comrie stared, then shook his head. 'If that's true, the situation is worse than I thought. The two of you must have been making eyes at each other at work, at my bakery, no doubt with everyone looking on and enjoying it.'

'No, never!' cried Viktor, his face a mask of anger. 'It was never like that, Uncle! How could you think that of us? No one knows, no one saw. We kept it secret, is that not so, Jinny?'

As he turned indignant blue eyes on Jinny, her own gaze fell. Of course, he hadn't been at the staff party so he didn't know what Senga had told her about the laughing and tittering that had gone on behind his back and hers, and she'd had no chance to tell him. But what could she say now? Mr Comrie's gaze was upon her, and with a sinking heart she realized he had correctly guessed the truth of the matter.

'Well, Jinny?' he asked impatiently. 'Do people know, or do they not?'

'They don't know,' she said after a pause, deciding it was better not to mention Ross's name. 'But I think some have guessed.'

'Guessed?' asked Viktor. 'Who says they have guessed?'

'Never mind,' his uncle snapped. 'It's plain to me that you've become the object of gossip – my own nephew who I had such hopes for! Well, it's got to stop – I won't have it. I'll phone your mother this evening, Viktor, and as you know what she'll say, I think you should arrange to go home as soon as possible. As for you, Jinny, your best plan is to forget this affair ever happened. It was never going to work out; you're both from different countries, you have no future together and that's all there is to it.'

'And did my mother's love for my father not work out?' Viktor asked quietly. 'They were from different countries and they've been happy together for years.'

Mr Comrie hesitated. He put his hand to his brow, and for a moment or two looked away from his nephew's level gaze.

'That was different,' he said at last. 'Your mother was willing to go to your father's country. What if Jinny doesn't want to? What if her father doesn't want it, either? I don't suppose he's happy about your seeing Viktor anyway, is he, Jinny?'

'He doesn't know Viktor.' Jinny suddenly turned a passionate dark gaze on her employer. 'But I do, Mr Comrie, and all I can say is that I want to be with him, wherever he is!'

'Oh, Jinny,' Viktor murmured. 'Jinny . . .'

But Mr Comrie was holding his head and almost groaning. 'God, what a mess, what a mess! I don't know what to say, I really don't. The thing is you've given yourselves no time. These things happen, they don't always last, and with you two – for heaven's sake, consider the difficulties! You don't even know which country you'd want to be in!'

'If you'll give us some time, Uncle, we can work something out,' Viktor said desperately. 'Let me stay until November, when I'm due to leave, and if we still feel the same—'

'What? What then?'

'Well . . .' Viktor's eyes went to Jinny, who was standing with her head down, her hands clasped together, looking suddenly so young, so vulnerable that he stretched out his hand to her as though his touch would give her strength. But she didn't take it, perhaps didn't see it, and he dropped it to his side.

'Then we make decisions,' he said in a low voice.

'Decisions,' Mr Comrie repeated. 'But have you forgotten your mother, Viktor? She will be very upset, very upset indeed about all this. She'll want you back home, and you should go.'

'I know what she wants, and I've no intention of doing it,' Viktor said with sudden firmness. 'I'm not going home to stay under her eye as though I were a child. If you won't keep me on here, Uncle, I can find a job elsewhere. I believe that there are other firms interested in what I can do.'

'Other firms? What other firms?'

With a slight shrug, Viktor mentioned two well-known names, at which his uncle became agitated. 'No, no, Viktor, that won't do! Your Viennese cakes belong with Comrie's! It was my idea to bring you over, and I've been the one to encourage and promote them. To make them elsewhere would be utterly disloyal!'

'You'd like me to stay on with you, then?'

'Yes. Yes, I would. It's only fair to me that you should!'

'So what about my mother, wanting me back home?'

Mr Comrie hesitated. 'I'll – I'll leave telling her for the moment. Maybe you're right – she needn't know the situation yet. It would only upset her.'

'You'll give us time, then, to make sure we know how we feel?'

'Until you are due to go home. And then, as you say, you make your decisions.' For some moments, Mr Comrie stared at his nephew. 'At least you are being sensible, Viktor. But you must promise me that you will keep your feelings to yourselves when you're at work. There must be no more scenes like the one at the station.'

'That was just a welcome home, Uncle. At work things have always been different, anyway.'

'Very well. There's just one more thing, and this is for you, Jinny. You say your father hasn't met Viktor. I think he should meet him as soon as possible. In my opinion, he has that right.'

'He has,' Jinny said bravely. 'It's whether he'll agree to it is the point.'

'Well, do what you can.' Mr Comrie heaved a great sigh. 'Now, I think we should get you home. What a day this has turned out to be!'

Viktor moved to stand next to Jinny. 'Thank you, Uncle. I'm glad we've made things clear. I'll take Jinny home – you needn't drive us.' His glance on her was tender. 'We'll take the tram.'

# Twenty-Eight

When they had settled together on the wooden seating of the Sunday tram that finally appeared, Viktor made Jinny turn her face to his and took her hand.

'You were very quiet back there,' he whispered, 'letting me do the talking.'

Her dark eyes were steady. 'Except when I told your uncle . . . what I did tell him.'

'That you'd be glad to be with me wherever I went?' Viktor pressed her hand hard. 'That meant a lot to me.'

'You knew it, anyway.'

'You put it into words.'

'And words are important.'

'*Liebchen*, what are you meaning? I haven't been saying the right things? Did I not say "*Ich liebe dich*"?'

She looked down at his fingers clasping hers. 'You did, and I know the translation. But what did you mean when you told your uncle that if we still felt the same after a certain time, we'd make decisions?'

Viktor gazed around the tram, which was only half empty yet still showed enough pairs of eyes and ears for him to look back at Jinny with some concern. 'Let us wait for our stop. This is not the place to talk, I think.'

'It's not,' she agreed, but withdrew her hand from his so that he would not feel it trembling.

It was better in the darkness of the street, when they'd alighted and could walk together without fear of being overheard, when there was just the two of them ready to face momentous things.

'What did I mean?' Viktor asked. 'It was what I had to say. That if we still felt the same about each other, we'd decide to be together.'

'You think we might not feel the same?'

'No! No, Jinny, of course not. I said that to please my uncle; I knew it was what he wanted to hear. That we were prepared to be reasonable.' He looked anxiously into her face. 'You understand my reasons, Jinny?'

'Oh, yes, yes, I do! But, you see, we've never talked about the future, have we?'

'You mean I have never put anything into words? I suppose that is true.'

'But why not, Viktor? Why not put things into words?'

'Because—'

He drew her to a halt, and took her gently into his arms. 'Because I suppose I was thinking that you are still so young, Jinny. I thought again today how young you seemed, how vulnerable, and that's what's always been in my mind.'

'I'm not young, Viktor! I mean, not too young. You're only a few years older than me, anyway, so what are you talking about?'

'Those years matter, Jinny. They've made me feel responsible for what I'm asking of you and I used to wonder sometimes if it was too much. I mean, expecting you to move into my life, giving up what you have here. I wanted you to be sure.'

'Well, now you know I am. I've never been so sure of anything before. I agree, we had to let your uncle think we needed time, but it's just like I said; I want to be with you, wherever you are.'

'But maybe it's still right, *liebchen*, to take this time my uncle is giving us. We'll take it and be happy. We will feel the same at the end of it, but we'll have proved to my uncle that we're right to make a life together.'

'So it's right in every way to take the time,' she whispered. 'I feel better now that we've decided what to do.'

'And maybe my uncle has done us a favour.' Viktor smiled. 'But let's not talk any more. Just let me kiss you.'

'In the street?' she asked teasingly. 'What will your uncle say?'

'The street is dark and there is no one to see us. But if you do not wish it—'

He was laughing, and so was she. They both knew what they both wished, and kissed long and passionately, time scarcely seeming to exist, except that they did eventually have to part and continue on their way to Fingal Street.

Here at last was the Hendries' flat; here were its windows that drew their gaze, as though they might see Jinny's father looking down. Of course, he wouldn't be, he'd be at the theatre, where another performance of the pantomime would be about to begin, and yet they felt his presence.

'Somehow I have to persuade Dad to meet you,' Jinny whispered. 'And he is very difficult to persuade.'

'Maybe I should be a surprise? One evening you should just bring me in and see what he says.'

'He's always at work in the evenings.'

'A Sunday, then. A Sunday afternoon?'

'We could try it, but there's no knowing how he'd take it.'

'I say we do try it. Next Sunday.'

'Next Sunday?' She gazed at him fearfully. 'All right, then, if you think it might work.'

'We must make it work. Even if he does not want to meet me, I want to meet him.'

After a long moment they stared at each other, then again went into each other's arms, and again for some time did not part. If only they could stay like this for ever, Jinny thought, but of course they lived in a real world, not a dream world. Next day they would be back at work, and how would things go for them then?

In fact, they went surprisingly well. Fortified by their secret knowledge that they would one day have a future together, there was a difference, a sort of confidence, in Jinny and Viktor that was somehow recognized by others at the bakery. There were one or two knowing smiles on the first day Viktor was back, but no one went further, no one made remarks, and even Senga only gazed warily at Jinny, perhaps wondering why she seemed so much more at ease.

Apart from Mr Comrie, no one, of course, knew about the scene at Waverley Station, but when Jinny returned to work the following day she was quick to tell Ross. He was his usual sympathetic self, commiserating with her on the shock of it and glad that nothing terrible was about to happen because of it.

'I'm so glad Mr Comrie is allowing Viktor to stay, Jinny, and that you'll have the time to make the right decisions. That's sensible.'

Decisions. That word again.

'Yes, well, you see, Viktor was serious all along, Ross. Everyone said I was storing up trouble for myself, that I'd be left heartbroken, but it's not going to be like that, not at all. All Viktor wanted was for me to be sure.'

'And, of course, be sure himself?'

'Both of us, yes, but this time thing is only a formality. We know how we feel. Why should we change?'

Ross hesitated. 'And at the end of this formality, what happens next?'

'We'll be together.'

'You mean marry? And live where? In Vienna?'

'In Vienna, yes. That's where Viktor will be working.'

'That's wonderful, then.' Ross smiled. 'For you, not for me. Where am I going to find another assistant?'

'There's some way to go before you need worry about that.' Jinny's expression had clouded. 'I haven't taken Viktor to meet my dad yet. There will be stormy weather ahead.'

'If he doesn't give his blessing, I suspect you will manage without it.'

'I want it, though, I do want it.' Jinny gave a heartfelt sigh. 'Wish us luck, Ross. Viktor's coming to meet Dad on Sunday.'

'Jinny, you know I wish the pair of you all the luck in the world.'

# Twenty-Nine

For some time before the fateful Sunday, Jinny, of course, was in a state of nerves, and when the day itself finally arrived she was on pins, watching her father and wondering about his plans.

The weather was wintry – he wouldn't want to go out, would he? On the other hand, May and Vi, who were both in on the secret, had to go out so as to leave the field clear, May to meet Allan, Vi to visit a friend. Maybe that would encourage Josh to go out too?

'He won't,' May told Jinny in her bedroom before she left. 'This is his time to relax and he'll sit in his chair reading the paper, just as he did before Allan came that time.'

'Allan? Oh, yes, he came on a Sunday, didn't he?'

'And all went well then, so it will today. Just remember that, Jinny. Dad had to accept Allan, didn't he?'

'But Allan's a Scotsman, Viktor's not.'

'Never mind. He's the one you want and Dad will have to see that. Courage, Jinny!'

'You do make me feel better, May.'

'There you are, then!' cried May, and hurried out to meet her own beloved.

At least she was right about what Josh wanted to do, for he did indeed sit by the fire and read his Sunday paper, snorting over news items that amused or annoyed him, while Jinny, her eyes on the clock, set out buttered scones and the remains of the Christmas cake for tea. Half past three was the time Viktor had said he would come, and at twenty-five minutes past, with a last glance at her father, Jinny left the living room and ran down the stairs to open the door.

Viktor was already there, waiting, his hat and overcoat covered in sleet, his face reddened with cold, but as she drew him inside, his eyes shone.

'*Der tag, liebchen*, the day is here. All will go well, I feel it.'

'I'm just so nervous, Viktor. It means so much, what happens.'

'Our luck will hold, you'll see.'

He took off his hat and kissed her quickly, then let her take his damp coat and lead him up the stairs, by which time his colour had faded and he looked, in spite of his brave words, as nervous as she felt.

'Dad,' Jinny said hoarsely, 'I've brought someone to see you.'

He looked up, his eyes a little unfocused, as though sleep was ready to claim him, but when he saw the tall blond figure in the doorway, everything cleared. Sleep was banished, the newspaper cast down, and Josh was sitting ramrod straight in his chair, his eyes alight with raw feeling.

'Who's this?' he cried. 'Have you invited that German into my house, Jinny? If that's who he is, he can turn round and go. I'll no' entertain him here!'

'Viktor is Austrian, not German, as you very well know, Dad, and, yes, I have invited him here. He wants to meet you.'

'I want that very much, Mr Hendrie,' Viktor said, stepping forward.

'Well, I don't want it at all. Just go, eh? You're no' welcome here.'

'Dad, we have something to tell you.' Jinny moved closer to his chair. 'It's very important. Please give us a chance and listen to us.'

'Please listen, Mr Hendrie,' Viktor put in. 'Please let me tell you that my intentions are good.'

'Intentions? I know what your intentions are!'

Josh stood up, his gaze on a level with Viktor's, his gaze unrelenting.

'You want to court my daughter to please yourself, be all lovey-dovey, take her out, turn her head, and then, oh, my, it's time to go! Goodbye, Jinny, goodbye! And that's that – except that my lassie is crying her eyes out!'

'It's not like that, Mr Hendrie.' Viktor's face was white but he was keeping himself well in control, his head up, his shoulders straight. 'I care for your daughter; she cares for me. We are planning to make a life together.'

Josh grew pale, his dark eyes widening as he looked from Viktor to Jinny.

'Is this true, Jinny?'

'Dad, it is.'

'We're going to give ourselves time, Mr Hendrie, before we announce anything,' Viktor went on, 'so that you and my uncle can be sure we know what we're doing. But you can see why I wanted to meet you. It's very important to us both that you're happy about our plans.'

'Important?' Josh repeated. 'I'll say it's important! But I already know all I need to know. You're a foreigner, you'll be leaving Scotland one day and there's no way Jinny will be going with you. She will never give up her family and her country, so all this talk of decisions and me being happy is just a waste of time!'

'My mother is Scottish, Mr Hendrie. She married my father from Vienna and made her home with him there. They've been very happy.'

'Maybe, but Jinny isn't like your mother, she'll never leave us for you, never!'

'Oh, Dad, that isn't true,' Jinny instantly wailed. 'I love Viktor and – and if he goes back to Vienna, I'm going too.'

'To Vienna?' Josh asked hoarsely, and at the look of desolation that swept over his face as he took in her words, for the first time, with a great inward pang, Jinny recognized just what she would be inflicting on him and her family if she left them for Viktor.

Was she being selfish? Yes, lovers were selfish, but she'd never really thought until then what effect her going would have on those left behind, and as her face crumpled and the tears pricked, she went to Josh and threw her arms around him.

'Oh, Dad, I'm sorry, I'm sorry! It's not what I want to do – to leave you and May and Vi – it isn't! But when you love someone, you have to follow wherever they go, eh? Wouldn't Ma have followed you?'

He shook his head, unable to find his usual flow of words to answer her, but held her close as she leaned against him, still holding back the tears, until she finally released herself.

'Let's not discuss this any more just now,' she whispered, dabbing at her face with a handkerchief. 'We have time ahead. I'll put the kettle on and we'll have some tea.'

'That would be very nice,' said Viktor, who had been standing apart, his eyes cast down. Josh, however, seemingly still stunned by Jinny's bombshell, simply sank into his chair and said nothing. Even the presence of Viktor, still in his house, failed to cause him to rally.

Jinny, glancing at her father as she set out the tea things, knew that he had never believed that Viktor could be serious about her, which was why he was now so shocked. He'd been like Mr Comrie, believing Viktor to be just playing around, but now he knew that that wasn't true and that she might one day go to Vienna, he couldn't take the blow. But she understood how he felt, oh, she did, and could no longer blame him. In this situation there was no way out from hurting somebody, and facing the fact that she would be doing the hurting, Jinny felt so bad she could have cried again over the teacups.

'Come and have some tea, Dad,' she called, trying to sound just as usual, and when he did stir to sit at the table, he finally managed to speak.

'Have you thought what'll happen if there's a war?' he asked, taking a buttered scone and studying it. 'It'll be no place for our Jinny to be if she's in a foreign country then. She'll be an alien.'

'I haven't heard that Hitler wants a war with Great Brtain,' Viktor said slowly. He too was studying a scone, which he eventually tried. 'I can't see that it would be of any advantage to him.'

'The papers say he wants world domination.'

'Oh, that's an exaggeration. All he wants is to give Germany some pride again, after what happened when they lost the war.'

'Well, from what I've read, he's keen to make your country join with Germany.'

'Our chancellor doesn't want that.'

'How about you?'

Viktor drank his tea. 'I'd prefer to remain as we are.'

'Let's not talk any more about Hitler,' Jinny said uneasily. 'Viktor, what do you think of my scones?'

'Excellent! I must introduce them back home, along with Mrs Fortune's shortbread.'

'If you like our baking so much, you might consider staying here,' suggested Josh, watching Viktor closely. 'Why not? Why not you stay in Jinny's country, instead of her going to yours?'

As Viktor opened his mouth to speak, Jinny leaped up to add water to the teapot.

'No more discussion,' she declared. 'We can talk another time. Dad, more tea?'

As he took the cup she had refilled, she touched his hand. 'Listen, I want to thank you – for letting Viktor stay.'

'I say the same,' Viktor put in quickly.

'Och, there's no point in fighting any more.' Josh's tone was heavy. 'What you've told me changes everything. For the worse.'

'Don't say that!' cried Jinny.

'What else can I say? It was bad enough when May fell for Allan, but at least' – Josh's voice shook – 'she's staying in her own country. I thought you'd be staying, too, Jinny. I thought you'd no future with Mr Linden. I thought I'd no need to worry—'

Suddenly he stood up and, looking at neither Jinny nor Viktor, moved away from the table.

'If you don't mind, I'm away to my bed. I just want . . . to rest.'

'Certainly, Mr Hendrie.' Viktor was on his feet, his face contrite. 'I'm so sorry if I've upset you.'

'Dad, try not to worry,' Jinny murmured. 'Nothing's been decided—'

But Josh had already left them.

On the stairs, where they were to say goodnight, Viktor put his hand under Jinny's chin and gazed into her face. 'My poor girl, you look exhausted.'

'So do you.' She took away his hand and stretched up to kiss his mouth. 'I'm so sorry, Viktor, it's all so hard for you – for all of us. You'll be wishing I was a Viennese girl in a *dirndl* and my hair in plaits.'

'I do *not* wish you were anyone but yourself, Jinny!' He crushed her to him, and as he released her his expression was bleak.

'Today, it has been good, though, that you have seen . . . how things might be. The reality of what we might want to do.'

'Viktor, it's all right.' She searched his face, her eyes tender. 'If I leave my family I'll feel bad, I know I will, but I'll still want to go with you – that's not going to change.'

'We have time ahead to be sure of that. Let's leave it for now, and try to be happy with what we have.' Viktor took a deep breath and smiled. 'I want to tell you that although he doesn't care for me, I liked your father. I think I understand him – and he looks like you. Or, of course, you look like him.'

'Viktor, that's nice of you. Fancy you saying you liked Dad when he wanted to throw you out! You will come again, then? Meet my sisters? They're dying to meet you!'

'Of course I will!'

As they clung together for one last passionate embrace, suddenly the future seemed very slightly brighter, and when they had to part, they knew they'd meet tomorrow.

# Thirty

In the end, rather than having Viktor come to the flat again, it was decided that he, with Jinny, should meet May and Vi one day for lunch.

'Just our usual place will be fine,' Jinny told him. 'May can easily walk there from the hat shop and if we make it in February, when Vi's taking a few days off, she can come too.'

'Vi is the one who works for a clothing firm?'

'Yes, in Accounts like me. She's very keen on social reform, very political. May's just calm and sweet.'

'Engaged to the nice watchmaker who found your brooch for me?'

'And, surprise, surprise, has been accepted by Dad. Sort of.'

'Me next, then,' Viktor said cheerfully, though both knew, of course, that his case was very different from Allan's.

A date was fixed for mid-February and on a dismal wet day, Viktor and the sisters gathered at the small West End café Jinny had suggested and, after they'd hung up their umbrellas and mackintoshes, introductions were made and they sat down to order.

Tomato soup, Welsh rarebit and macaroni cheese were the choices, plus Viktor's sausages, and as they ate they all made easy conversation, with May and Vi covertly sizing up Viktor, while he remained his usual courteous self.

He likes them, thought Jinny with relief, and they like him. Even Vi, always less outgoing than May, seemed to be resting her dark eyes on Viktor's handsome face with approval, though of course she'd be reserving true judgement on him until she knew more of his views on how the world should be run. So far, so good, though, with May really seeming charmed, and Viktor the same.

'So sorry you had a bit of trouble with Dad,' May told him, as she finished her Welsh rarebit – a dish that had intrigued Viktor because of its name. 'He'll come round, though, I'm sure. He has with Allan, anyway.'

'I understand his worries,' Viktor replied. 'The situation is not easy.'

'People can alter situations,' said Vi. 'Depends if they know what they really want.'

'That's what's not easy,' put in Jinny. 'Sometimes you want everything.'

'I'll get the pudding menu,' Viktor said smoothly. 'They do a very nice jam tart here.'

'Tell you what I've been seeing lately in the papers,' Vi remarked when the puddings had been ordered, 'and that's the name of your chancellor, Viktor. Kurt Schuschnigg?'

'Vi always reads the foreign news,' May confided. 'More than I do, I'm afraid.'

'Yes, he's been in the news lately,' Viktor agreed. 'For his meetings with Hitler.'

'Looks like they haven't gone well,' said Vi. 'Seemingly, Hitler wants this *Anschluss*, and your chancellor doesn't.'

'What's an *anschluss*?' asked May.

'It means "union",' Jinny told her, with some pride. 'So, here, the union of Austria with Germany. I looked it up.'

'That's correct.' Viktor's smile was strained. 'I hope it will not happen.'

'Doesn't Hitler usually get what he wants?' asked Vi.

'Well, there's talk of our chancellor organizing something to find out Austrians' views. If most people don't want it I don't see how Hitler can force it through.'

Vi raised her eyebrows. 'You don't? From what I've heard he's good at forcing.'

'Whatever happens, I wish I could have been there.' Viktor glanced quickly at Jinny. 'Only to vote, I mean. This is so important.'

'Oh, yes,' she agreed, but a coldness was running down her spine and it was with obvious effort that she asked if he would be going home. 'Just for the vote,' she added hastily.

'No, no, I don't think I can do that. I'll just have to rely on others to do the right thing.' Viktor's expression brightened. 'I see our puddings are on the way. I'll order coffee to follow, shall I?'

'Brave man,' said Jinny, feeling better. 'Viktor has a problem with our coffee,' she told her sisters, who laughed.

'Suppose you know why we're a nation of tea drinkers, then?' asked Vi. 'Maybe you should start serving coffee along with your *Sachertorte*, eh?'

'A brilliant idea,' said Viktor.

Everything was so relaxed, so pleasant, that when they stood outside under their umbrellas they agreed they must all meet again, next time with Allan.

'And our treat,' said May. 'It's been so nice, Viktor. We're so glad we've met you and we want to thank you, don't we, Vi?'

'Certainly do. I say we should all go to the theatre as well. Get some tickets from Dad. He likes us to take an interest in his handiwork.'

'I'd like that very much,' Viktor told them, raising his hat as May set off for her hat shop and Vi went to catch a tram. 'Jinny, I mean that. Your sisters are delightful – I'd be very happy to meet them again.'

'So glad,' Jinny replied, taking his arm as they turned to make their way to Comrie's. 'I can tell they were very impressed with you.'

'Can't believe that. But May, she's so lovely – and Vi, she's like you! Very sharp, too, I should say. I can see her doing well in politics.'

'Anything that will let her make things better for ordinary folk.' Jinny glanced up at Viktor as they splashed along the streaming pavements. 'Viktor, I'm sorry you're so worried about things back home. I can tell you are, but it may all work out well, you know. You're right, I'm sure – Hitler can't force a union of Germany with Austria if the people don't want it.'

'Yes, that's what I think. Or, at least, I hope.'

But only a few weeks later they had to read in the paper that Hitler and his Nazis had marched in triumph into Vienna and been accepted by the Austrians. Hitler had cancelled the peoples' plebiscite, Chancellor Schuschnigg had resigned and might be facing imprisonment, and the *Anschluss* was now a fact. Austria and Germany were one.

# Thirty-One

'I can't believe it,' said Viktor, sitting with Jinny in the lounge bar of a West End hotel, his face so pale, so distraught, he seemed quite strange. They had planned to go to the pictures, but when he met Jinny from work he seemed so low in spirits that as soon as he asked if they could go for a drink first, she'd agreed. After all, the hotel was not a pub, where women would not generally be welcome, and though she knew her father didn't like her drinking out, a glass of wine wouldn't hurt. He wasn't to know about it, anyway.

'I knew you'd be upset when you saw the papers today,' she said, studying Viktor worriedly, after the waiter had served their drinks – a sweet German wine for her and a Scottish beer for Viktor. 'You were hoping it wouldn't happen, weren't you? This *Anschluss*?'

'Of course I was. I never thought Austrians would welcome Hitler the way they did.'

'Though you've never said much against him yourself, Viktor.'

'Not while he didn't try to interfere with my country. But uniting us with Nazi Germany makes me see him very differently. There's always been talk against him, of what he's doing to Jewish people, for instance, but I never knew quite what to believe. Now I think I can believe anything.'

'I read it was the Austrian Nazis who welcomed him to your country. Did you know about them?'

Viktor sighed heavily. 'Oh, yes. My uncle let me telephone my father today. He feels as bad as I do, but he told me a lot of his customers are Nazis and are very keen for the union. So they're the ones who've let it happen.'

'And what does your mother think of it all?' Jinny asked after a pause.

'Oh, she's absolutely furious! She's never wanted to be part of Germany – she remembers the war too well.' Viktor gave slight smile. 'She wants me to go home, of course.'

Jinny set down her glass, her face showing her feelings. 'Viktor you won't, will you? You won't go back home yet?'

'It's just that everything's so uncertain, Jinny. Our fate is tied up with Germany's now. What they'll do, what we'll do, and if there's a war—'

'There won't be a war, Viktor! There's no need for you to go home early. We agreed, didn't we, that we'd give ourselves time before we made things official, and how can we do that if you leave me now?' While she kept her gaze fixed on his face, she was close to tears, fighting not to let them fall. 'Tell me you won't go!'

'*Liebchen*, don't worry, I'm not making plans to go back yet.' He reached across to press her hand. 'I've discussed it with my uncle and we've agreed I should stay on unless there is a real threat of war.'

'Thank God,' she said simply, withdrawing her hand from his so that she could wipe her eyes. 'I don't know what I'd have done if you'd left me now. I mean, I'm not ready – not prepared—'

'But Jinny . . .' He hesitated. 'You do realize that if Germany does start a war, I'll have no choice but to go back? Now that we are part of Germany, I'll be eligible for war service.'

'On their side? Oh, Viktor! How can you fight for Germany when you don't trust Hitler?'

'What else can I do? I'll be conscripted.'

As the words sank in, Jinny shivered. 'I never thought you'd be talking about fighting – I mean, at all. It's like a bad dream, a nightmare—'

'But may not happen in real life, Jinny.'

'It might.'

'I was painting the darkest picture, that's all.' Viktor sat up, straightening his shoulders, running his hand across his brow. 'Look, I'm sorry, *liebchen*, it seems I've been unloading all my fears on to you, and I shouldn't have done because we don't know what's going to happen. I may have been frightening you for nothing. There may be no war, no question of my going into the army. Please forgive me.'

At once she brightened, a smile lighting her whole face, her eyes softening with a look of love as she touched his hand. 'Viktor, there's nothing to forgive! If you aren't going home yet and we can just follow our plan – oh, that's all I want!'

'I want that too.' He looked down at their glasses. 'Would you like another drink, Jinny? Or should we still go to the cinema and see that picture you mentioned?'

'I don't want another drink, thanks, but I'd love to see the picture. Just to relax for a bit . . . move into another world.'

'What's it called, then?'

Jinny looked a little embarrassed. '*The Divorce of Lady X* – sounds silly, but it's supposed to be a comedy.'

'About divorce?'

'I think it all ends happily. Merle Oberon's the star – she's lovely – and Laurence Olivier.'

'And he's handsome, I suppose?'

When they'd put on their coats, hats, scarves and gloves against the winter wind outside and Viktor had paid the bill, he opened the double doors of the hotel and held them wide for Jinny.

'Come on, then, let's move into this other world and forget ours for a bit.'

'Not all of it,' said Jinny as she took his arm, and together they ran down Princes Street for their tram.

# Thirty-Two

As the year 1938 progressed through spring to summer, it seemed strange to those worrying about possible war that everything seemed so normal. Though Hitler's name appeared in the papers often enough, it was usually in connection with Czechoslovakia or the Sudetenland, and didn't, to the general public, seem to involve Great Britain. What, after all, was the Sudetenland? Something to do with Germany? Nothing to worry about, anyway.

In Scotland, there was the British Empire Exhibition, opened by George VI in Glasgow in May, to provide excitement and pride, and even though the weather was dismal, crowds flocked to see the handsome 'palaces' and stands concerned with arts and trades, while all thought of the international situation was put aside.

Certainly, no one discussed it at Comrie's Bakery, where life continued as usual, except that Viktor's cakes became ever more popular and he and his assistants had to struggle to meet demand. Which seemed, in fact, to suit Viktor, who threw himself into his work with so much dedication he began to look far from well and excited the motherly attention of Mrs Arrow, who said he needed beef tea and glasses of stout to 'build himself up', while Mabel Hyslop even went so far to speak to Jinny about it.

'It's really worrying to see a young man look so run down,' she remarked one coffee break. 'I really think you should have a word with him, Jinny.'

'Why me?' Jinny asked, flushing and avoiding meeting Ross's eye.

'You're the one to do it, dear – everyone knows you two are close.'

Jinny drank her coffee. 'As a matter of fact, I have told him he's doing too much, but he – well, he has a lot on his mind at the minute.'

'Oh, yes, I can quite see that, poor boy, being in a foreign country and so on. I expect he'll be wanting to get home.'

'He's due home in November, Mabel.'

'Yes, but he might want to go earlier – just in case anything happens. Though it all seems to have gone quiet, eh?' Saying she'd better get back to work, Mabel collected the coffee cups for washing and removed herself, at which Jinny gave a sigh of relief.

'Poor Mabel,' said Ross. 'She's only trying to help.' He gave Jinny a meditative look. 'I take it Viktor is not going home yet?'

'No, he isn't. But it's true what I said – he does worry.'

'About the *Anschluss*? I can believe a chap away from his country would be worried if it suddenly became part of another one. But you're worried too, aren't you, Jinny? You're not looking a whole lot better than Viktor.'

'I've got Dad to think about,' she said after a pause. 'He was upset before, to think I might go to Vienna, but now it's a part of Germany he thinks the worst has happened.' She sighed and looked down at the column of figures she should have been adding up. 'He always did call Viktor a German – says now he was right all along.'

'I'm sorry, Jinny. Look, if you ever want a shoulder to cry on, you know mine's available.' Ross studied her, concerned.

'I do, Ross, and thanks.' She gave a weak smile. 'But listen, you might be able to tell me something – I don't want to ask Viktor as I'm trying not to talk to him about Hitler. But what is this Sudetenland Hitler's so interested in?'

'The Sudetenland? Well, I'm no expert – only know what I've picked up from the papers – but apparently it's a part of Czechoslovakia. About three million Germans live there from the time it was Bohemia, and Hitler wants them to have self government. The problem is that the Czechs say no.'

'And Hitler's annoyed?'

'You bet, but we and France are on his side and they've told Benes – he's the Czech President – to do what Hitler wants. Instead, Benes has started mobilizing troops.' Ross shrugged. 'Can't see Hitler accepting that.'

'He'll go to war?' Jinny asked fearfully.

'He might.'

Germany could go to war? Jinny's heart plummeted. That meant Austria would also go to war. And Viktor too? He'd said nothing, but maybe he was already thinking again of going home? Of becoming a soldier? No wonder he seemed so low recently.

'Hitler hasn't declared war yet,' she said, trying to appear calm. 'Maybe he won't?'

'Well, we'll do all we can to prevent it. But if you're worrying about Viktor, I think he'll be all right. He's over here, that's the good thing.'

'But he might want to go home.'

'He needn't, unless there's a definite declaration. There'll be a lot of diplomatic activity going on behind the scenes, and the whole thing could be sorted out without war. You could tell him that, Jinny.'

'I will, but whether he'll listen or not, I don't know.'

As they'd arranged to meet at lunchtime, at least she'd have a chance to speak to Viktor then, for which she was grateful. Returning at last to her work, she knew she could not have got through the day without knowing what she had to face.

But it was all right. As soon as Viktor saw her anxious face, he held her hands outside the bakery and managed a smile.

'*Liebchen*, what have you been thinking? That I'm planning to go home again? No need to worry – I'm not.'

'But Ross was saying that Hitler might be going to declare war on Czechoslovakia, and that would mean—'

'I know what it would mean, but I speak regularly now to my father and he says the talk at home is that Hitler will be holding his fire. Nobody knows, of course, what's in his mind, but there's every chance he doesn't want to start a war at present.'

'Viktor, that's wonderful! Wonderful! I've been so worried – and you've been looking so down lately. I thought you were sure to want to go back—'

'Not yet. Come on, let's have something to eat.'

Over a secluded table in their usual café, Jinny studied him, seeing beyond his smile the lustreless look of his fine eyes, the dispirited air that had replaced his confident manner, and she shook her head.

'You are feeling low, aren't you? People seem to be noticing . . . Are you ill—'

'I know, I get advice on all sides. Should have a holiday, should have beef tea, should have milk stout, whatever that is!' He shrugged. 'But there's nothing wrong with me. It's just that I feel weighed down by what's happened to my country. And that my people let it happen. You can understand that, Jinny?'

'Of course I can! It's no wonder you feel bad, when Austria has lost its independence.'

'Not just its independence.' Viktor's voice was low. 'It's lost its heart.'

They ordered their usual soup but were without appetite, and afterwards had only coffee and called early for the bill.

'I'd better get back to the bakery,' Viktor told Jinny outside the café. 'We are having so many orders now we have to work flat out to keep up.'

'It's too much, Viktor. You're doing too much.'

'No, it's good to be busy. Helps me to forget for a while.'

'You know what I think?' she asked, with an attempt at lightness. 'You should help yourself to a great slice of your own *Sachertorte* – that would be better than Mrs Arrow's beef tea or milk stout!'

'*Sachertorte?*' Viktor gave a genuine laugh. '*Liebchen*, have you never realized that I don't like cakes? Especially my own. I am like someone in one of your sweetshops who never eats a chocolate.'

'Oh, Viktor, it's so good to see you laugh! Promise me we'll be happy again one day, when all this is over!'

'When I think of you, Jinny, I'm happy now,' he said seriously, and touching his thin cheek, she wondered – could she believe him? But as they separated, he to return to the bakery, she to Accounts, she knew in her heart that at that time it would take more than thoughts of her to make him happy.

# Thirty-Three

She found only her father and Vi at home when she let herself into the flat, May being out with Allan, but Vi was busy cooking and Josh was listening to the wireless.

'Let's just get the news,' he told Jinny, meaning she was not to talk, which was no hardship as she didn't feel like talking anyway. Vi, though, was ready to chat when Jinny joined her at the gas cooker, first asking how poor Viktor was, as he'd been so down in the dumps when they'd all gone to a play recently. And then, keeping her voice down, she reported that she was sure something was up with May.

'How d'you mean?' asked Jinny, beginning to strain the potatoes ready for mashing.

'Well, when she went out she just seemed, you know, all agog about something.'

'She's usually in a happy mood when she's meeting Allan.'

'Aye, but this was something special. I didn't ask her what was going on – she was in a hurry – but we'll see how she is when she comes back.' Vi was opening the oven and inspecting her fish pie. 'This looks done – thought I'd give you a change from my fried haddock. Let's serve up and get on – I've a meeting tonight.'

Oh, good, thought Jinny as they served the meal and called to Josh to the table. It looked like she'd have a nice quiet evening to herself, maybe do her mending, listen to the wireless and try not to think how much she'd rather have been with Viktor. Down in the dumps he might be, but he was still the one she wanted to be with, and always would be. Lucky May, out with her dear Allan!

Lucky May indeed, for when she came home – quite late – she brought Allan with her and a piece of good news too, as her family only needed to look at her to realize. Josh was back from the theatre, Vi from her meeting, and Jinny, feeling virtuous, had finished all her mending, but all eyes were on May, looking so flushed and lovely in her blue jacket and matching dress as she stood in the doorway next to a smiling Allan.

'What is it?' Josh asked shortly. 'What's happened?'

'Oh, Dad, Vi, Jinny – we have something to tell you!'

'Not that it's really news,' put in Allan.

'It's official news,' said May, and she held out her left hand, on which a ring was glittering. 'We're engaged!'

There was a short silence, then Vi and Jinny sprang to their sister and hugged her, while Josh rose slowly to his feet.

'Engaged,' he repeated.

'I know I should have spoken to you first, Mr Hendrie,' Allan said hurriedly, 'but I think you knew what was going to happen, didn't you? We did say, right from the beginning, didn't we? I'm afraid I told May I'd be collecting the ring today, and when we met I couldn't resist putting it on her finger.'

'Collecting the ring?' Josh repeated. 'It's no' from your shop, then?'

'Oh, no, I've nothing in stock I'd want to give May. I knew the very one she liked – we'd seen it in the window of a jeweller's in town and I had her finger measurements, so I went back and got it, and here it is!'

Everyone, even Josh, studied the diamond ring on May's finger, which was beautifully set in a little circlet of pearls and was, apart from Jinny's Edelweiss brooch, the prettiest thing they'd ever seen.

'It's truly lovely,' Jinny said softly, and kissed first May and then Allan. 'And we're all so happy for you, aren't we, Dad?'

'Come on,' ordered Vi. 'Congratulate them, or at least Allan. Isn't that what you're supposed to do?'

'You are happy, Dad?' May asked, her voice trembling. 'I want you to be pleased – so much.'

'Aye, all right, then,' he said gruffly. 'If you're happy, I'll . . . I'll say I am.'

'Oh, Dad!' She threw her arms round him and kissed him, while Allan stood waiting to shake his hand.

'Pity we've nothing to offer in the way of celebration,' said Vi. 'You should have given us warning.'

'Don't worry, we've got a celebration planned for Sunday at my place. May's going to do lunch for us and you're all to come. Right?'

'As though we'd say no!' cried Vi, and everyone laughed as Jinny said she'd make the usual tea, which would have to stand in for a celebration for the time being.

It was while she was making the tea that Allan told her quietly that if she wanted to bring Viktor on Sunday, he'd be very welcome.

'Oh, but what about Dad?' whispered Jinny. 'We wouldn't want to cause trouble.'

'Ask Viktor first and see what he says, then we'll speak to your father.'

It sounded such a wonderful idea, Jinny couldn't believe it the next day when Viktor said he was most grateful but he really didn't think he should come. Just as Jinny herself had feared, he didn't want to cause trouble on her sister's lovely day, but he sent his congratulations and wished her every happiness.

And so do I, thought Jinny sadly. My lucky sister, May.

All she could hope was that she and Viktor would be happy too. There was no alternative she could bear.

# Thirty-Four

As the wet, dreary summer progressed, May's happiness was all that cheered Jinny. She and Viktor still met when off duty, going around together to cinemas, cafés and so on, just like any couple who might soon be ready to declare their love to the world. Except that Jinny never felt they were like other couples in that way at all.

She knew how things had been for her and Viktor before his country had been annexed by Germany, and could tell the difference between how he'd been then and how he was now. He'd been so happy in those early days, running to meet her, his blue eyes shining, desperate to spend time with her. Whilst now, though he still wanted to be with her – yes, she was sure of that, sure he still loved her – now a change had come over him, cancelling out that delicious anticipation and making him seem preoccupied with a world that was outside theirs, a world she couldn't know.

They had stuck to their plan of waiting until November before telling the world of their love, but how were they to know now how their love would be affected by what had happened to Viktor's country? Or by the anxiety caused by Hitler over possible war?

In spite of all this, she had to believe that when the time came they would still be able to marry and that she would go to Vienna, for even if the international situation worsened, she was determined that she and Viktor would be together. How it would all work out, she didn't know, but if they loved each other, which they did, it would work out somehow. Whatever change had come over Viktor, of that she was certain. The important thing was just to keep going as normally as possible and see what happened. Just what everyone else was doing, no doubt, in Great Britain and in France.

In August, though, things took a turn for the worse. Reports came out that thousands of German soldiers were massing on the Czech border, and though no action was taken, there was a feeling in the air that trouble was simmering and might soon come to the boil. In September, Hitler made a speech at the huge Nuremberg rally, guaranteed to stir the pot by calling Czechoslovakia a 'fraudulent state'. It was after this that the British Prime Minister, Neville Chamberlain, asked for a personal meeting with Hitler, which was granted, and on the fifteenth of September he arrived at Berchtesgaden, Hitler's home in the Bavarian Alps. The people of Europe held their breath.

'What do you think will happen now?' Jinny asked Viktor, whose face wore its usual look of strain.

'Nothing good, I'm afraid.'

'Why do you say that? We've got a great empire and Mr Chamberlain's our prime minister – why shouldn't Hitler listen to him?'

'He might listen, but he'll still do what he wants to do. And he won't care about your empire, except to conquer it.'

'You used to say he wouldn't be interested in attacking us!'

'That was before he took my country,' Viktor said bleakly.

There was nothing left to do but wait to see what the papers said after Chamberlain had returned home, and when they appeared, it seemed that there might be some hope of a settlement. But it was not to be. Though Czechoslovakia had eventually agreed that parts of the Sudetenland could be returned to Germany and Hitler had seemed to be satisfied, only a week or so later he demanded all of the Sudetenland. After another trip to see him, Chamberlain admitted that the stage looked set for war.

Gas masks were being issued, air-raid shelters were being built, and everyone was beginning to fear the worst, but there was one last hope. Mr Chamberlain, it was reported, had left for yet another meeting with Hitler, this time in Munich. If it were to fail, well, the abyss might be waiting, but no one cared to think about that.

The thirtieth of September was the day Mr Chamberlain was due back, and, like the whole country, staff and customers at Comrie's were agog for news. Being a Friday and wages day, Jinny, as part of her routine, went with Terry as usual to the bakery, where of course her eyes instantly sought out Viktor.

He was at his work table, surrounded by layers of sponge cake and bowls of an elaborate egg and butter cream, seemingly completely oblivious to his surroundings as he poured caramel syrup over one of the sponge layers which he then set aside and called, 'Bob!'

As Bob came hurrying over, Jinny moved forward, smiling. 'Viktor?'

He looked up and for a moment stared, as though he couldn't take it in that she was near him, then returned her smile. 'Jinny! What are you doing here?'

'Don't expect Viktor to know it's pay day!' cried Senga, coming over from her work icing small cakes to laugh with Terry, who had sauntered along to join her. 'He doesn't have to think about it like the rest of us!'

'Pay day, of course,' Viktor only replied mildly. 'Nice to see you, Jinny. Just wait till I get Bob to pour this caramel over another layer.'

'We're doing a *Dobertorte*,' sandy-haired Bob announced proudly as he picked up a pan of caramel syrup. 'That's the Hungarian cake with layers, you ken, and the Devil's own job to make – aye, and we're doing two!' He rolled his eyes.

'Oh, yes,' Jinny said hurriedly, nodding coolly to Senga before fixing her eyes on Viktor again. 'It's not just pay day today, though, is it? Mr Chamberlain's coming back from Munich and he might have good news, Aren't you excited?'

'You bet,' said Bob.

'Sure,' said Terry, 'I'm walking on pins till we hear.'

'Me, too,' said Senga.

But Viktor's blue eyes on Jinny showed no excitement, no shine, and after a moment he looked away. 'There is no point in getting excited, as there will be no good news.'

'You don't know that!' cried Jinny.

'Whatever Mr Chamberlain brings back from Hitler, it will not be peace.'

He sounded so definite, and yet so defeated, they all stared at him in surprise, Jinny with a hollow feeling inside, as though she'd been expecting something good and been refused.

'I don't understand—' she was beginning when she heard Mr Whyte's voice calling to her.

'Jinny, have you got the wage packets? How about coming to my office?'

'On . . . on my way!' she called, turning, then looking back at Viktor, at which he moved swiftly to her side. Disregarding interested eyes, he put his hand on her arm.

'Jinny, may I see you this evening?'

'We don't usually meet on a Friday.'

'I know, but I'd like to, tonight.'

At the urgency of his tone, the appeal in his eyes, she knew she could not refuse.

'All right. I'll ring May at the shop to say I won't be home.' She hesitated. 'You'll come to Accounts?'

'Outside. Let's meet outside.'

'Till tonight, then.'

Now the appeal in his eyes had faded as his face took on its defeated look again, but Jinny had to move on, into Mr Whyte's office, leaving Viktor to return to his table.

At first he did not speak, only stared down into a bowl of butter cream, then raised his eyes to Bob.

'Finished covering that top layer?'

'Aye, I hope it'll be OK. This is no' ma favourite cake to make, you ken. Too fiddly.'

'You're doing very well, Bob. I am confident you will be able to take over from me when I leave.'

'Oh, God, Viktor, that's no' yet, is it?'

'We'll just let the caramel on the top layers almost set,' Viktor replied smoothly, 'and then we can begin assembling the cakes. Six layers for each. Think you remember what we do?'

'We fill the cakes with the butter cream, and just before the syrup sets on the top layers, we cut it into sections.' Bob groaned. 'And hope it doesna crack, eh?'

'If you oil the knife it shouldn't crack.' Viktor smiled. 'Well done, Bob. Don't forget to ice the sides of the cakes with the butter cream and finish off the tops with a few twirls of icing.'

'Don't move away until I've done all that, eh? Cutting thae sections, it's nerve-racking!'

'Don't worry, you'll be fine,' Viktor told him, clapping him on the back. 'I promise you!'

'Bit of a pessimist, young Viktor,' Terry remarked when he and Jinny were on their way to Morningside. 'According to him, we can't win, whatever happens.'

'If there's no war, he'll be pleased,' Jinny declared. 'I know he will; he couldn't be anything else.'

'Well, if he isn't happy, the rest of us will be, that's for sure. I reckon folk'll go mad with relief if we get a promise of peace. I mean, who wants another do like the last one?'

# Thirty-Five

Terry was proved right, for when the news came through that Mr Chamberlain had arrived at the airport declaring there was to be 'peace for our time', the BBC reported that the whole country appeared to be going wild. As he waved the piece of paper Hitler and other politicians had signed, promising that there would definitely be no war, the cheers for him echoed. He was called a hero; he was summoned to Buckingham Palace to meet the king and queen; he was cheered again in Downing Street, feted everywhere he went on the day that no one had dared to hope would ever come.

For Comrie's, the news came before closing time and, like everyone else, staff and customers were hugging and shaking hands, some even shedding a few tears – Jinny, for one. As she and Mabel hugged Ross and shook hands with a beaming Mr Comrie, she felt her eyes smart, but she'd never been happier, for in the euphoria of the moment she was sure that Viktor's depressing thoughts would not survive the really good news they'd all heard. 'Peace for our time' – what could be more wonderful?

Now the two of them could go ahead in the knowledge that the future held no fears, and Viktor would realize that her love for him was as strong as it had ever been.

Although Mr Comrie regretted that he couldn't provide drinks for everyone, he declared that Accounts people at least should have a wee dram of his good whisky, or maybe sherry, if Jinny and Mabel would prefer?

'I think I'd better have the sherry,' Mabel said, giggling. 'I'm sure to feel a bit tipsy, anyway.'

'What better day than today to feel tipsy?' asked Mr Comrie and, as Jinny also opted for sherry, Ross caught her eye and winked, indicating he thought Mr Comrie had already sampled his own whisky. Why not, though? For this was a very special day.

'It's so good to see you looking so happy,' Ross whispered to Jinny as they moved to the windows to look down on crowds of shoppers stopping to shake one another's hands. 'All seems to be going right at last.'

'Oh, yes, I couldn't feel better, and I know Viktor will be feeling the same.'

'No doubt of that.' Ross drank some whisky. 'This news will have special meaning for him.'

'And for me, Ross!'

'Yes, but I'm thinking of his country. Now it won't be drawn into a war alongside Germany. And his country does matter to him, doesn't it?'

'Very much,' she answered, looking into her glass. 'Ross, mind if I use the office phone to ring May? I'm meeting Viktor instead of going home.'

'Of course you can ring her. And I'm not surprised you and Viktor want to go out tonight. This is a time for celebrating.'

'Will you be, too?' Jinny asked with unashamed curiosity

'Oh, yes! I promised that if we got good news I'd take Lorna out for a meal.'

'Lorna?'

'My cousin, you remember? Came up at Christmas with my uncle and aunt, but she's on her own this time. A friend got married here last week and Lorna's stayed on for a few days.'

'Oh, nice,' remarked Jinny, remembering the pretty redhead at the Christmas party. And she was genuinely pleased that Ross would be out 'on the town' that evening. Was he really coming out of his shell at last?

'More sherry, Jinny? Mabel?' asked Mr Comrie. 'Another whisky, Ross?'

They thanked him but refused, as it was in fact already time to finish work. What a relief! Though even Mabel wasn't tipsy on one drink, they really felt quite intoxicated with the events of the day and their avoidance of the abyss. Though they would all have to be back at work on Saturday morning, the evening was theirs to enjoy, and as Jinny began to run down the stairs she felt on wings, she was so happy. Until, suddenly, her steps slowed.

A memory of Viktor's face as she had last seen it – so depressed, so defeated – flashed into her mind and drew her eventually to a halt. Supposing . . . Supposing, when she saw him, he appeared just the same? If, in spite of so much joy on every side, he hadn't changed? No, it wasn't possible. Now that there was a definite agreement for peace from all who'd signed Mr Chamberlain's document, including Hitler, Viktor must be happy about it. He must be feeling as she was feeling . . . mustn't he?

She moved slowly onwards, down the stairs as far as the door to the street. When she went through that, if Viktor was there, waiting, as soon as saw him she would know. Yes, just from his face, she would know. And sure enough, when she pushed open the door and saw him waiting in the street, she did.

# Thirty-Six

As soon as she saw him waiting, wearing a light overcoat over his suit and a dark trilby hat over his fair hair, she knew he hadn't changed. He hadn't been won over by Mr Chamberlain's paper. There would, in his opinion, be no peace. All this she knew from his face, though its look was different now, being neither depressed nor defeated, but unhappy – which did not deter her from deciding to argue the case for Hitler's wanting peace as soon as she got the chance.

'Viktor, you're here already!' she cried as cheerfully as she could. 'Not getting wet, are you?'

'I believe the rain has stopped,' he replied, holding out a hand. 'But do you have your umbrella?'

What were they talking about? Rain? Umbrellas? When the world might be righting itself around them and they should be celebrating?

'Sorry, I never thought about it.' She slipped her arm into his. 'So, where are we going? Our usual place?'

'I've booked at Ritchie's in the Old Town. You said you liked it when we went before.'

'Oh, yes, but it's a bit smart. I'm not dressed for it.' She looked down at her everyday blue coat and put her hand to her blue beret. 'I see you've put on your suit.'

'You look lovely, you always do.'

'Ritchie's is more expensive, too.' Her face brightened. 'Viktor, are you celebrating, after all? I should tell you, I've already had a sherry from your uncle.'

'A sherry? What next?' He laughed as they made their way through good-humoured Princes Street crowds towards a tram stop, though it seemed to her that his laughter was not quite natural. Or was she seeing things that weren't there? Maybe, but she didn't believe he was celebrating – at least, not in the way he should be. If she could only get him to believe what everyone else was happy to believe, how much happier he'd be . . .

They were early at the restaurant but glad they'd booked for it was unusually busy, with many people deciding to dine out in recognition of Mr Chamberlain's heroic act in saving the country from war. Wine was flowing and the talk was loud, but Viktor, ordering a bottle of a German wine he liked, said it was all to the good if people were noisy.

'If we want to talk, no one will be listening,' he explained, studying the menu as Jinny studied him. Though the restaurant lights were far from bright, she could see now that he seemed not just unhappy but also on edge, his eyes staying on the menu, evidently unwilling to meet hers.

'Are we here to talk?' she asked lightly. 'Because I do want to say a few things myself.'

'Oh?' At last, he looked at her. 'What sort of things?'

'Well, I can tell that you're not going to accept we now have peace, and I'm going to persuade you to change your mind. Be like everyone else, Viktor! Be happy that Hitler is sincere and doesn't want war, and let's get on with our lives!'

Very carefully, he laid down the menu and again rested his eyes on her face. 'Jinny, please listen to me. It's not true what you say about Hitler and it will do no good to believe it. I only wish it were otherwise.'

As Jinny opened her mouth to reply, a waiter appeared to serve their wine, followed by another, who asked if they were ready to order.

'Are we?' asked Viktor. 'Any preferences, Jinny?'

They settled on a melon first course, followed by a poultry dish, and breathed a sigh of relief when both waiters had gone.

'Now I can answer you,' said Jinny eagerly, but Viktor held up his hand.

'Let's leave it for now. There's a lounge here, if you remember, where we can have coffee and won't be disturbed. That will be best.'

Suddenly she was afraid, with a coldness surrounding her heart that was not soothed by the wine she began to sip. 'You really do want to talk to me?' she asked hesitantly, keeping her eyes down when he said he did.

Better not try to read his face. And better not drink any more wine, in case a clear head were needed. *Thud, thud, thud* went her heart, and it was with relief that she saw their waiter arriving with their first course. Now there would be something to do, thank God, other than worrying about what Viktor wanted to say.

# Thirty-Seven

All too soon they were together in the lounge, coffee on the table before them, no one else around except a couple in the corner who had no eyes for them. Only a nearby mirror seemed to show another couple, but it was just their reflections, Jinny's and Viktor's, both looking pale, their eyes dark smudges, even his – but that must have been a trick of the light.

'Mind if I smoke?' he asked, as Jinny turned her gaze from the mirror.

'You know I never mind. Is this coffee all right for you?'

'Not bad at all. Better than most.'

'That's good.'

Watching him light a cigarette, she saw that his hand was trembling. He was nervous, then. Nervous, and unhappy.

'What is it you wanted to say?' she asked, drinking her coffee, her own hand trembling as she held the cup.

'I – the truth is – I don't want to say it.' He drew on the cigarette. 'Perhaps you've guessed what it is, anyway?'

'Just tell me.'

'Jinny – *liebchen* – I have to go back to Vienna. Quite soon. It's not much earlier than I would have gone anyway, but I don't want to delay.'

Silence descended. The couple in the corner rose and went out. No one else came. Jinny did not speak.

'Please,' Viktor said at last. 'Please, say something, Jinny. I know how you must be feeling, I feel so bad myself—'

'I'm trying to take it in, Viktor, what you've told me. You've made a decision to go home? And that's yours alone? I thought we were going to make a decision together? Isn't that what we said?'

'Things have changed. We don't have the same choices now.'

'Why? All that's changed is that there's going to be no war. I'd have thought that'd make things easier for us.'

He shook his head. 'Jinny, please, listen. It's as I said, Mr Chamberlain has not achieved peace, whatever is written on his paper. Hitler has no intention of honouring his promise and, when he's ready, he will strike. I have to be in my own country when that happens. I can't afford to be trapped here, where I'd just be interned as a foreigner. You do see that?'

'No, because I don't know why you're so sure that Hitler wants war. How do you know? You can't know!'

'I do know,' he said wearily, and with a last draw on his cigarette, stubbed it out. 'I know because my father has told me what his Nazi customers have told him. Hitler has no respect for Chamberlain, he finds him irritating and foolish, and will have no hesitation in going to war with Great Britain when the time comes.' Viktor stretched out his hand to take Jinny's. 'So you see, my dearest, why I must go home.'

'Yes, I see,' she said quietly, staring down at their clasped hands. 'You have to go, so you must take me with you.'

It was Viktor's turn to fall silent. He withdrew his hand from Jinny's and ran it over his face as she sat watching, her eyes alight, her lips parted.

'Why not?' she cried. 'Why not, Viktor? If we love each other?'

'Oh, Jinny, we do, we do! But there is no way you can come with me to Vienna the way things are. You'd be a foreigner, from a country likely to be an enemy – it would never work out. I could never let you do it.'

'But if we were married? I'd be with you, part of your family—'

'It would make no difference – you'd still be under suspicion. And how would your family feel, if war comes, as it will, and you were living in an enemy country? You could never put them through that.'

She was silent, coming face-to-face as never before with the difficulties, the near impossibility, of sharing the life of the man she loved in the present situation. If he was right and war between their two countries came about, he would not even be with her in Vienna but in the army, fighting her countrymen and women. She would be alone, regarded as an alien, an enemy, maybe even interned, as Viktor said he would be if he stayed in Scotland. There was no hope, no hope at all, of their being together, whichever country they were in.

Great tears began to fill her dark, tragic eyes and then slide silently down her cheeks. With a long sigh wrenched up from her unhappy heart, she dabbed at the tears with her hankie and rose to her feet.

'I think I should go home now, Viktor.'

'Of course.' He leaped up to be near her. 'I'll just get the bill and call a taxi.'

'A taxi? What are you talking about? We never take taxis.'

'Tonight, we will.'

'No, I'm taking the tram. You needn't come, Viktor. I'd like to be on my own, to sort out things out in my head. Where's my coat, then?'

His face quite white, he ran after her as she moved to the main restaurant, where a waiter helped her put her coat on and she pulled on her dark blue beret.

'Wait, Jinny, wait!' Viktor cried, scrambling into his raincoat. 'I have to pay the bill—'

She halted, shrugging. 'Be quick, then.'

People were staring but it was all right, she was not embarrassing him, they were not having a tiff at the end of their evening as lovers sometimes do. What was going wrong for them went much deeper than that, and it would have been childish not to leave together.

'Thank you,' Viktor said as they walked fast to the tram stop. 'Thank you for waiting, Jinny.'

'Thank you for dinner.'

'Oh, God, Jinny, you're not going to stop me taking you home, are you? I know how you are feeling, and I feel terrible about it, but it's not the end for us. We'll write, we'll keep in touch, and when it's all over we'll be really together. Truly together.'

'What are you saying, Viktor? We're engaged?'

He hesitated. 'You know we are. Not formally, maybe—'

'Not formally at all.'

'There is a reason, for that.'

'What reason?'

'Jinny, this isn't the time or place to talk. Let me come with you now—'

She turned her head, saw a tram in the distance, and sighed. 'All right, then, all right. I give in.'

'Thank God,' he said simply and, when the tram arrived, climbed on with her and sat close on the wooden seating. Both were exhausted and did not speak until they were in Fingal Street, outside the Hendries' flat.

Jinny said quietly, 'Tell me the reason, Viktor. Tell me why we can't be formally engaged.'

'It's difficult, Jinny. I don't want to sound too . . . pessimistic . . . but you have to think of the . . . situation.'

'If you're talking about the war, that shouldn't matter.'

'I'm talking about going to war, and—' He stopped. 'Look, you must know what I'm trying to say.'

'Going to war and not coming back?' she asked huskily. 'Viktor, that's why we should be engaged. So that I'd always have that, always know that's what we both wanted.'

'No,' he said definitely. 'No, if anything happens to me, I want you to have your own life. A properly fulfilled life, not just a string of memories. That's why I'm not going to let you tie yourself to me until we can be properly together.' He drew her into his arms and kissed her gently. 'So, let's just think of that happening, *liebchen*. Being together, making love – and don't ask me how often I think about that – but secure. In a world without war. That's what we have to work for, because it's all that matters.'

She leaned against him, her tears returning, wondering how she could have thought of not letting him be with her to say goodnight. It was the pain, she supposed, of his deciding to go home without her – it had been so hard to bear, especially when she'd been so happy thinking there could be something so different for them, now that there was peace. But Viktor did not believe in Hitler's peace. He was looking ahead to war and going off to fight, even accepting that he might not come back, and working out how things might be for her if he didn't.

Thinking of that, she clutched him compulsively, kissing him with all her strength and love.

'I think about making love, too,' she whispered. 'And sometimes I've wished – I've wondered – if we could be together like that. I mean, why not, Viktor?'

'You know why not, Jinny. Afterwards you might think differently, have regrets—'

'No, no, I wouldn't. If we were engaged.' In the light of the street lamp, her drenched eyes were tender. 'It's not too late, you know.'

'It's too early,' he said softly. 'Our time will come, though, I promise you. One day it will come.'

After they'd held each other in a vain attempt at comfort, Jinny slipped from his arms and took out her key.

'Would you like to come in for a minute, Viktor? No one's home yet – there's no light on.'

'I . . . maybe I'd better not. If your father were to see me he'd be upset.'

She was about to say not to worry, but instead smiled a little ruefully and waved at three figures in the distance.

'I see my sisters and Allan,' she murmured. 'They must have been out celebrating. But you must still come in.'

He didn't, though, and instead, when the sisters and Allan arrived and there'd been laughter and hugs, said he must get back.

'Oh, what a shame!' cried May. 'We've been over to Allan's to celebrate – had some of the neighbours in and had a wonderful time. Didn't we, Allan? Didn't we have a grand time?'

'With mine the only dissenting voice,' remarked Vi. 'Well, I had a grand time too, but shouldn't have done, really, seeing as I think Mr C. should never have signed that document with Hitler. Giving him everything he wanted! It was disgraceful!'

At which May said she was calling time on any more of that talk and now they must all go inside and she'd put the kettle on. Did Viktor really have to go?'

'I'm afraid so, but it's been wonderful to meet you all like this. Jinny, I'll see you tomorrow?'

Their eyes met.

'Tomorrow,' she agreed, and watched as he went down the street until she could see him no more, when she turned to join the others and hoped they wouldn't notice she'd been crying.

# Thirty-Eight

Within three weeks, Viktor had gone. The worst three weeks of Jinny's life, she'd thought them. Until she said goodbye to him at Waverley Station and walked unseeingly back to Comrie's. It was then she realized that every day ahead was to be like this, filled with the searing pain of loss, and felt her knees almost buckle and her head swim, as though she had some sort of flu.

That Viktor felt the same – and she knew he did from his anguished face at the train window – gave her no comfort. In a way, it only made her feel worse, for his unhappiness seemed to make it clear that there was no real hope for them. If he could have been cheerful, telling her that this parting was only temporary and they would meet again soon, she might have been able to rally to cheerfulness too.

But of course, he couldn't pretend things weren't as they were, or that his clear-sightedness was mistaken – otherwise they would not have been saying goodbye. Even though they promised to write, and Jinny even said she'd be taking German lessons at evening class, they both knew this parting could be one of sorrow only, for there were no guarantees they would ever meet again.

How kind folk were, though! Jinny had never imagined her situation would bring such sympathy. Even her father, who was so relieved she was not going to Vienna, had taken her in his arms and said, 'Lassie, lassie, don't cry, he'll be back, eh? If there's no war, you'll see him again,' and she'd sobbed but been so grateful that he should try to help her.

And her sisters, of course, did all they could, trying to think of things to cheer her, pointing out that Viktor might have got it all wrong and there'd be peace after all, though Vi did not believe it, and May couldn't stop wondering what she would have done if she'd been left as Jinny had been and her Allan had gone to foreign parts.

The staff at Comrie's, though, were the most surprising to Jinny, for she knew there'd always been those who'd prophesied disaster for her if she went out with a foreigner, as well as those who'd teased and laughed, or felt a certain envy, and they might have taken a gloomy satisfaction in seeing her as she was now – abandoned, as it were. Yet that hadn't been the case at all. They'd all made a point of showing sympathy – from the bakery workers to the shop and café staff – with even Senga strangely showing some heart. Especially when she and Terry, out of the blue, announced their engagement at Christmas, and Senga, showing her ring, had whispered to Jinny, 'I'm that sorry, Jinny, I am, honestly.'

At which, Jinny, astonished, almost burst into tears, but with true sincerity wished her and Terry every happiness.

As for Accounts, her own workplace, it was here that she gained the most comfort. Not from Mr Comrie, who never seemed to want to look at her, perhaps because of feelings of guilt that his nephew had departed. Nor from Mabel, who was always shaking her head as though she'd known all along that something like this would happen. No, it was from Ross that the most comfort came.

The difference between him and everyone else was that he knew the whole background to her love affair with Viktor, had in a sense been through it with her having always been there, always ready to listen. Sometimes, it was true, he'd felt it necessary to warn her of possible future unhappiness, but usually he'd accepted her love and understood what it meant to her. And now that Viktor had gone, though his love hadn't died for her, as she'd been able to explain to Ross, if not to others, he knew just how much she was suffering, being now alone.

'You're so kind,' she told him once. 'You understand how I feel, but you don't keep asking me how I am or telling me I'll soon feel better or anything. I appreciate that.'

'Well, I know from experience that it's pointless telling people they'll feel better one day. They probably will, but it takes time. In your case, though, there is hope, isn't there? That you and Viktor will be together again one day?'

'Hope? I don't know. I have a feeling that I'll never see him again.' Jinny caught her breath. 'But it's much worse for you, Ross. I shouldn't be complaining to you.'

'Actually, I'm at last feeling better,' he said, after a pause. 'I'm not forgetting – I'll never forget her, but I'm . . . beginning to live again, you might say.'

'Ross, that's wonderful! Oh, I'm really pleased for you.'

She would have liked to know if his pretty cousin, Lorna, had anything to do with Ross's return to the world, but could scarcely ask that. Perhaps it was just a coincidence, anyway, that he'd been seeing her when he was getting better.

'Teatime!' cried Mabel, appearing in the office with a tray of cups of tea and a plate of biscuits. 'I'll just clear a space on your desk, Ross. Jinny, are you all right, dear? Feeling better?'

'Yes, thanks, Mabel,' Jinny said with a sigh.

'Oh, dear, poor Mabel,' Ross said, when she'd gone. 'She means well, though.'

'You always say that.' Jinny managed a smile. 'Look, do you want to OK these bills? I've put them in order if you want to look through them.'

'Fine. Let me just ask you, though – how are your German classes going? You finding them useful?'

'Oh, yes, I'm not doing too badly. Don't think I'll be able to write my letters to Viktor in German any time soon, though.'

'You do write to each other?'

'Of course. Not every day or anything, but yes, we write. It's our lifeline.' She smiled a little. 'Even though Viktor's written English isn't as good as his speech. Sometimes his sentences sort of look like German, if you know what I mean.'

'The main thing is you're in contact.'

'Like I say, we have our lifeline.'

# Thirty-Nine

At least Jinny had that. A lifeline, made up of Viktor's letters. And though she didn't know if she would ever see him again, as Ross had said, she had hope. Hope, and her job, and peoples' kindness – she could manage. As long as they still had peace.

And peace they seemed to have. Maybe it really was true that Hitler didn't want war. And if it were – Jinny hugged the thought – she might have more than hope . . .

Until, that is, the news came on 15 March 1939 that Hitler had attacked what was left of Czechoslovakia. Then her hope died – and not just hers. The whole world saw the move for what it was – a beginning and an ending. The ending of peace; the beginning of World War Two.

For it was plain enough that Hitler would not stop at taking Czechoslovakia. He had his sights set on Poland, who would not give in to his demands on territories, and though Chamberlain had finally agreed that Great Britain would stand up to him, along with France, they had little hope that he would listen to them.

It was on 1 September that he invaded and bombarded Poland, and it was on Sunday, 3 September that Great Britain, having promised to support Poland, sent Germany an ultimatum. If, by 11 a.m, there had been no end to hostilities, war would be declared. No reply was made; no hostilities were ended. Therefore, at 11.15 a.m, Mr Chamberlain broadcast to the nation that Great Britain and Germany were officially at war.

Still grouped around the wireless after that fateful message had ended, the Hendries and Allan Forth sat for some time without speaking, only their eyes revealing their shock. Finally, Josh cleared his throat and looked around at his family.

'So, where do we go from here?' he asked. 'Back to 1914? The trenches? I canna believe it.'

'There won't be trench war this time,' Allan responded. 'This time it'll be the turn of the bombers.'

'Oh, no!' cried May. 'What'll we do?'

'Find the nearest air-raid shelter,' said Vi. 'They've been building 'em all over the place.'

'You canna fight a war just from the air,' said Josh. 'There'll have to be battles and troops, just like always, before we're done.'

'Oh, agreed.' Allan glanced at May. 'But this time they won't wait for volunteers. There'll be conscription – for men of the right age.'

'And women, they say, sooner or later,' put in Vi. 'Which is only fair.'

'Never!' cried Josh. 'You mean you lassies'd have to go to war? That'd be a piece o' nonsense, eh?'

'I wouldn't mind going,' Jinny said quietly. 'Like Vi says, it's only fair.'

As her family looked at her, May stretched out a hand to touch hers.

'What about Viktor?' she asked softly. 'You haven't mentioned him lately.'

Because she hadn't heard from him since he'd said he would be joining the army. Although he hadn't spelled it out, clearly he would find it more difficult to write to her then, and now that war had been declared between their countries, neither of them would be able to write. Maybe that was easy to understand, but it didn't make it any easier to bear.

'I don't expect to hear from him now,' she said after a pause. 'Now that he's in the army and we are at war.'

'In the army?' Josh repeated. 'You mean the German army?'

'Of course she means the German army,' Vi snapped. 'What else?'

'And you say he's no' a Jerry?' Josh asked. 'I always said he was, and now you see I was right.'

'He's an Austrian!' cried Jinny. 'That's all he wants to be. It's not his fault that his country's part of Germany now!'

Everyone waited for Josh to make some sharp riposte but when he didn't, only sat and filled his pipe, his face grey and weary, May rose to her feet.

'Come on, girls, let's get on with the Sunday dinner. Might as well have something good to eat.'

'While we've got it,' said Vi, joining her on the way to the kitchen.

But Jinny's thoughts, as she slowly stood up, were far away from roast beef and Yorkshire pudding.

# Part Two

# Forty

It was 1940 and a day in late June – a time of summer, when the Princes Street gardens Jinny could see from Accounts were in full bloom, and people hurrying by were lightly dressed and looking just as usual. Except that they weren't, of course; they were people at war, people under threat, people more vulnerable than they'd ever been in their lives. For France had fallen.

Jinny, totalling up figures on her adding machine, still could not believe that France had surrendered and that a British expeditionary force, originally sent to help, had earlier had to be rescued by boats from the German army now in control of Europe. It just didn't seem possible that Hitler had been so triumphant, taking – as well as France – Norway, Belgium, Luxembourg and Holland, so that all that remained to be conquered was Great Britain. Just across the Channel.

'Aye, it'll only be a matter of time before Hitler's here,' her father had said when the news about France's defeat had come. 'What's to stop him, eh? That wee strip o' water where our laddies were rescued? Forget it. We'll just have to prepare ourselves for what's going to happen.'

'Dad, you shouldn't be so defeatist!' Vi had cried robustly. 'We've got our defences, we've got an army; we won't be just giving in and opening the door for Hitler.'

'That's right.' May had added, with a voice that shook, 'Allan hasn't been called up for nothing.'

Poor May, her family thought as she looked down at her wedding ring. Still only a newly-wed, really, for her quiet registry office wedding had taken place in April, and she was now on her own in Allan's house while he'd been called up and was in Aberdeen doing basic training. Everyone had been happy that wedding day, except for Josh, though he'd surprisingly done his best not to show his feelings. But after only a weekend's honeymoon in the Borders, Allan had had to report to his unit. After which there'd been one terrible piece of news after another, culminating with the fall of France. It was when that news had broken that May had come over, so that they could be together as a family and discuss what they might do. As though there was anything they could do!

First would come the bombers – that was Hitler's practice – then the troops. There would be resistance, as Vi had said, and Mr Churchill, who'd taken over as prime minister from Mr Chamberlain in May, would no doubt be planning with his service chiefs their contingency plans at that moment. But why should Great Britain succeed in blocking Hitler when everyone else had failed? All that was sure was that the British people stood alone against a so far unstoppable army. For how long?

What am I doing? Jinny suddenly asked herself, putting down her pen and looking round the pleasant accounts office, at that moment filled with sunshine. This was all crazy, eh? Carrying on as though everything was normal? Any minute now, Mabel would come in with their tea and they'd all take their break as usual, yet Jinny had only to look across to Ross's desk and see Mr Lennox, Ross's replacement, checking some invoices to know that she was right and that nothing was at all normal.

Oh, how she missed Ross! He'd been gone since September, having volunteered for a Scottish regiment soon after the outbreak of war, and his place had been taken by Hugh Lennox, an old friend of Mr Comrie's and a retired accountant. After Ross's training, Jinny had felt she could have managed the office herself, and might have said so once, but now just let it go. Of course, it was good to have Mr Lennox anyway and he had certainly lost none of his skills, but every time she looked at him – and he was quite handsome in his way, with smooth grey hair and strong features – she was reminded that he wasn't Ross and that the old, pleasant way of working had gone and might never return.

Other things had changed, too. Comrie's, for instance, which was struggling to provide a service to its customers under difficult wartime conditions. There was a shortage of supplies, of course – flour, sugar and eggs, and pretty much everything else. There were new rules and regulations that had to be followed, such as the replacement of all breads by a so-called 'national loaf', a solid, wholemeal affair few people liked, and had the extra disadvantage that it could only be sold when a day old. The official intention was so that folk wouldn't try to eat too much when it was new, which as Mr Comrie said was a piece of nonsense if ever there was one!

As for his staff, Mr Comrie was in despair. Of his bakers, only Alf, who was over forty-one and not eligible for call-up, was left, which meant that Norah Mackie had been required to help out.

Imagine Norah, a woman, being a professional baker! But she was happy enough, her own work of decorating cakes being no longer required, there being so few cakes made and those only of the plainest type.

It was just as well, perhaps, that Trixie had departed to work in munitions, for there might not have been enough work for her, and certainly not for Senga, the trainee, though she was now married to Terry and 'expecting', while Terry no longer drove the van, for which there was no petrol allowance anyway, and was now serving in a Border regiment.

Not only Trixie had left to work in the munitions factory at Portobello – Audrey from the Princes Street shop was another who'd gone for the better money, leaving Mrs Arrow with only Fiona and Joan to help, about which she bitterly complained even though the café, at least, was no longer anything to worry about, Mr Comrie having closed it in 1939.

'Aye, there was no way we could keep that going, what with all the rules and regulations and nothing much to offer,' Mrs Arrow had said at the time, but she still liked a little moan to Jinny about her difficulties.

'So little to sell in the shop!' she would sigh as Jinny stood waiting to eat her sandwiches at lunchtime. 'I mean, compared to what we used to have!'

Of course she never mentioned Viktor's Austrian cakes, as there was no Bob to make them, even if they'd had the ingredients, and they wouldn't have made them anyway, would they? Who'd want Jerry cakes now?

In fact, no one ever spoke Viktor's name – certainly not to Jinny, and certainly not to Mr Comrie, who must be feeling bad enough that his nephew was probably fighting with the Germans by now. How Jinny was feeling it was thought better not to ask.

How was she feeling, then, on that apprehensive day so soon after the fall of France? She wasn't even sure herself.

# Forty-One

How did she feel? Glancing over to Mr Lennox again, Jinny saw that he was still absorbed in his work, and after a moment's wait she picked up her bag from under her desk and took from its inside pocket a small box and a photograph. Removing the lid from the box, she looked down at her brooch, her Edelweiss, and as she remembered her joy, her utter happiness a the time it had been given, tears pricked her eyes and blurred the white flowers, so beautifully made, resting on the fine gold stem.

Would she ever have believed, when Viktor had given her the brooch, that she would be afraid now to be seeing his countrymen marching with Germans down Princes Street, as they would have marched in Paris and all the places they'd overrun? Might she even see Viktor himself? Oh, no, that wasn't possible! He wouldn't let that happen. He wouldn't be like those Nazis, so triumphant . . .

Yet as she put the brooch away and turned to his photograph, a snap she'd taken herself on one of their city walks, she had to admit that she didn't really know what Viktor was like now. He had not wanted to fight for Hitler before he went home, but time had passed and he might have changed. People did change, didn't they? And she had not heard from him for more a year. Time enough maybe for him to no longer be the man she had loved.

For she was no longer sure she still loved him. There was her problem and her pain, which was not the same as that she'd suffered when she was first without him. Then she'd felt only loss. Now she felt guilt. How could she not love Viktor just as much as ever when they'd been so happy together? Shared a love that was true? A year was a long time to manage alone, maybe, but how was it possible that she could allow the memory of his face, once so beloved, to begin to fade?

As her eyes again studied his photograph to remind herself of his fine, handsome face, she felt a great stab of grief cut through her heart like a knife, and as she thrust the photograph back into her bag she gave an involuntary sob. Oh, God, had Mr Lennox heard? He had.

'All right, Miss Hendrie?' he called.

Miss Hendrie . . . He always called her that, saying he was far too old fashioned to use colleagues' first names, which only made Jinny miss Ross all the more.

'Fine, thanks, Mr Lennox,' she answered, pushing her bag under the desk again as Mabel brought in tea, followed by Mr Comrie, who said he was on his way out to a doctor's appointment.

'All this stress and strain – it's not good for me,' he announced as Mabel gave Jinny and Mr Lennox their tea. 'Arthur Whyte's just rung to say there's more trouble over our flour allocation – I mean, what does anyone expect? We feed the nation on fresh air or what?'

'You're sure you don't want tea before you go, Mr Comrie?' Mabel asked as he clamped his trilby hat down on his head and strode to the door.

'No, no, I'd better get on my way. Though why we're worrying about anything I couldn't really say, after the news about France. What hope is there for us, Hugh, eh?'

After a quick glance at Jinny, which seemed to warn her against mentioning his nephew – as though she would! – Mr Comrie finally departed, allowing Mabel to sink into a chair and fan herself with her handkerchief.

'Mr Comrie talks about stresses and strains,' she remarked, 'as though he's the only one suffering. But I'm sure we're all on edge, eh? I feel quite bad myself, thinking about an invasion.'

'He's in charge, he has the responsibility,' Mr Lennox replied rather coldly. 'And these worries take their toll.'

'That's just what I'm saying – on all of us.' Rather pink in the face, Mabel stood up. 'May I take your cup, Mr Lennox?'

'Thanks, but I'm not quite finished. I'll bring it through.'

After she'd left, her head held high, Mr Lennox gave Jinny a slight smile. 'I'm afraid I've upset her, haven't I?'

'I shouldn't worry about it, Mr Lennox. As Mabel says, everyone's on edge at the moment.'

Why indeed worry? she asked herself, draining her own cup and setting it down. Why be touchy about things that didn't matter, when for all they knew they might have no future. At least, not as an independent country?

How she wished she could get away! Away from Mr Comrie and Mr Lennox and Mabel, and the flour allowance and the sugar shortage, and who would do what to help Mrs Arrow or Mr Whyte at the bakery. Was there not something else she could do? Something more worthwhile? Something that would put all these worries at Comrie's into perspective?

And maybe put her guilt over Viktor's fading image into perspective, too?

But what could she do? Where could she go?

With a sigh, she collected Mr Lennox's cup and her own and took them through to wash them, but with this little duty done and returning to her work, no answers to her questions came to mind.

# Forty-Two

As the evening was so warm and close, Vi – whose turn it was to do the tea – announced that they were going to have salad and Dad would just have to put up with it.

'We're lucky to have it, *and* the boiled ham I managed to find, so don't go complaining,' she told him as they sat down to eat, at which he shrugged.

'Who's complaining? If I think salad's rabbit food, it's still food, eh? I know we're lucky. As long as Herr Hitler's no' crossing the Channel yet.'

'Don't!' cried Jinny. 'Don't joke like that!'

'Only way to get by, pet. Joking, I mean.'

'Nothing on the wireless yet?' asked Vi.

He shook his head. There'd been no news of movements across the Channel so far. Not that they could take comfort in that. It was still early days and no doubt Hitler was perfecting his bombing plans so that Great Britain would be attacked from the air before the troops came over. London, of course, would be his first target, but Scotland would not be forgotten. The Scots would be sure to need their air-raid shelters, just like folk in the south.

'I don't feel very hungry,' Jinny said, putting down her knife and fork. 'Sorry, Vi.'

'Oh, come on!' Vi had drawn her dark brows together. 'That's just silly talk! We have to eat; we have to keep going. And I got some lovely raspberries at the market – no cream, of course, but there's a wee bit of sugar. Just have to be careful.'

'Anything Jinny doesn't want you can give to me,' Josh said cheerfully. 'I need my strength for this farce we're putting on at the minute. Talk about scene changes! I feel I've run twice up Arthur's Seat by the time we've finished!'

'Full house?' asked Vi.

'You bet! To think they closed the theatres at the beginning of the war! Soon found out that was a bad idea!'

'I think I'll have some of the raspberries, anyway,' said Jinny, who was feeling slightly better seeing her father in a good mood, which was probably his aim.

After he'd left for work, the sisters washed up and turned on the wireless, but there was no news to alarm them, only a woman's educated voice talking about a wonderful 'response'.

'Response to what?' asked Vi.

'Ssh, I think she's telling us,' said Jinny.

'The number of young women responding to the Princess Royal's call for volunteers – "Your King and Country Need You!" – has been most gratifying,' the broadcaster was continuing. 'And I can assure everyone that they will be doing a thoroughly worthwhile job in the ATS, working alongside our brave soldiers and meeting new people, knowing they are responding to the call to help their country in her time of need. Now, it only remains for me to thank—'

'Think we'll cut out the thanks,' said Vi, switching off the set. 'But that's interesting, eh? All those lassies running off to join the ATS?'

'ATS?' Jinny repeated. 'What exactly does that stand for?'

'Auxiliary Territorial Service – it's the women's army.'

'Doesn't sound like it's for women.'

'No, I think I read there'd been trouble finding the right name. The women's air force and the women's naval service have got W for women in their titles – WAAF and WRNS – but nobody worked out how to put it in for the army. Still, what's in a name, eh?' Vi smiled. 'Fancy volunteering?'

The two pairs of dark eyes met.

'You know, I just might,' Jinny said slowly.

'You what?' Vi's mouth had dropped open. 'You don't mean it? Why would you want to leave Comrie's until you have to? We'll probably all be called up when they get round to passing an act for it.'

'I just felt today that I couldn't stick it any longer. I know it's nobody's fault, but the young men are away fighting and the rest of us are just going on about rations and how much flour we can have and all the rest of it. I know it's important – folk have to eat – but I'd like to get away, do something that matters.' Jinny smiled nervously. 'Couldn't think what – and then just now, hearing the wireless—'

'And you decided to join up? Well, I'm struck dumb, I really am!'

'Struck dumb, you?' Jinny tried to laugh. 'Do you think I shouldn't go for it?'

'Oh, I don't say that. If you're really fed up with Comrie's, why not? But Mr Comrie won't want to lose you, will he? How's he going to manage?'

'He's got his old buddy, Mr Lennox, working there instead of Ross, so he doesn't need me. There isn't as much to do as there used to be. We've had to cut down so much.'

Vi's look was dubious. 'And Dad? Have you thought what he'd say if you joined the army? He doesn't think women should go to war.'

'I don't suppose they'll be letting women really go to war. We'll probably just be back-up.' Jinny leaned forward. 'But it'll still be worthwhile to join up, eh?'

'Yes, I think it will. Remember, we said it was only fair that women should be conscripted like the men.' Vi took out a packet of cigarettes and lit one. 'I wouldn't mind volunteering myself.'

'Why don't you?'

'Until I'm officially called up I think I'd better stay with the firm. Since the changeover to uniforms we've been snowed under with paperwork and most of the men have gone, leaving you know who to carry on.' Vi studied her cigarette. 'Besides, we can't both leave Dad, can we?'

'Why, I never thought I'd hear you say that!' cried Jinny. 'You always say that men should be able to look after themselves and not depend on women to do everything for 'em!'

'I know, but he's lost May, and if he loses you too he'll be in a state. It'll be better if I stay on till I get the call.'

'You're just a great softie, after all,' Jinny said, laughing. 'Now it can be told!'

'None of that!' Vi grinned and offered her cigarettes. 'Here, have a smoke to celebrate your new life, eh?'

'No, thanks, I don't fancy smoking. You know I never have.'

'Wait till you're in the forces – you'll be smoking like a chimney! I'm told everybody does.'

Their talk had been so absorbing it had quite taken their minds off the danger that might be coming their way, but when they tuned into the BBC at nine o'clock, there was still no news of German bombing or invasion, and once again they breathed sighs of relief.

They were not to know that, within a few short weeks, everyone in the country would also be heaving sighs of relief, for it had become clear that Hitler would never invade Britain. He had gambled on winning a battle of the air in the skies over England, beginning in July and ending in September with defeat for him and his air force. The young British pilots, in their Spitfires and Hurricanes, had brought respite from fear for their countrymen and women, and though their cities had to endure German bombing, they no longer needed to picture German troops marching through London, or, indeed, Edinburgh.

'Never in the field of human conflict has so much been owed by so many to so few,' said Winston Churchill of the Battle of Britain, and the words of gratitude echoed throughout the land.

But in late June, when Jinny sat with her sister, planning her new future – all that lay ahead. Her immediate problem was how to break the news, first to her father, then to Mr Comrie, that she would soon be going away. In theory, they should be prepared for it, as all young unmarried women would certainly be conscripted sooner or later. In practice – well, in spite of what she'd told Vi, she didn't know how her news would be taken. With some apprehension, she watched Vi calmly smoking, and decided she must just wait and see.

# Forty-Three

Jinny told her father first. On the following Sunday, it being a fine afternoon, it was decided she and Josh should take a tram to the Botanic Gardens, stroll round the extensive grounds, maybe look in at the hot houses and have a cup of tea. Finding cafés open on Sundays in Edinburgh was not easy, but it was possible to have tea at the Botanics, even if there probably wouldn't be anything much to eat.

'Very nice,' remarked Josh when they were sitting in the crowded tea room, looking out at trees and lawns. 'I appreciate this – I don't see enough greenery in my line o' work.'

'More tea?' asked Jinny.

'Aye, please. It's thirsty work, all this walking, and that hot house nearly finished me. Shame Vi's not with us, though. She should see a tree or two, eh?'

'She's out with her friend – you know, Marion,' Jinny told him, knowing of course that Vi was under her orders to be elsewhere while she broke her news to her father. When she had passed him his tea, she cleared her throat and took courage to speak. 'Dad . . . there's something I want to tell you—'

'Oh?' His dark eyes, so like hers, were instantly alert. 'Something good?

'It's just I've been thinking – well, no, I've decided, really – to volunteer for the ATS.'

He set down his cup. 'You've what?'

'Decided to volunteer, Dad. Seemingly, they want ten thousand women for the service. The Princess Royal came on the wireless and asked girls to join. For king and country, she said, and I thought . . . I thought I'd like to do something to help.'

'For king and country?' Josh raised his eyebrows. 'That's why she wants you to go? All I can say is that half the fellas that went last time for king and country never came back, and the rest were never the same again. I should know; I was one.'

'I know, Dad, it was a terrible war, a terrible waste, but this one is different. We have to fight Hitler because he's a tyrant; he's trying to enslave the world. That's why I want to do my bit.'

As he said nothing, she went on eagerly: 'But I won't be fighting like the men, you know, Dad – no one's saying that. I'll just be helping, that's all, doing back-up sort of jobs.' She laughed a little. 'Nothing in the front line!'

'What'll they say at Comrie's if you go?' he asked after a few quiet moments. 'Why can't you just stay there till they bring in this bill to conscript women? You'll be needed, eh?'

'Mr Comrie's got a retired accountant to stand in for my boss. They'll be able to manage without me. And I'm tired of what I'm doing there; I want to do something useful.'

Suddenly seeming to tire of her efforts to persuade her father to see her point of view, Jinny sat back in her chair and sighed, at which Josh shrugged,

'OK, if it's what you want – go ahead. Volunteer. Might be for the best.'

She jolted herself upright, staring at him with large, astonished eyes. 'You won't mind, Dad?'

'I don't say that, all I'm thinking is . . . it might be a good thing for you to meet other people.'

'Other people? Well, of course I'd be meeting other people!'

'Other men, Jinny.'

She was mystified. He had never wanted his girls to meet 'other men', to have lives away from him – why should he so suddenly have changed? Then it came to her. Because of Viktor. The men she would meet would be soldiers. British soldiers, men Josh might relate to, but that wouldn't matter. All that mattered was that any man she met in her new life would not be a foreigner who might take her away to live in his country. She would not be lost to her own country, to her own family, to Josh. She could now understand his thinking, but of course he didn't know anything of her present feelings for Viktor. How could he, when she didn't even fully know them herself?

'To meet other men is not my reason for joining the ATS,' she said, a little unsteadily, her heart beginning to ache at the thought of Viktor and how she didn't know whether he was alive or dead. 'But if you don't mind me going, it'll make me feel a lot happier.'

'Aye, well. maybe I shouldn't have mentioned the men, Jinny. It was just a thought. Thing is if you do join the ATS it'll give you a new life and if that's what you want, so be it.' Josh rose to pay for their tea and gave an uncertain smile. 'We'd best get going, eh?'

As they returned home, she couldn't really believe her luck – that she'd so easily got through the hurdle of telling her father her plans. If he liked to think she might make new relationships that would break her attachment to Viktor, best let him think so. If she had no thoughts of making new relationships herself then that wasn't something he needed to know.

All she had to do now was brace herself for her interview with Mr Comrie, and hope he would not think she was deserting Accounts for no good reason.

In the event, he took the news of her intentions so well that she was a little taken aback. Was she not to be missed at all? But when he expressed surprise at her decision to volunteer for the services, yet no real regret, she knew it was not because her work was inferior, only that he was confident his friend, the male and professional accountant, would manage very well without her. Of course, she should have expected that sort of reaction, Mr Comrie being the sort to believe a man always had a head start on any woman where work was concerned, and she had to admit Mr Lennox was very well qualified and experienced.

Still, it would have been nice if Mr Comrie had seemed genuinely sorry to lose her. He had said, of course, that her job would be waiting for her when the war was over, and patted her kindly on the shoulder when she turned to leave his office – she must make do with that. At least she could take comfort from the fact that others at Comrie's seemed sorry she was going – Mabel, for instance, who said Accounts just wouldn't be the same, and Norah Mackie and Mr Whyte, who were quick to lament over the departure of another familiar face. As for Mrs Arrow and her bakery staff, they made her promise to let them see her in her uniform as soon as she got some leave.

'But no getting wed to some soldier laddie and disappearing altogether!' Mrs Arrow cried on Jinny's last day.

'No fear of that!' Jinny answered.

And, of course, no one mentioned Viktor.

# Forty-Four

The worst goodbyes were to her family, events having seemed to move so quickly that no sooner had she been accepted for the ATS than she was ready to go, those last kisses and hugs with her dad and sisters bringing tears to her eyes but quickly over and her new life coming up fast.

To begin with, as had been explained to her, there would be four weeks' basic training at one of the many camps, with an issue of uniform, or as much as was available, as there were usually shortages of various items. There would also be injections and checks for hair lice and social diseases – 'Nothing personal!' the woman officer who had been informing Jinny of what lay in wait for her had said with a laugh. 'We just have to be careful, you know.'

'Oh, yes,' Jinny had agreed, blushing, and thinking she'd be glad when all that was over. Where would she be sent first was the question. It turned out to be a training camp near Berwick-upon-Tweed, so not too far away. She might have had to go anywhere, from Aberdeen to the south of England.

Even though easy to reach, it was daunting to arrive at the spartan camp and meet up with a crowd of strange young women, all eyeing each other up and down before being directed to an army hut where they collected bedding and made up their own beds.

Surely she would never get to know any of these girls, thought Jinny as she and the other 'rookies' struggled to put together the three thin mattresses that made up what were known as 'biscuits', the look of which boded ill for comfort.

Her eyes went over those girls nearest to her – the tall, thin one with glasses, for instance, and the little, snub-nosed, sandy-haired girl who looked quite petrified; the couple of blondes who had already gravitated to each other, and the plump, cheerful young woman who had declared that if she could sleep on that terrible 'biscuit' on her bed, nothing would surprise her more.

Oh, but there were so many others, all speaking with different accents, all wearing different clothes: some smart and expensive, others shabby and well worn – all, except maybe the little sandy one, trying to put on a good front and at least finding something to laugh about when they tried on their army underwear.

'Help, will you look at me in these khaki knickers?' one of the blonde girls cried. 'I bet even my old granny wouldn't be seen dead in 'em!'

'Well, let's hope we're not either,' the tall girl with glasses retorted. 'Actually, I think the shoes are the worst – talk about clodhoppers!'

'And they've run out of khaki stockings,' the plump girl reported. 'We're going to look a bit odd in uniform wearing the ones we came in, eh?'

'Can't be helped,' snapped the woman sergeant overseeing their uniform allocations. 'The main thing is to remember to look as smart as possible with whatever you've got. Buttons polished, shirts and skirts ironed, hair neatly tucked into your cap. And not too much make-up!'

'Oh, dear, I'm not looking forward to the drill,' Jinny heard someone whisper, and as she was rather apprehensive about that herself, she was relieved to know they would not begin square-bashing until tomorrow. For now, they could go along to the cookhouse for a break, try what tea tasted like in enamel mugs and chew on the thickest ham sandwiches they had ever seen.

All very wearying, that first day, but at last, when they gathered in their off-duty room, some names began to be attached to the girls around Jinny, making her feel a little more at ease.

The tall, thin girl was Brenda, who had been working in her father's pharmacy and would eventually train in pharmacy herself, while the blonde couple were Georgina and Verity, not known to each other but with the same idea that being in the ATS would be 'fun'. 'Hope you're not disappointed,' commented Molly, the plump one, adding that she wouldn't mind a bit of fun herself, although her reason for volunteering from her office job was because she wanted to contribute to the war effort.

'That's a bit like me,' said Jinny, giving her name and explaining her background, and as Molly grinned and shook hands, she felt she might have already have made a friend, if only for four weeks.

Although there was a wireless and a gramophone in the off-duty room, most of the girls were so tired they didn't mind being told to go to bed, where they would learn the worst about their mattresses when they tried to sleep. Next day, there'd be PT and various lectures, as well as the dreaded drill – better be prepared.

'Don't worry about oversleeping,' the corporal who was supervising them said with a laugh. 'I'll be in early to call you – "Wakey, wakey, rise and shine" – and that means your shoes!'

# Forty-Five

Jinny's bed was at the end of the hut, next to that of the little sandy-haired girl, who had said scarcely a word since she arrived and seemed most desperately shy. Poor kid, thought Jinny, resolving, once they were in their issue pyjamas, to speak to her before 'lights out'.

'Hello, I'm Jinny Hendrie from Edinburgh,' she whispered across. 'Are you settling on all right?'

The girl gave a timid smile. 'Oh, hello. I'm Sukie Woodman, from Worcester. I thought you were Scottish – I could tell by your voice.' She hesitated. 'To tell you the truth, I'm a bit scared. I've never been away from home before.'

'Nor me. I bet most girls here haven't, unless they were away at school, or something.'

'Bet those blonde girls were.' Sukie murmured. 'They don't seem a bit worried by anything.'

'That's blondes for you.' Jinny smiled. 'But it's a bit of a shock for most of us, being here, I'd say. Still, we volunteered, eh? Can't complain.'

'I never thought what it would be like. I just wanted somewhere to go.' Sukie shivered a little and tried to draw her thin blanket more tightly over her, but it was clear that she'd already found that nothing stayed tightly around the 'biscuits'.

'I live with my auntie,' she said after a moment. 'Me mum and dad are dead, you see. And it looks like me job in a shoe shop'll not be lasting much longer – the manageress says there's not enough work for both of us now, and Auntie'll never want to me to stay if I can't pay me keep.'

'Oh, surely—' Jinny began, but Sukie shook her head.

'No, no, I had to find somewhere else and when I heard the ATS wanted volunteers I thought it'd be for me, but now I'm worried I won't be able to keep up and they'll throw me out.' In the gloomy light of the hut, Sukie's hazel eyes were large and woebegone. 'Then what I'll do, I don't know.'

'They won't throw you out,' Jinny declared. 'No need to worry about that. They need you. And you'll be fine – remember, none of us knows anything. We're here to be trained and once you're trained you'll be posted and do a good job, I promise you!'

'You really think so?'

'Certainly do!'

'Lights out!' called the corporal. 'Everybody try to get some sleep. Need to be fresh as daisies tomorrow, eh? Goodnight, all.'

Well, she'd done her good deed for the day, Jinny thought as she listened later to the sound of Sukie's regular breathing. Fingers crossed, all would go well for that poor girl who'd so far had so little good luck.

But what of herself? As she lay awake in the long dark hut, shifting uncomfortably on her 'biscuit', aware of strangers all around and that home was much farther away than just a trip from Berwick might seem, Jinny wondered. Had she done the right thing, giving up all she knew in order to do something that might or might not be useful? Tears pricked her eyelids as she thought of her usual nights spent sharing a room with dear, prickly Vi. Of her father, back from work, in his chair smoking his pipe and sounding off about items in the newspaper. Of May, away from her old home, yet still so often popping in, always ready with a sympathetic ear, even with such real fears of her own about Allan.

Why had Jinny left them? To have a change from Comrie's? Well, in spite of Mr Comrie being so indifferent to her leaving, she'd been doing a good job there and she should maybe have continued to do it, until her conscription came. If, in fact, it ever did. The government hadn't even got a bill together, had they?

Round and round her thoughts whirled, until suddenly – it seemed no time at all – she opened her eyes and it was daylight.

'Wakey, wakey!' the corporal was crying as girls were leaping out of bed, complaining that they hadn't slept a wink, hurrying to wash and dress in their new uniforms, trying to be ready for all that lay ahead.

Maybe things didn't seem so bad as in the night, Jinny decided. She too hurried around, pausing to smile at Sukie and wave to Molly. She too was asking what was for breakfast in the cookhouse along with everyone else. And how the devil did you get these 'biscuits' to stay together?

Of course, come the night, she guessed she'd be tearful again, thinking of home, but the cure for daytime seemed to be to keep as busy as possible, and there was no problem there.

# Forty-Six

It was said – the girls had heard it – that senior officers were constantly surprised at the way a group of young women 'rookies' could, in only four weeks, be transformed into a smart, well-trained marching squad that could equal that of the men.

'Equal?' the girls would have cried if they'd had the chance. 'We're better than the men!'

Well, no one would go as far as that but there was no doubt that at the end of their basic training the girls were a credit to their instructors, had mastered all fear of the drill and were even prepared to admit that their introduction to army life hadn't been as bad as they'd thought it might be.

Of course, the discipline was always there, and could be irksome – 'far too much nit-picking and fussing over regulations' was a common complaint, and why did there have to be so many pamphlets dealing with everything under the sun? When they thought about it, however, it did seem to make sense that every category of army life was covered, which meant you at least knew where you were and could quote 'regulations' if need be.

The best thing for most of the rookies was that as the days went by they got to know one another, made friends and felt a shared comradeship that was particularly helpful, especially if anyone was feeling homesick or worried.

Sukie, for instance, was still very unsure of herself in the early days, in spite of encouragement from Jinny. But the more she discovered she could do what was required of her the better she performed her tasks and she visibly gained in confidence. It was true she was the despair of the PT instructor, being so small and slight, and seemingly unable to master the handling of the gym equipment, but she did her best and, as Jinny told her cheerfully, there was no question of her being 'thrown out' just because she couldn't leap over the vaulting horse! Plump, good-natured Molly had the same problem, but didn't let it worry her, and Sukie, who'd done so much better in her new life than she'd ever believed she could, showed her new spirit by not worrying either.

'Everyone's been so kind,' she told Jinny. 'I'm really surprised, you know.'

'Well, apart from a sergeant I won't name and one or two officers, I think I'd say the same,' Jinny answered.

Of course, there were always folk you didn't like – you just had to put up with them – but on the whole, Jinny found she got on with the people around her very well, learning everyone's names and backgrounds, and sometimes felt rather sad that at the end of their basic training they would all be saying farewell and moving on. Who knew where?

By this time, they had all have been assessed for the jobs that would suit them most, with their postings soon to be announced. Then would begin their real work for the army, and they would discover just how much they could offer towards the war effort. Before that happened, however, a dance was organized with the soldiers of one of the Border regiments, and great excitement reigned as the girls gave up worrying about where they might be posted to concentrate instead on looking attractive, finding some decent make-up and getting their hair right.

'But won't it feel odd to go to a dance wearing uniform?' asked Verity, frowning. 'That'll be a first.'

'Oh, what's it matter?' Brenda retorted. 'We are supposed to be soldiers.'

'When it comes to dancing I don't feel a soldier at all!' said Georgina.

'I'm not really looking forward to it,' Sukie confessed to Jinny, her face taking on her old woebegone look. 'I've never been one for dances.'

'But why not, Sukie?'

'Well, I always think no one will ask me to dance.'

'Oh, what a piece of nonsense, as they say where I come from. The chaps will be sure to ask you.'

'I don't look like you, Jinny. I . . . don't get noticed.'

'All you need is a bit of lipstick and your hair swept off your face and you'll be fine. Trust me.'

'You always cheer me up,' Sukie said, managing a smile.

The dance went well. The soldiers, smart in tartan trews, were eager to see the new 'talent', as they called the latest intake of rookies, and wasted no time in taking partners for the opening quickstep, played by a local band. One of the first on the floor, Jinny was gratified to note, was Sukie.

'The lipstick must have done the trick,' she remarked to Molly, just before they were themselves being asked to dance, at which Molly laughed and told her she'd done a good job there.

'Poor little Sukie – she's like a different person from the waif that first arrived, thanks to you.'

'Not just me. I think we've all been changed by joining up. Shame we'll lose touch, eh?'

'Let's see where we get sent – we may meet up again.'

At that point they parted to join the crowd on the floor, and from then on there wasn't much time for talking. For one strange moment Jinny thought of Viktor when a tall, fair-haired soldier danced by with Georgina, and though his looks were not really like Viktor's, they were similar enough to make Jinny catch her breath and feel the familiar stab of pain for lost love she always felt when she remembered Viktor.

'Hey, penny for 'em!' asked her partner, a ginger-haired corporal, having noticed the far-away look in her eyes. 'Where've you gone, then?'

'Oh, sorry, I was just remembering something—'

'Something you should've done?'

'No, no.' She gave a quick smile. 'Nothing to worry about.'

'That's a relief. You're supposed to be enjoying yourself, you know.'

'And I am!'

When the music drew to a close and they stood clapping, Jinny felt it was true, she was enjoying herself – as long as she did not look back.

The interval brought a curtain of cigarette smoke and the usual thin coffee and thick sandwiches, but as the drill hall had no licence there was no alcohol, which meant everyone behaved themselves, laughing and flirting until the band struck up again.

'Oh, I'm having such a good time,' Sukie whispered to Jinny before she returned to the floor with the cheerful young soldier who had first asked her to dance. 'You were so right, you know. Right about everything.'

'Oh, that's me!' laughed Jinny. 'Always get things right – I don't think!'

Still, when she and the rest of the girls were dancing again and she was being careful not to think about anything but the present, it did seem to Jinny that so far her new life was working out well. 'So far', however, being the key words here. So much depended on where she and the others were sent next, and they wouldn't know that till Monday, they'd been told.

But when Monday came and Jinny knew where she was going, she rather wished she didn't.

# Forty-Seven

'Royal Army Pay Corps,' she told her family when she arrived home for a week's leave and had put aside her uniform for a pretty dress. 'Can you believe it? I spend half my time in Civvy Street doing wages, and when I join up for a new life where do I get posted? The Pay Corps!'

Josh and Vi, who'd taken time off work to welcome Jinny home, exchanged glances with May, who'd come over from the hospital where she was now working as a nurses' aide, the hat shop having closed for the 'duration'.

'Seems to make sense to me,' Vi observed, shaking the teapot before topping up Jinny's cup. 'I mean, you won't need much training, will you?'

'That's right,' said Josh. 'And they probably thought you'd be good at the work.'

'Well, I don't know, I think I agree with Jinny,' put in May. 'When you sign up for a new life you don't expect to be doing the same old thing.'

'It might be quite different work,' Vi suggested. 'Maybe more interesting. Where did other girls get posted, anyway?'

'Oh, all over the place,' answered Jinny, thinking back to that day when everyone found out where they were heading. How Sukie had been told she'd be joining the Royal Army Ordnance Corps to be dealing with all kinds of stores and was delighted, while Verity and Georgina would both be doing anti-aircraft work with the Royal Artillery and declared themselves thrilled. As for Brenda and Molly, their postings appeared to be top secret, probably deciphering codes, others had guessed, but they were both brainy girls so it was expected that they'd be selected for something like that.

In fact, the whole intake seemed to be going to do something interesting, except for Jinny, who sighed as she thought about it.

'Daresay I was the only one who wasn't too excited, but I expect it'll work out all right,' she said lightly. 'Like Vi says, the work might be different from what I did before. I'd better not complain.'

'Shame you can't work in Scotland, though,' said Josh. 'Are there no pay offices here, then?'

'Oh, they never like to send you close to home,' Jinny told him. 'So I'm going to Chester in Western Command. There'll be ATSs there, but any men'll probably be unfit for combat – so I've been told. They've probably been wounded. Not badly enough to be invalided out, but not able to fight.'

A silence fell as they all considered Allan, who had yet to be tried in battle, but who must face it sooner or later and then must trust to luck. Better not think about it.

'I should get back to the ward,' May said, rising with a sigh. 'But it's been so lovely to see you again, Jinny. That four weeks you were away seemed like forever.'

'You can say that again,' muttered Josh, also getting up. 'I'll be away and all, but it'll be grand to think you'll be here, pet, when I come back for tea. Come here and give me a hug, eh?'

'It's grand to be back,' said Jinny, hugging and kissing May and her father. 'Can't tell you how I missed home to begin with. Your letters were a big help, but the tears were often flowing, I can tell you!'

'And to think you needn't have gone yet,' commented Josh, shaking his head. 'But that's water under the bridge, eh? You're in the service now, and it seems to suit you. Did they get you marching in your training?'

'You bet, and we thought we beat the fellows hollow!' Jinny laughed. 'Oh, it was all a lot better than I thought it would be. I made some good friends and we had some grand times.'

'So, I've nothing to fear?' asked Vi, shrugging. 'I won't do as well as you, Jinny. I'm not your easy type, that's for sure, but I am wishing I could get away like you and do something useful.'

'Oh, don't say it,' groaned Josh, making for the door. 'I don't want to lose you as well!'

'Away with you, Dad! I'm not going yet, anyway. May, will you come back for your tea? I'm cooking for Jinny tonight – and yes, it's fish!'

'Oh, yes, I'll be back!' cried May as she and Josh hurriedly left and Jinny stood up, stretching, and said she'd unpack her few things.

'Nice to be back in civvies again – do you know, we had to wear our uniforms for the dance – they were all we had.'

'So, you went to dances?' asked Vi. 'They wouldn't be for me, but – don't tell Dad – I've changed my mind and am seriously thinking of volunteering. It might be some time before they start conscripting women and I want to get on with it.'

'As I said, you'll enjoy it, Vi, as I have so far, but still, you know, it's grand to be home.' Jinny smiled. 'And I've a whole week here before I need worry about the Pay Corps. Tomorrow I think I'll look in on Comrie's – see if the place hasn't fallen down without me, eh?'

In the bedroom where her bag was waiting to be unpacked, she first opened the little drawer under the dressing-table mirror where she kept her few pieces that were precious. Her mother's locket, a last present, was there, with a necklace or two and a ring that had been her grandmother's, but what Jinny was taking out now was the Edelweiss brooch Viktor had given her. Every so often she liked to look at it, though she never wore it and certainly would not take it with her on her ATS posting.

Why remind herself of happiness that was gone? She couldn't answer that, except perhaps that she felt it was right not to block everything from her mind. She didn't actually know what had happened to Viktor. They could still meet after the war, even though that might be years away, and if it was true his image had faded, the memory of it could still surprise her. Take Saturday night, when she'd seen the fair-haired soldier dancing with Georgina and been reminded of Viktor. How that look had sparked off the old pain again, until she'd been brought back to the present! Just as the lovely Edelweiss was bringing it back now.

After a moment, Jinny replaced it in its box and turned to begin her unpacking. It was strange to be at home again, the training camp already a memory! As she put away her few things she purposefully began to sing a popular song, reassuring herself that she felt better, able to look forward to the future. There was no point at all in thinking about the past.

# Forty-Eight

Comrie's. There it was, in busy Princes Street, looking not too different from when she'd last seen it. Jinny, smart in a dark green dress and navy jacket, stood for a moment looking at her old workplace, remembering how things had used to be. Of course, by the time she'd left, change had already come – the windows were almost empty instead of displaying the selections of mouth-watering scones and cakes as in pre-war days, the staff so reduced in size as almost to be described as 'skeleton'.

And now there was something she'd never seen before outside Comrie's and that was a queue. The shop had always been busy, of course, the girls kept on their feet serving so many customers, but queues? No, there'd never been queues, but Jinny knew she should have expected one. Queues in wartime were a fact of life, especially for food. At the baker's, at the butcher's, at the grocer's, for if you could reckon on receiving foods that were rationed, any extras in short supply had to be queued for, which made life difficult for those at work, such as Vi.

'Had to take time off to get that fish we had,' she told Jinny. 'There's something to be said for being in the forces, eh? All food found!'

'Such as it is!' Jinny had retorted.

Feeling a little self-conscious now, she was wondering how she could get into the shop to say hello to the staff without being accused of queue-jumping. People were said to be cheerful about the problems of their changed lives, but some of the women outside Comrie's were looking pretty glum – Jinny doubted that they'd take kindly to a girl pushing ahead and trying to take their place, as they would see it. Still, she'd have to get in somehow.

Plucking up courage, she spoke to those at the front of the queue.

'Mind if I go in? I don't want to buy anything, I'm on leave from the ATS and just here to see the people I worked with.'

Without smiling they stared at her, taking in her great dark eyes, her pretty dress and jacket, and then looked at one another.

'Aye, let the lassie in,' one said. 'She's doing her bit, eh?'

'Go on, then,' another said, 'but if we catch you putting any teacakes into that handbag of yours, you'll be for it!'

'There was laughter as Jinny said, 'No teacakes, I promise!' and with a relieved laugh made her way into the shop.

Inside, there were still people queuing right up to the counter, where Joan and a young girl Jinny didn't know were darting about, putting items into paper bags, while Mrs Arrow was calling in a sergeant major's voice: 'Only *one* fruit pie per customer, please. We're going to run out as it is.'

'And what's the good of one wee fruit pie for a family?' someone in the queue demanded.

Mrs Arrow retorted, 'Take it or leave it! We can't sell what we haven't got.'

'The pastry's just like cardboard, anyway,' another voice muttered, and there were sighs and laughter, but by then Mrs Arrow had spotted Jinny and rushed round the counter to greet her.

'Jinny, is it really you – looking that well, eh? My, it's grand to see you!'

'I've only been away a month,' Jinny murmured, embarrassed, 'though it does feel like more!'

'Well, we're really pleased to see you, anyway. Still got Joan, you see?'

'Hello, Joan!' cried Jinny, waving, as Joan looked up from putting a large pallid loaf into a flimsy paper bag and smiled, as the unknown young girl, thin and fair, smiled too.

'That's Peggy,' Mrs Arrow whispered. 'A school-leaver I managed to get, not doing too badly, though terrified of the customers. But just imagine what it's like trying to satisfy 'em, Jinny. It's terrible, I'm telling you! I mean, take thae fruit pies – there's never enough and it's true what they say, 'the pastry's just like cardboard', but we canna get the ingredients to make it any better, and Mr Whyte feels that bad. Even the fruit's out o' tins and nobody'd eat it if there wasn't a war on, but there you are, we have to do the best we can, eh?'

'I'm sure you're doing a wonderful job, Mrs Arrow, and it's grand to see you, it really is.'

'I wish I could give you a cup o' tea, but as you can see, we're rushed off our feet—'

'That's quite all right—' Jinny was beginning when her eyes widened and her lips parted as a copper-haired man in a sports jacket and tweed trousers came into the shop from the stairs, and Mrs Arrow waved.

'Ross, look who's here!' she cried. 'Jinny's come visiting, too!'

'Jinny?' he cried.

'Ross?'

Like the old friends they were, they hugged and shook hands, then burst out laughing.

'Talk about snap!' said Ross. 'I never thought to see you here, Jinny, and looking so well. You're a sight for sore eyes!'

'And you're looking well, too, Ross. Are you on leave, then?'

'I am, thank the Lord.' Ross's brown eyes were shining. 'But it's just so nice to see you, Jinny, I can't believe my luck. I came in to see how everyone was and to have a word with Hugh Lennox, but I never imagined I'd see you!'

'And I never thought I'd see you.' Jinny's eyes were as bright as his. 'I've just finished my basic training and I'm on a week's leave, so thought I'd call in here.'

Noting the interested eyes of Mrs Arrow, and all around her, Ross took Jinny's arm. 'We're a bit in the way here, how about going for a coffee? If we're lucky we can get one at Logie's.'

'I'd love to, Ross, but I was going up to see Mr Lennox and maybe Mr Comrie—'

'Ah, you can see them later. Come on, we've some catching up to do, haven't we?'

'All right, then, let's go! 'Bye, everybody.'

''Bye, Jinny, pet, and Ross!' cried Mrs Arrow. 'Or, should I say, Lieutenant MacBain?'

'Lieutenant?' repeated Jinny, remembering how Ross had liked to call Viktor that so long ago, or so it seemed.

'It's only second lieutenant, as a matter of fact,' Ross was saying. 'And I'm just Ross to you, Mrs Arrow.'

'An officer, though?' said Jinny. 'Well done, you.'

'Come on,' he said hastily. 'Let's go to Logie's.'

# Forty-Nine

Logie's being Logie's, the best department store in the city, there was still a certain pre-war feel about the restaurant with its white-clothed tables and attentive service – even if the waitresses were either very young or rather old, the coffee weak and there were only biscuits, no scones. None of that mattered to Jinny and Ross as they sat at a window table, ready to exchange news and enjoying being together.

'This reminds me of when we used to share the office,' Jinny remarked after the waitress had brought their coffee and shortbread. 'Sometimes we'd have a good old talk. Usually when you wanted to give me advice, I seem to remember.'

'That's all you remember? My giving you advice?'

'No, of course not. I'm joking. I know we talked about lots of things.'

Ross was silent for a few moments while sampling the shortbread. Perhaps he was remembering that she had rarely taken his advice, except on work matters, thought Jinny. Perhaps he wanted to ask about Viktor, for his advice had often concerned him, but if that were the case he didn't put his question into words.

'I did hear you'd volunteered for the ATS,' he said at last, 'and now you say you've finished basic training. How did you like that?'

'It wasn't too bad at all. Och, you should have seen us marching! We thought we were so wonderful – much better than the men, we said!'

'Bet you were, too.' Ross passed the shortbread. 'Like one of these? I don't suppose they've much butter in 'em but can't expect it these days. Did you hear all Mrs Arrow's groans? If you see Mr Whyte he'll bend your ear about shortages as well. But tell me, where've you been posted?'

'Would you believe, the Pay Corps! Just because I used to do the wages! I'm pretty disappointed, really.'

'Is it a command pay office, or a regimental one?'

'A command one, near Manchester.'

'Ah, well, that'll be different work for you. You won't be paying out soldiers' wages, more likely dealing with public monies for military services. Might be more interesting.'

'It certainly sounds it! Thanks for telling me that, Ross – it's quite cheered me up. But now you must tell me what's been happening with you. It's not hush-hush, is it?'

He stirred his coffee, his face suddenly bleak. 'No, I think everyone knows about the evacuation of Dunkirk.'

'Dunkirk? You were involved in that, Ross?' Jinny's voice was hushed. 'I'm so sorry.'

Like most people, she had heard about the chaotic scenes that had taken place after the Allies, who'd been trapped by German forces following the Battle of France, were rescued by all sorts of little ships. It hadn't been possible to take the men off from the shore, and some had had to spend hours wading though the sea while waiting for an enemy attack which fortunately had not come. But though the evacuation had been something of a miracle, it could never be called a triumph, especially when it was remembered how many Allied soldiers had been killed earlier and how much equipment had been lost. It was no wonder that, as he recalled it, Ross's face was dark.

'No need to be sorry for me and the rest of us who were saved – we were lucky. All I can think of is the men who died before.'

'But have you been all right, Ross? I mean, have you recovered?'

'I'm fine, and I haven't been anywhere dangerous since. At the moment, my battalion is stationed in the south but we steer clear of London. That is not the place to be in the Blitz – it's taking a pasting, all right. But let's talk of other things.'

With some effort, Ross smiled and caught the eye of their waitress. 'How about another coffee? Then you must tell me about your family.'

'They're very well. Except that May is always worrying about Allan, of course. I'm not sure where he is at the moment. Dad's working flat out at the theatre which is selling out every night, but Vi is pretty discontented. I think she might volunteer too.' After a pause, Jinny asked casually: 'And how about your cousin? Lorna, wasn't it? Have you seen her lately?'

'Lorna? No, no. She's another volunteer – she joined the Wrens some time ago. She's down in Portsmouth. I haven't seen her for a while, though she writes now and again. Which reminds me, why haven't you and I been writing? You must give me your new address.'

'Oh, I will.'

Fresh coffee arrived and Jinny sat back in her chair, feeling strangely relaxed. In spite of their distressing talk of Dunkirk and the London Blitz, being with Ross again was so very pleasant she could almost say that she felt . . . not happy, she couldn't go as far as that, but at least at ease. As though she could put her worries behind her.

'What are you smiling at?' Ross asked, smiling himself.

'Was I smiling? I didn't even know.'

'I was hoping it meant you were feeling happier.'

At that, she sat up, knowing that his remark was more of a question – one she should answer. When she did, her voice was low. 'I still think of him. Viktor, I mean.'

Ross's brown eyes were steady on her face. 'Of course. It's natural that you would.'

'I think of him because I want to know what's happened to him, and because he meant so much. But . . . I don't know how to put it . . . I don't want to sound cold . . . and fickle . . .'

'I know you're not, Jinny.'

She shook her head. 'But I have changed, Ross. I never thought it would happen, but I don't feel the same. Viktor was everything to me, and now he seems . . . so far away. A sort of shadow.'

She looked away, to the people in the street below, all hurrying somewhere so purposefully, unaware of one another's troubles – and everyone would have troubles. Oh, yes, today they would. 'Sorry, Ross,' she murmured, 'if I don't seem happier.'

'I understand. I've been through something of the same myself.' He raised his hand to the waitress. 'But let's not talk of that now. I'll get the bill, shall I?'

Out in the street, amid all those hurrying people, they stood together, their eyes meeting, their faces serious.

'Ross, it's been lovely,' Jinny told him. 'It's a wonderful treat to see you again.'

'And for me to see you.' Ross put her arm in his. 'I'll walk back with you to Comrie's, if that's where you're going?'

'Yes, I'll look in on Mr Lennox – maybe see the bakery folk another day.'

But Comrie's came into sight too quickly. Although there was no longer any queue to observe them, they had no wish to say goodbye within sight of the shop window, and drew to a halt before they reached it.

'Jinny, I was wondering . . .' Ross began with an unusual

awkwardness. 'If you're on leave and I'm on leave, could we perhaps meet again? It would be a shame not to.'

'I'd like that very much, Ross, but are you sure it'd be all right?'

'Why shouldn't it be?'

'We'll, you're an officer and I'm not. We're not supposed to mix, are we? Bad for discipline, they say.'

'Oh, come, we're old friends, we've a right to mix on leave. And we're not in the same unit – that's when the discipline problem crops up.' Ross grinned. 'Same old conscientious Jinny! Look, apart from anything else, we'll be in civvies – I don't see any military policeman reporting us.'

'All right, then, if you're sure. When shall we meet?'

'Tomorrow night? There's a play I wouldn't mind seeing at the Raeburn – not your dad's theatre, I'm afraid, but I think you might find it interesting.'

'What is it?'

'*Time and the Conways* by J.B. Priestley. He's pretty good, usually. What do you think?'

'I think I'd like to go. Thank you, Ross.'

'Great. I'll book tickets. Starts at half past seven – shall I call for you a bit for that?'

'Our flat's right out of your way. I'll meet you at the theatre.'

'I'll call for you, it's no trouble,' he declared so firmly she didn't argue.

'OK, I'll be waiting, then, Ross. But now I'll pop in to see Mr Lennox, and then go and queue at the butcher's – Vi told me he's got some sausages.'

'Good luck!' he called, laughing, and they parted, after a cloud or two, in sudden sunshine.

# Fifty

Ross was early coming to collect Jinny, but she didn't mind. She was ready, anyhow, and had given the living room a tidy up too, which was a bonus.

'Come on up,' she told him when she'd run down to answer his knock, and with alacrity he followed her up the stairs, looking well-turned out in a dark suit and carrying a bunch of mixed flowers.

'Jinny, you're looking lovely!' he exclaimed when she'd shown him into the living room. 'Such a pretty dress! Is it new?'

'No, it's ancient – hard to get new clothes these days.' She glanced down at her rose-pink dress, one of her favourites, which suited her colouring so well, and laughed. 'I often wear it – you must have seen it loads of times.'

'Sorry, but that's me – a hopeless case. Please accept this little bouquet as a peace offering.'

'Ross, they're beautiful!' She took the flowers, putting her face close to smell their scent. 'Wherever did you find them?'

'There's a wee florist's still open on the south side, and as I couldn't get you any chocolates, I thought these anemones and such would do instead.'

'I'm thrilled,' she answered, feeling at his mention of chocolates another little reminder of Viktor, a memory she quickly put from her mind. 'Just let me put them in water and then I'll get my coat, but we've plenty of time – you're nice and early.'

'That's me again, always catch the train before the one I want,' he answered jauntily, his gaze moving round the living room, taking in the well-filled bookcase, the heavy sideboard and chairs, the long window with pretty curtains, and the open fireplace that was so attractive compared with the usual kitchen range.

'Nice room, Jinny,' he called as she set a vase containing his flowers on the table. 'But are you on your own? I thought I might meet Vi.'

'Och, she's out at a meeting – or is it her evening class? Vi's rarely in, and May, of course, doesn't live here now. She and Allan have a bungalow his parents left him.'

'And your dad's at the Duchess?'

'Yes.' Jinny had taken her coat from a peg, and smiled thanks as Ross helped her into it. 'I wish he could have met you, Ross. I know you'd get on well.'

'Maybe another time,' said Ross, and as she waved him through the front door which she then locked, she noted his words.

Another time, did he say? Was this theatre outing not to be a one-off? Perhaps he wanted company? He was, of course, on his own.

They took a tram to the theatre in Morningside, as Ross had no petrol for his car, and taxis were mainly for emergencies, as he said with some apology, which made Jinny laugh.

'Why, we never take taxis, anyway, Ross! What an idea!'

'Only the best for you,' he said, grinning.

'Which is a dear old tram. Look, we're at the theatre already!'

The Raeburn, where a crowd was already gathering, was a small, old-fashioned building, known in recent years for its adventurous programmes, although, as Ross remarked, the Priestley play might well have appeared at the Duchess, J.B.'s work being so popular.

'*Time and the Conways* is one of his time plays,' he explained when they were settled in their seats in the stalls. 'He's written several, all based on the theory that time is sort of simultaneous, the past, present and future being one. I'm not sure I go along with it.'

'I think I've read about it,' Jinny said, studying the programme. 'But J.B. Priestley didn't invent it, did he?'

'No, that was a chap called J.W. Dunne. Cynic that I am, I can't help wondering if Priestley just saw the theory as a new peg to hang his plays on. But let's see what we make of it, anyway.'

When the curtain went up on the first act, set in 1919, with the Conway family feeling happy and optimistic, Jinny found herself thinking how agreeable it was to be beside Ross, different though it might be from the first time she'd gone to the theatre with Viktor.

How excited and strung up she'd been then, when they were watching Agatha Christie's *Black Coffee*, whereas being with Ross, her one-time boss and her old friend, was, of course, very different. Everything was so easy and pleasant and in no way nerve-racking. Yet, in its way, it was exciting, too. For this evening out was so much a departure from everything they'd known when they'd worked together, it had rather made them seem different people. Just as nice, though, in the case of Ross, who no longer felt like her boss.

Better concentrate on what was happening in the play, she decided at last, so that she could talk intelligently about it when they had coffee in the interval. But, oh dear, by the time she got to it they'd reached the second act, set years after the first, and everything, it seemed, was going wrong for the characters. How was Time going to help there? Only, as someone explained, if people can see it as something that does not progress in a line but includes the past, present and future, and helps them to overcome their suffering.

'Gives them a second chance?' Jinny asked doubtfully when she and Ross were having their coffee in the interval. 'I must say, I don't really understand what Priestley's getting at.'

'Nor me,' Ross admitted. 'Though I'm all for second chances.'

'That's because you have a generous nature.'

'Have I?'

'Of course. You don't go in for judging people, do you?'

'I have my prejudices, all the same. Remember how I didn't like Viktor at first? And I'd really no reason for that.'

'I remember,' said Jinny, smiling a little. 'Well, maybe that shows you're human, after all.'

'Hey, was there any question of it?' Ross laughed and stood up. 'There goes the bell. Let's see how the third act works things out – if it does.'

# Fifty-One

The third act, like the first, was set in 1919, with the Conways and others appearing to be in their original optimistic mood. It soon became clear, however, that already there were signs of future disaster, with the play seeming to suggest that it could be avoided if only the lessons of Time could be learned. Somehow, one or two of the characters found hope and it was on that brighter note that the curtain fell, leaving the audience to make of it what they could.

'Happy about that?' Ross asked cheerfully as they joined the crowd leaving the theatre. Seeing the look on Jinny's face, he added, 'No, can't say I am, either. Yet it was interesting, wasn't it? I mean, it gave us something to think about.'

'Oh, yes, I enjoyed it,' she said quickly, 'it was different.'

'But we still need convincing that Time's going to make things easy for us?' Ross put his hand on Jinny's arm. 'I see a tram on the horizon. We'd better get to the stop.'

'You're coming back to Fingal Street with me?'

'Of course! No arguments, please.'

'I'm not arguing. I'd like you to come.'

That was true. Even though Jinny knew the shadow of Viktor would be with her as they made their way to Fingal Street, she was happy to be with Ross.

Outside the flat, there was the usual halting by the streetlight, the gaze up at the windows, the hesitation before the goodbyes. With Viktor, of course, there had been much more – desperate kisses, fierce embraces – all the delight and sadness of a parting between lovers. With Ross, there would be . . . what? A handshake, a friendly peck on the cheek?

'Why don't you come in?' Jinny cried suddenly. 'Just for a minute? Vi should be back, and probably Dad, too. You could meet them.'

'I'd like to very much – if you think it's not too late?

'No, no, come on – I'll open the door.'

Josh was indeed back, sitting in his chair by the fireplace, being brought tea by Vi and just about to switch on the wireless when Jinny and Ross walked in.

'Hello, Dad!' cried Jinny. 'I've brought someone to say hello to you and Vi.'

'Nice,' said Vi, setting down Josh's cup and advancing to shake Ross's hand. 'So you're Ross? We've heard so much about you.'

'Groan,' he said lightly, but his gaze was on Josh who had risen, pipe in hand, to fix him with a hard stare.

'We got your note, Jinny – knew you were going out with your boss. A Priestley play, eh? We've had a couple of his things at the Duchess. Mr MacBain, how d'you do?'

'Oh, please, Mr Hendrie, call me Ross.'

Josh nodded and sat down again, drawing his cup towards him. 'Well, you'd better have a cup of tea,' he said gruffly. 'Jinny, get your boss a cup.'

'He's not my boss now, Dad – we're both in the army. Ross is a second lieutenant.'

'That right? First over the top, in my day, the officers, but war's different now, eh?'

'You'll have a cup of tea?' Jinny whispered to Ross, but he said perhaps he should be going.

'I'm sorry to look in so late, Mr Hendrie, and Vi – may I call you that? But I'm very glad to have met you both. I've heard a lot about you, too, you know.'

'All glowing reports, I'm sure,' said Vi. 'But it's been good to meet you.'

'Aye, very good,' put in Josh. 'Take care now, Ross. Do your best against Hitler!'

'I will indeed, Mr Hendrie,' Ross answered, smiling, as he was steered to the door by Jinny. When they had reached the street she gave a huge sigh of relief.

'What a hit you were with Dad!' she cried. 'You know what he can be like. So, what's your secret?'

'I think we were just two soldiers together – both with going to war in common.'

'Well, it was grand to see.' Jinny took Ross's hand. 'Thanks for the evening, Ross. It was lovely, I really enjoyed it.'

'Me, too.' He hesitated. 'Maybe we could meet again? I don't want to monopolize you – I know you've your family to see – and friends—'

'Well, I'm going to Glasgow with Vi tomorrow. We're hoping to see if they've got anything in the shops that we haven't.'

'I see.'

'But I'm free the next day.'

He brightened. 'You are? May we meet, then?'

'I'd like to, Ross. Where shall we go?'

'Think it'll have to be local. Travel's so difficult these days. Trams, buses – they've either got reduced timetables or they're packed out.' Ross smiled ruefully. 'And the entire coastline seems to be a restricted area.'

'Still plenty to see in Edinburgh.'

'That's right. Look, I have to see my lawyer tomorrow – he's doing the paperwork for my tenant's new lease – but I could come later, about two? How about we decide then where to go?

'That'd be fine. But I didn't know you had let your house, Ross.'

'Oh, it's been let since I joined up. Not much point in keeping it empty except for my leave.'

'I did see it once, when you asked us all round once at Christmas.'

'And I wish you could have seen it again. Unfortunately, I don't live there any more.

'Where've you been going to, then, when you've left me?'

'I'm a member of the Northerner Club – I can stay there.' Ross laughed. 'Don't worry, I'm not on the streets. Not yet, anyway. Look, I'll see you the day after tomorrow then, at two?'

'The day after tomorrow.'

'Goodnight, Jinny.' He gave her a quick kiss on the cheek. 'Have a good day in Glasgow.'

'I don't suppose we'll buy a thing. Goodnight, Ross.'

Oh, I do hope they don't say anything about him, she thought, returning to the flat. I just can't face a great interrogation.

But as soon as she went into the living room, Vi asked, 'Are you sure Ross is just your boss, Jinny?'

'Was. That's all over for the duration.'

'Well, he seems pretty friendly for a boss.'

'Ross is a friendly chap. We always got on fine at Comrie's.'

'Seems a grand Scottish fellow to me,' Josh put in. 'Ready to fight for his country – that's the thing.' He tapped out his pipe on the grate. 'A big improvement on the last man you brought here, Jinny.'

'He's not to be compared with Viktor, Dad.

'You can say that again.'

As she lay in bed later, going over the evening, she thought how right she and her father had been. Ross was not Viktor, and if at one time that wouldn't have been in his favour, things were different now. Being with him, she had been able to relax, feel calm and know all was well, yet there was no consciousness of dullness or boredom. No, there had been that little spice of excitement brought about by the change from all they'd known before in their surroundings, an excitement that made the thought of the day after tomorrow – well, quite exciting too.

# Fifty-Two

At two o'clock on the dot, Ross arrived to collect Jinny for their afternoon out, looking cheerful in casual clothes and without a hat. his copper hair glinting in the sun.

'How was Glasgow?' he asked, as Jinny, wearing her navy jacket with matching skirt, hurried down the stairs to meet him. 'Any luck finding anything?'

'Yes! I got soap and make-up and two tea towels.' She laughed as they stood outside the flat in the autumn sunshine. 'Imagine being thrilled at finding tea towels! But everything's so short these days, you're lucky if you find anything.'

'Too right. By the time this war's over we'll all be dressed like scarecrows. And you'll still look, as they say, like a million dollars.'

'Ross, what a lovely compliment!' She slipped her arm in his. 'So, where are we going?'

'How about a gentle walk up Calton Hill?'

'Gentle suits me. I like Calton Hill – wonderful views without climbing.'

'And easily followed by tea – if we can find any. We'll away, then.'

Sitting together in the tram, there came again that wonderfully pleasant feeling of ease in each other's company. And when they began to walk up Calton Hill from the east end of Princes Street, there was still that feeling of rightness between them, of affinity shared.

Of course, there was nothing new for them to see on Calton Hill – they were both Edinburgh people, they knew it well – but the object of their day out was not to see something new as though they were tourists, just to enjoy time together. As they had in the past in the office, but that, of course, was different.

Often, as they followed the road up to the highest point, from where there was the magnificent panoramic view over the city, their eyes kept meeting, as though to say, 'isn't this the life?'

'Beats being on the parade ground,' said Ross, looking across the city to the Forth. 'I really am grateful to you, Jinny, for taking pity on an old guy on leave.'

'Old guy!' She laughed. 'You're only thirty!'

'Must seem old to you.'

'Of course it doesn't!' She took his arm. 'Come on, let's go down and see the monuments – if you can manage without a stick!'

'Cheek! I'll race you down, if you like.'

'No takers.'

Laughing, they made their way down the hill to see the famous monuments again: one to the dead of the Napoleonic Wars, always called 'Scotland's Disgrace' because it was never finished, another a great tower devoted to Nelson.

'See the time-ball at the top of the tower? Ross asked Jinny. 'That comes down at one o'clock to give the time signal to shipping. The one o'clock gun is its supplement. Which, of course, I'm sure you know.'

'I don't mind being told again.'

He laughed. 'That's the only problem with going to places in Edinburgh – we've seen them all before.'

'Yes, but don't you think it's worth coming here just for the air?' Jinny had taken off her blue beret and was breathing deeply as she shook her dark hair free. 'I mean, you're not far from Princes Street, yet you might be miles away in the country.'

'Let's sit for a while, then,' said Ross. 'We could take that bench over there if you're not too cold.'

'No, I'm warm after our walk.'

They took their seats on the bench, sitting close and not talking at first, just appreciating where they were. People passed them on the way to the top and they smiled and waved, so full of wellbeing, and equally full of goodwill to strangers.

'I like this,' Ross said after a while. 'Being here with you.'

'We've been together often enough.'

'You mean, in the office? You must admit, Calton Hill is different.'

Or are we different? wondered Jinny.

'What did you mean?' she asked aloud, 'when you said you understood about my change of feeling towards Viktor?'

Ross looked away for a moment. 'I was thinking of Annette,' he said at last. 'When she died, I thought the place she'd left could never be filled, that I'd always be missing her. For years, I thought that. But then, as I told you once, I began to feel better, as though I was back in the world again. What I didn't tell you was that I found, as you did with Viktor, that her image was fading.'

Ross, still looking away, gave a long sigh.

'Then I felt guilty. I thought it shouldn't happen, but gradually, as I began to think of her without pain, I realized it was natural. She had gone, I was still here, and life had to move on. I knew I would never forget her, that what we'd had would always be precious to me, but I had to realize it was over.' Ross turned his eyes on Jinny. 'Finally, I did – realize it.'

'You really felt better? There was no more guilt?'

'The guilt went with the pain.'

'You should never have felt it, anyway.'

'Nor should you, over Viktor. For whatever reason, he's no longer in your life. You must move on, too.'

'But I don't know what's happened to him, Ross. That's what different for me. He might still come back.'

'And if he did? You think you might care for him again?'

'No, Ross, I don't.' Her dark eyes were suddenly full of pain. 'But he did seem wonderful, didn't he?'

'So you thought,' Ross said shortly.

'Yes, well he was different from anybody I knew. So romantic, you see, coming from Vienna, and everything. I truly did believe I loved him. Well, I did, I know I did, but maybe we were never meant for each other, things were too difficult for us.' She shook her head. 'Whatever it was, it's over now. There's no way of going back.'

When she had finished speaking, a silence fell between her and Ross, while the sky began to darken as the clouds rolled over the city from where no lights could be seen.

'Time to go,' announced Ross, rising and giving his hand to Jinny, who stood beside him, straightening her skirt and pulling on her beret. 'What shall we do about finding some place to eat?'

'We can always get a cup of tea somewhere.'

'It's a bit late for teashops, and I feel like something more than tea. There's a place in Thistle Street sometimes has a menu to offer. Want to see what they have?'

'It's worth a try,' said Jinny.

# Fifty-Three

They were in luck, the Thistle Street restaurant could offer two choices for their early supper – a beef casserole and baked haddock. Both chose the haddock, having had too much tough beef in army cooking, and when the waiter had taken their order, sat back, relaxing, yet also covertly eyeing each other with special interest.

Do we look different? Jinny wondered. She'd asked herself the question in the restaurant cloakroom when she'd combed her hair and splashed her face before putting on a little powder, and decided that they must. After all, they seemed different now from those two people who worked in Accounts. Something must surely show in their faces? Not really, it seemed.

Somehow, Jinny couldn't resist talking of Lorna again, as though she thought her something of a threat. A threat? she asked herself. Why should she regard any woman Ross might be interested in as a threat? She didn't bother to work it out, but as soon as they were eating their fish and drinking the pre-war wine Ross had chosen, heard herself saying, 'You know, Ross, at one time I thought you were keen on Lorna.'

'Lorna?' He stared in surprise. 'You're not serious? She's my cousin.'

'Cousins are sometimes attracted to each other. And she's a lovely girl.'

'She is, but she's the nearest I have to a sister. I could never think of her in any other way.' Ross smiled. 'Imagine your thinking I might!'

'I'm sure a lot of other people at Comrie's thought the same when you brought her to that staff Christmas party.'

'They understood when they knew she was my cousin. I thought you would have done, too.'

'Well, yes, only I did get the impression you were interested in her, and I suppose I was a bit surprised. But I knew I wanted you to be happy, so I was happy too – for you.'

'You wanted me to be happy?' Ross gave a wide smile. 'Jinny, that was nice of you. You always were a caring sort of girl.'

'But I was wrong about you and Lorna?'

'Wrong to think there was any sort of romance between us. I'm sure Lorna would be amused at the very idea. If I think of her as a sister; she probably thinks of me as an uncle!'

'A very attractive uncle, then,' said Jinny firmly, which brought another smile from Ross.

Reaching Fingal Street again to say goodnight, their steps were slow as they approached the door to the Hendries' flat. When they finally stopped, Jinny looked up at Ross and asked him what he was thinking.

'You seem worried. Is anything wrong?'

'Not at all, Jinny. I'm just getting the courage to ask you what day you go back.'

'Tuesday. What about you?'

He sighed deeply. 'Monday.'

'Oh.'

'I've got one more day.'

'Sunday.'

'And I suppose you'll be seeing your family then?'

'Yes, May's asked us over. She's managed to get a joint. It's a big treat.'

'I see. Well, your family comes first, of course. Can't expect you to see me again – you've been very good as it is.'

'Ross, I've had a wonderful time.' Jinny stood in thought for a moment or two, then her face lit up. 'I know, Ross! You could to come to May's as well! You said you'd like to meet her.'

'No, no, thank you, I wouldn't intrude. It's a nice idea, but I couldn't ask it of your family.'

'Seems a shame not to say goodbye tomorrow. If you're worried about sharing the joint, how about if we met in the evening?'

'The evening?' Ross's brown eyes were bright. 'You think we could?'

'Yes, why not?' Jinny was searching her handbag. 'I'll just give you May's address. You can come to her house and have a cup of tea with us, then we can go out somewhere. Got a pencil?'

When the address, written on a scrap from Ross's notebook, had been safely put away, they stood for a while, not seeming sure how to say goodnight. Then Ross gave Jinny one of his quick kisses.

'Until tomorrow, then.'

'Until tomorrow.'

'We're good friends, aren't we?' Ross asked. 'Special friends?'

'Special friends.'

'Goodnight, Jinny.'

'Goodnight, Ross.'

Special friends? Her family would think so, Jinny thought, when she told them Ross was not only coming to tea but spending the evening with her – again. So, what did special mean? Hard to be sure what was in Ross's mind, or in fact in her own, and soon they would be far apart, anyway. But at least they needn't say goodbye until tomorrow.

# Fifty-Four

'May, that was grand,' Josh said, sitting back in Allan's armchair in the comfortable sitting room of the bungalow. Sunday dinner was over and had been a great success, with the joint so like something pre-war that they couldn't believe their luck.

'Can't think how you got it,' Josh went on. 'Was it a miracle or what?'

'Sweet-hearting the butcher, maybe.' Vi laughed. 'Blue eyes are such a help, eh?'

'Vi, what a thing to say!' May cried, for once losing her calm. 'As though I'd go around sweet-hearting, as you put it!'

'Oh, I didn't say you'd do it deliberately – just give a smile or two.'

'Now, Vi, stop your teasing,' Josh said easily. 'You know May would never go making up to the butcher – let's have our tea in peace.'

'Listen, I'd just like to say something.' Jinny cleared her throat. 'Ross is coming round later to call for me and meet May. It's his last day of leave and we thought we'd go out.'

'To meet me?' May smiled. 'That's nice. I've heard so much about your boss, Jinny.'

'On a Sunday?' Josh asked, sitting up straight. 'Where will you go?'

'Oh, there's always something open – with so many folk about these days.'

'I've never heard there was anything open.' Josh was now staring hard at Jinny. 'You've been seeing a lot o' this Ross this last week, eh?'

Jinny hesitated, glancing at her sisters, who were quietly watching. 'Yes, I have. We've enjoyed meeting up again.'

'As friends, eh?' asked Vi.

'Yes, why not? He has no family and he's glad to have a companion.'

'And that's all there is to it?' asked Josh.

'Oh, yes.'

'I haven't met him yet but he's always sounded very nice, from what Jinny's told us,' said May.

'He is nice,' Vi told her. 'Dad likes him.'

'Aye, I do,' said Josh, sitting back in his chair. 'He's a Scottish laddie, keen to fight for his country. That's the sort I like.'

'Why didn't you invite him to share our roast?' asked Vi. 'Bet he'd have enjoyed that.'

'He said he didn't want to intrude,' Jinny replied. 'He'll just have a cup of tea.'

'And be very welcome for that,' said May.

He was early, of course, that being his way, but, as May had promised, he was made very welcome, first being introduced to her, then greeting Josh and Vi again with his easy, natural manner.

'You'll have a cup of tea?' May asked.

'Thank you, I'd like that.'

Ross was looking round the pleasant room that had been furnished by Allan's parents but already bore some of May's touches – new curtains and cushions and lamp shades she had covered herself. He turned back, complimenting her, but she only sighed a little.

'I had great plans once, though I was lucky to get as far as I did. Now, of course, Allan's away and that's all I can think about.'

'May, you're doing good work at the hospital,' Josh put in. 'Don't forget that.'

'Might I ask where Allan is?' Ross asked May gently.

'Well, I'm not sure. He did mention Crete when he came on leave, but in his letters he never says.'

'Must be difficult for you, May, on your own.'

'Oh, we're all in the same boat, aren't we? And I've got Dad and Vi. Miss Jinny, though.' May smiled and rose, saying she'd make the tea, and when her sisters went out to the kitchen with her, Josh looked at Ross.

'Your regiment is still in this country, eh?'

'That's right, Mr Hendrie.'

'Can't say where, I suppose?'

'Oh, I think I can tell you it's the Isle of Wight.'

'Way down a bit from here, that. Where d'you think you'll go next, then?'

'Ah, well, that I can't say. But it will be abroad.'

'Not to fight Jerry?'

'Not yet.'

'But there'll be fighting wherever you go. Take care of yourself, if you can.' Josh put out his hand, which Ross shook. 'I'll wish you all the best.'

'Thank you, Mr Hendrie. I appreciate that.'

'Now, here come the girls – let's see if they've rustled anything up for tea. May told me she'd only one egg. Now, what can you make with that?'

'Scones!' May called across, setting down a tray. 'No cake, though, I'm sorry to say.'

'Home-made scones? What could be better?' asked Ross, smiling at Jinny and her sisters, savouring the family atmosphere he had not himself known for many years.

# Fifty-Five

When he and Jinny prepared to leave May's some time later, there were more good luck wishes for Ross, as well as hopes that they might find something open for their last night out.

'Aye, what there'll be on a Sunday night in Edinburgh, I canna think,' Josh told them. 'There's nothing open, eh? Dead as a door-nail – that's Auld Reekie on a Sunday.'

'As a matter of fact, we do have a place to go,' Ross told him. 'My dad belonged to the Northener club in Abercromby Place, and I took out membership too. You can get a meal there, even on a Sunday, and women are welcome, as guests or members.'

'You're taking Jinny to the Northener?' cried Vi. 'Help, she'll be about thirty years younger than everybody else, if what I've heard is true.'

'Hey, what about Ross?' asked Jinny. 'He's not old!'

'Probably the youngest member,' admitted Ross, 'but you must admit, it's handy, having a place to go on Sunday evening!'

'You know what?' asked Jinny a few minutes later on the tram. 'I haven't even begun to think about my new posting. I thought I'd be so nervous, but it's all just gone out of my mind.'

'You'll be fine with the pay office, Jinny. You certainly don't need to be nervous, anyway.'

'Think I'll get a stripe?'

'You're sure to. You'll be a lance corporal in no time. The sky's the limit for you.'

'I don't think so! But listen, I'm getting nervous now, going to your club. I mean, am I dressed right?

'In your navy suit? You're perfect.'

'Is it true that everyone's ancient?'

'Well, they won't see twenty-one again. But they're OK. Middle-aged, mostly.'

'As you say, it is a place to go.'

'That just about sums up what clubs are for,' Ross said wryly.

The Northener, as it turned out, was a comfortable, well-kept establishment, without the subdued atmosphere usually associated with men's clubs because of its mixed membership. Certainly, the women Jinny saw when she entered the dining room with Ross were talking freely, and though well-dressed, not so smart that she felt she needed to worry.

'The food's not particularly exciting,' Ross whispered as they were seated at a corner table for two. 'But they've got their problems with rationing the same as everyone else.'

'I'm not worried about the food. After May's roast I'm not really hungry.'

'We can just have a ham salad, then, if you like. And some wine?'

'Oh, no thank you, no wine.'

'Just coffee to follow, then.'

The ham in the salad turned out to be corned beef, but it wasn't too bad, and the coffee served to them when they'd moved to the lounge was good and strong.

'Nice,' commented Jinny. 'It's not often you can get coffee like this. Even pre-war, Viktor was always complaining about our coffee—' She stopped and coloured, but Ross shook his head.

'You don't have to worry about remembering Viktor,' he said

gently. 'He was an important part of your life and memories don't just disappear. I should know. I lived on them for long enough.'

'It's just a bit disconcerting for me, that's all.' Jinny finished her coffee and set down her cup. 'Better make a move, I suppose.'

'I don't want to. When we go we'll be on our way to saying goodbye, and I'm not looking forward to that.'

'Nor am I.' Jinny rested her eyes on Ross's face. 'These few days have been so nice, Ross. I've really enjoyed being with you.'

'Tell me something.' He leaned forward a little. 'Do you see me – after these few days – in a different light?'

'From the office?'

'Yes, from the office.'

'It's odd, but you've just put into words what I've been thinking. I do see you in a different light. Is it the same for you with me?'

'Very much so. That gap away from each other, away from the office seems to have made us into two different people.'

'Two new people,' suggested Jinny.

'New people after years of already knowing each other and liking each other – does that seem crazy?'

'No, just special.'

'And we did say we were special friends.'

'We did.'

For some time, they stayed where they were, studying each other, then Ross reluctantly stood up.

'Think we'd better go or they'll be turning down the lights. I'll just sign the bill.'

# Fifty-Six

Outside in the elegant New Town street, where they could hardly see each other's faces in the blackout, Jinny sighed and slipped her arm into his.

'I don't know that I want you to take me home, Ross. It's too sad.'

'Come on, we have to say goodbye.'

'Maybe I could come to the station?'

'That'd be worse. I hate station farewells. I know what they're like. No, Fingal Street it is. Back to the tram stop.'

'It isn't as though I even know where you're going,' Jinny said when they were together on the wooden slatted tram seat. 'I mean, I know you're in the south, but you won't be staying there, will you?'

'We don't stay anywhere for ever, but I'll be writing to you. You'll know where I am then.' He moved his hand to take hers. 'And I'll be sure to get more leave one of these days, and when I do, I wanted to ask you – would you be willing to try to wangle leave yourself? So we could meet again. Would you want to do that, Jinny?'

'I would, though whether I'd get it just when I wanted it I don't know.'

'As long as you want to see me again, that's all that matters.'

'I don't know why you have to ask, Ross. We are special friends, aren't we?'

He pressed her hand hard. 'That's right. We are. As well as old friends who seem new. So we said.'

'And it's true,' said Jinny.

Though they put it off as long as possible, the time came when they reached the Hendries' flat again and stopped in the darkness of Fingal Street, below the blacked-out windows.

'This is it, then,' said Ross. 'Goodbye time. Or, we could just make it *au revoir*?'

'That does sound better,' Jinny agreed, looking up into his face that was so hard to see.

'And we are going to try to meet again, aren't we?' Ross took her hands. 'I just want to thank you again, Jinny, for making this leave so special – there goes that word again.'

'It was special for me, too.'

'But you had your family to see, yet you spared time for me. That's what I appreciate.'

'I had a wonderful time, Ross. I want to say thank you, too.'

They were silent for a while, waiting to make the final farewell.

'Wish I could see you better.' Suddenly, Ross drew Jinny closer, and the thought came to her: now he would kiss her, with one of his friendly little pecks . . .

But a friendly little peck, it wasn't. As his mouth met hers, she was so taken by surprise at the passion of the kiss that she did not at first respond, but as it lengthened and deepened she found herself kissing him back with a pleasure she'd never expected to feel. Could this really be herself and Ross?

'Special,' he whispered, as they finally drew apart. 'That was special. You didn't mind?'

'No, I didn't.'

'Oh, God, I think I'd better go. The longer I stay the more difficult it is to leave. Look, I'll write to you and we'll meet again. Promise?'

'Promise.'

'*Au revoir*, then, Jinny.' He smiled in the darkness. 'I'll be seeing you, as the song says.'

'*Au revoir*, Ross.'

She watched him as best she could – saw him straighten his shoulders, wave and walk away, but soon he swallowed up into the darkness and all she had of him was the sound of his footsteps ringing out until there was silence. All she could do then was to open the front door and climb the stairs.

'Guess what?' cried Vi as soon as she saw her. 'I've done it!'

'Aye, she's done it,' Josh said from his chair. 'She's written her letter.'

'What letter?' asked Jinny.

'My letter of resignation,' Vi said grandly. 'I'm joining the ATS, like you. Oh, I can't stick around here any longer – I have to do something.'

'And what I'm going to do, I don't know,' said Josh glumly. 'I mean, who's going to do my tea? Who's going to take care o' the house?'

'I'd have to go anyway, Dad. They'll be calling the women up next year, that's for sure. And May says she'll come over and do some cooking for you. She won't have to go in the forces – she's married.'

Vi looked across at Jinny. 'How d'you get on at that posh club, then? Och, I bet it was like having a meal in a graveyard, eh?'

'It was very nice and very comfortable.' Jinny took off her jacket. 'I enjoyed it.'

'You look a bit down, all the same. Saying goodbye to Ross, eh?'

'It was a bit sad. But I've still got a day of my leave left. Maybe we can do something?'

'Aye, I'm taking the day off for that. After I've been to the recruiting place we'll fix up something. Cheer you up before you've to go to that Pay Corps place.'

'That'll be difficult. I'm terrified.'

'You'll be fine, a clever lassie like you,' Josh said, rising. 'Now, I'm away to my bed. Wish I could be with you tomorrow, Jinny, but I canna make it. You get leave again, soon, eh?'

They all, unusually, kissed goodnight, and then Jinny was lying awake thinking about Ross, about that surprising kiss, about where they were going, if anywhere. And then her nerves came back and it was some time before she could sleep, worried as she was about her posting.

# Fifty-Seven

Within a week, the worries were over.

Hard to believe when Jinny remembered how nervous she'd been when arriving on her first day at the rather splendid Pay Corps premises, so anxious, so wearied by the crowded train trip. Cigarette smoke had hung like a pall in the carriage and was still in her hair when she reported to the ATS sergeant, along with two other newcomers she'd met at the entrance. Turned out they'd managed to find a taxi from the station, where Jinny had followed instructions and taken the bus.

'You going where we're going?' one of them, a lanky young woman with reddish hair had asked, before introducing herself as Josie Marriott and her companion, thin and fair, as Pauline Sanders. 'Reporting to Sergeant Abbott?'

'That's right. I'm Jinny Hendrie.'

'From Scotland?' asked Pauline.

'How did you guess?'

They laughed as a soldier who had to let them in took their names, ticked them off on a list and escorted them to plump, black-haired Sergeant Abbott, in a room where there were uniformed girls but only two men. All looked up from their work and smiled.

After that, it had become hazy. Just as it had on Jinny's first day at the training camp. So many different girls' faces, so many different heads of hair – fair, dark, ginger, mousy. So much to take in all at once.

I'll never get this lot sorted out, thought Jinny, but at least the two men stood out, and Captain Norton, the officer in charge, was easy to distinguish, he being a man too – tall, with a limp and metal-framed spectacles. He shook their hands, said he was sure they'd enjoy their posting, and handed them back to Sergeant Abbot, who in turn had brought forward a girl with two stripes on her sleeve who said she was Corporal Holt and would be taking them to their billet.

'It's a country house not far away,' she told them. 'Mind walking?'

They said they'd be glad of the fresh air and, as they only had small kitbags to carry, there was no problem.

'Be prepared, usually, to march to the office and back,' Corporal Holt added crisply. 'But you'll all be good at marching, eh? Being straight out of basic training?'

'Don't know about that,' said Josie.

'Oh, I hope so,' said Pauline.

'Right then, quick march!' said the corporal. 'No, I'm only joking.'

The billet was really rather grand, or had been before it was requisitioned. The rooms were large and high-ceilinged, the fireplaces made of marble, the floors parquet blocks, and the windows, covered in anti-blast strips, were long and elegant. Even the dormitory where the three new girls were given beds showed signs of its former splendour as the upstairs drawing room.

'Not bad, eh?' asked Josie, slinging her bag on to her bed. 'Gracious high living, except for the furniture.'

'We could certainly do a lot worse,' Corporal Holt remarked. 'The pay office was custom built and it's a nice place to work, but for us they've just got to find accommodation where they can. Sometimes in schools or colleges, old houses with leaking roofs and no bathrooms. I tell you, you're lucky here.'

When they'd washed and unpacked, they were returned to the headquarters to have a cup of tea at the canteen and were told to report back to Captain Norton.

'But don't worry,' the corporal said, before leaving them, 'real work'll start tomorrow. The captain'll just give you an introductory chat.'

'Phew, I could do with this,' sighed Pauline, drinking her tea. 'Been on the go since crack of dawn.'

'Where from?' asked Jinny.

'Essex.'

'And I'm from Dorset,' put in Josie, lighting a cigarette and avoiding, like the others, the appraising looks from a couple of soldiers eating doorstep sandwiches at the next table. 'But I'd just like to get started, find out what we have to do. I was in the accounts office of an insurance firm so I reckon I should be OK, but I'd just like to know.'

When Jinny had said that she too had accounting experience, Pauline cried 'Snap!', which made Josie declare that it was plain to see why they'd all been selected for the Pay Corps.

'Maybe, but I'm still feeling nervous,' Jinny admitted. 'I'll be happier when I know what's expected.'

That was discovered soon enough, when Captain Norton outlined what the work of the command pay office entailed.

'Not dealing with pay parades,' he had told the newcomers, 'but the paying of all bills, handling all the public monies involved in military services, the payments for requisitioned houses and land, renewal of equipment, or special reasons for replacing uniforms and so on. The office also gives advice on technical matters and on various costings of establishments. So, you see, we have a wide remit and plenty to do.'

He gave a mild smile and removed his glasses for a moment to rub his eyes.

'And of course there'll be all the routine bits to learn as well – how invoices are handled, who signs what and that sort of thing, but I know your backgrounds and I don't think you'll find anything you're asked to do too difficult.'

'How many ATS girls are here, sir?' Josie asked him as he replaced his glasses.

'Eighteen, counting you three. All very friendly – you'll soon get to know them.'

Maybe, Jinny had thought, but so it had turned out, and by the end of the week she had indeed got to know a number of her colleagues and agreed that they were friendly. She'd also found her way around the headquarters, taken a trip into town to look at the shops, received a letter from Vi all about her recruitment, and had found time to write one in reply. There was nothing, as yet, from Ross, but she knew a letter would come. No doubt of that.

As for the work, Ross had been right – it was more interesting than doing the bakery wages, or paying out soldiers' pay. In fact, she was fascinated by the variety of the jobs that came her way and had no trouble in learning the routine.

'Shouldn't be surprised if you get your stripe soon,' Sergeant Abbot commented, and Jinny thought, now, that would be something to tell them back home . . . and Ross, of course.

# Fifty-Eight

Waiting to hear from Ross, she had been wondering what sort of letter he would write. Friendly, cheerful, or . . . romantic? After that farewell kiss of his, she wasn't sure what to expect. Just how far did 'special friends' take them? Not so far as love letters, she guessed, and so it turned out, for when his first letter arrived, it was as Ross himself had always seemed to her – kind and understanding, generous of spirit, with the added bonus here of humour and descriptions of life on the Isle of Wight without giving too much away. He did, however, sign the letter 'with love', which didn't necessarily mean anything. People would sign Christmas cards 'with love' when there was no actual love involved.

Still, it was a lovely letter, and she wasn't at all sure that she could equal it. She'd never had to write many letters and felt she didn't have the skill to write amusingly of her routine at the pay office, or her not very exciting daily life.

All the same, she was relieved in a way that Ross's first letter had not been romantic. There was certainly something special between them, something they had not shared when they worked together, and it had been hard to say goodbye. Maybe they were moving towards a true relationship, but it was easier, maybe, as things were in their unsure world, to let that develop gradually and take things as they came until they could be very sure themselves. After what had happened between herself and Viktor, and how her feelings had changed, the one thing she wanted was to be sure.

At least, the way Ross had written to her, she knew what style to aim for in her reply, and spent a whole evening trying to produce something that would equal his for lightness of touch and humour, several times tearing up efforts that did not satisfy until, finally, she achieved a short account of her new life that might interest him. She sealed it up before she could change her mind and put it ready to post on her bedside locker.

'Finished it?' asked Josie, getting up from her bed on which she'd been lying, reading a magazine.

As Jinny only stared, Josie came over and nodded at the letter to Ross. 'I mean your letter. My, you had problems, eh? Or, am I speaking out of turn? Sorry, just ignore me.'

'I'm not much of a letter writer,' Jinny said stiffly.

'Nor me. And letters to young men are always the worst, eh? My chap is much better at writing than I am – I'm for numbers, not words – but letters are important to fighting men and you have to do your best.'

'I know.' Jinny hesitated. 'This one was to my ex-boss. We're . . . good friends.'

Josie's narrow grey eyes appeared a little amused, but she only asked if Jinny would like to go for a cuppa in the canteen.

'Yes, all right, I could do with something.'

'After all that effort,' Josie said with a smile.

The canteen was, as usual, wreathed in smoke and full of ATS girls, all known by now to Jinny, who knew their names, their backgrounds and their interests, just as they knew hers. How quickly it could happen, she reflected, that you could become absorbed into a crowd you hadn't known existed before! And here they all were now – Barbara, Alice, Shirley and the rest, some talking to each other and some to soldiers, though these were in short supply. Jinny knew their names, too, but not so much about them. Girls were always more forthcoming – they liked to talk, Jinny supposed.

'None of the fellows here is able-bodied,' Josie whispered to Jinny over their pale coffee. 'I mean, if they were able-bodied they wouldn't be here, they'd be on active service.'

'I suppose they've all been injured already.'

'Well, Captain Norton was, in France before Dunkirk, I've heard, but often I think if they end up here they're just not that fit.' Josie lit a cigarette, offering the packet to Jinny, who shook her head. 'I suppose that's where we come in – we certainly seem to be in the majority at the pay office. How're you liking it, then?'

'Fine, I've settled in pretty well, I think. I was nervous to begin with, especially with so many strange faces around, but it's as it was in basic training – I soon got to know everybody.' Jinny sipped her coffee. 'I've even got one girl writing to me now.'

And that was Sukie, still grateful to Jinny for her help and doing well, it seemed, in her own posting.

'Is that right?' Josie laughed. 'Bet you find it easier to write to her than your ex-boss, eh? Oh, dear, there I go again – sorry, none of my business!'

'Here's Pauline,' said Jinny, glad to be changing the subject as Pauline came up to join them with tea on a tray, a cigarette dangling from her lip.

'Hey, you two, you're ahead of me!' she cried, setting down her tray and stubbing out her cigarette on a tin ashtray. 'I just nipped out to the chemist's to get myself some shampoo. "Light Touch" it's called – guaranteed to make me a blonde bombshell. What do you think?'

'I think your hair's fine as it is, said Josie. 'Who's to notice here, anyway?'

'Why, there's an engineers' regiment putting on a dance at the weekend!' Pauline cried. 'They're outside Chester but Sarge says they're laying on a bus for us. We'll all be going, won't we?'

'When is it?' asked Josie.

'This Saturday. Jinny. You want to go?'

Jinny hesitated. 'I suppose so – if everyone else is – but I don't know if I'm all that keen.'

'Come on, it'll make a change,' said Josie. 'You don't have to go out with any guys if you don't want to, though they'll be sure to ask you. Just have a night away from here, I say.'

'I wouldn't mind going out with somebody,' Pauline murmured. 'I know you've got your young man, Josie, but at the moment I'm fancy free, and that's not as much fun as it sounds.'

'Wait till you appear as the blonde bombshell – the lads will be queuing up!'

'Oh, Josie, you're such a tease,' said Pauline, finishing her tea and laughing. 'You never know, I might surprise you all.'

Why didn't she want to go to the regimental dance? Jinny wondered as she went to bed that evening. Somehow she couldn't summon up any enthusiasm, though everyone in the dormitory was talking about it. Catching sight of the letter still on her locker, she thought of Ross with a sudden, warm feeling of remembrance. Was he the reason? Was she worried that he might not want to see her dancing with other men? No, she didn't really think so. Ross was Ross, not the type to get worked up. He knew how to kiss, though – and there was another memory. Smiling a little, as the lights went out, she prepared to sleep.

Better go to the dance, anyway, she decided – she didn't want to appear as an outsider – and as her eyelids grew heavy and she could hear Edith in the next bed beginning to snore, wondered if she should have her hair trimmed, or if it would do.

# Fifty-Nine

Cigarette smoke, of course, was already hanging over the improvised dance floor in the sergeants' mess when the pay office staff arrived on the following Saturday evening to join the waiting soldiers and girls from other ATS units. An army band was tuning up in one corner, eyes were being cast around at possible partners, and for those sitting out there were wooden chairs placed round the walls. It was all very similar to the dance at the training centre, but larger, thought Jinny, who had in the end had her thick dark hair cut, but like everyone else had not had to worry about what to wear, as they were all in uniform.

'Doesn't seem like a proper dance, does it?' whispered Pauline, whose hair was now a strange straw colour that had had her running around earlier, asking everyone if they thought it looked OK. 'Be honest now, just say,' she'd implored, but as no one had wanted to be honest and they were all as polite as possible, she'd decided not to try to re-do it and was 'hoping for the best'. By which she meant success at the dance, which was not like a proper dance, in her view, as they had no dresses to wear.

'We'd never have got 'em in our kitbags,' Josie reminded her, her eyes busy looking round the room. 'This is wartime, don't forget. But here comes the CO to start things off.'

After a few words of welcome from the commanding officer, the band began to play a foxtrot, partners were selected and the dance began. There was no shortage of soldiers for the girls, some chaps indeed having to wait their turn, and were already cheekily turning the dance into an 'excuse me', which caused a few dark looks, though the girls were not complaining. Pauline, in fact, was truly enjoying herself. Jinny, pleased for her, smiled as she saw the blonde head in the distance, turning from side to side, quite like a professional, as the dance progressed.

She herself was much in demand, soldiers calling her 'dark eyes', and 'gorgeous', and didn't object too much until a tall, raw-boned sergeant with a high-bridged nose and piercing grey eyes claimed her for a quickstep and told her he wasn't having any of that 'excuse me' nonsense.

'I've been waiting for a chance to dance with you,' he told Jinny. 'Saw you come in and thought, "Wow, what a looker!" and then lost out till now – so watch out, other guys, they'll be on fatigues if they try to interfere.'

'Heavens, it's only a dance,' Jinny said uneasily. 'People are just enjoying themselves.'

He looked down at her coldly as he expertly guided her round the floor. 'I've told you – no one cuts in with me.'

And no one did, though Jinny caught plenty of glances from soldiers coming his way and moving on with haste. Obviously, he was a tough one; not many would care to trifle with him.

'You're from the pay office, that right?' he asked her. 'And Scottish, eh? How d'you like being in England?'

'This part is lovely.'

'I'm from Manchester myself. Name's Bart Randall. And you are . . . ?'

With some reluctance, she told him. How long was this dance going on? She was beginning to feel trapped.

'Jinny,' he repeated. 'Well, Jinny, how about a trip to the pictures with me sometime?'

As his sharp gaze rested on her, she couldn't think what to say. She was never going to go anywhere with him, but how was she to refuse gracefully? How avoid the full battery of those cold eyes meeting hers?

'Oh, that's – that's very kind of you,' she heard herself murmuring, 'but—'

'But what?' he asked starkly.

'Well, I don't really go to the pictures much.'

'Come off it, everybody goes to the pictures. What else is there to do? What you're saying is that you don't want to go with me, is that it?'

The dance at last had come to an end, with the bandsmen putting aside their instruments. It seemed it was the interval, thank God – now she could get away . . .

'Thank you very much, it was nice dancing with you,' she said quickly, 'but I see my friends over there—'

'Wait a bit, wait a bit.' He took hold of her wrist, not hard but with definite intent – it was clear he wasn't going to let her go without a struggle. 'Just why don't you want to go out with me? You don't like sergeants, or what?'

'I have someone,' Jinny snapped, her dark eyes suddenly flashing. 'I don't want to go out with anyone else. And now, would you please let go of my wrist?'

'I don't see any engagement ring, Jinny.'

'I didn't say we were engaged. And it's nothing to do with you, whether we are or not!'

'All right, all right.' Slowly he let go of her wrist and shook his head at her. 'Quite the firebrand, aren't you? Well, I don't want to take another guy's girl – if he exists. All I'll say to you is you don't know what you're missing.'

With which parting shot, he marched across the dance floor as though he were on the parade ground, leaving Jinny to hurry across to where Josie and Pauline were standing, Pauline looking flushed and excited, her hair seeming brighter than ever, and Josie looking at Jinny with interested eyes.

'What was all that about? Thought you were going to have a stand-up row with that sergeant!'

Jinny shivered, not looking round in case she saw Bart Randell again, and as Josie drew on a cigarette she almost wished, if it would calm her nerves, that she could have one herself.

'He was awful,' she whispered. 'Wanted me to go out with him and, when I said no, took it as a personal insult.'

'They do, they do – it's a question of manly pride, dear. "Who are you to turn me down?" Et cetera, et cetera. I hope you told him what to do.'

'I did my best, but he held my wrist and I thought he might not let me go, but of course he did in the end. I just hope I don't have to see him again.'

'What a shame!' cried Pauline. 'Now the fellow I was dancing with just now is so nice. Did you see him? Curly hair, lovely smile . . . He's getting us some coffee. You want one, Jinny?'

'I'll say,' said Jinny.

When Pauline's cheerful dancing partner had passed her one of the coffees he'd brought, she felt better, though still alarmed at the thought of meeting Bart Randall again. There was also a certain amount of wonder in her mind that she'd been so quick to mention she had 'someone', and that the someone she'd thought of had been Ross. Should she have described him like that? Well, they were, after all, special friends. More than friends, you might say, though it was true they had not really spelled out what their feelings might be, despite their passionate kiss. Ross had been keen, though, for them to meet again, and that kiss . . .

Oh, whether or not it had been right to describe him as her 'someone', she knew, as she sipped her coffee, how much she would have given to have been with him then, how much she did in fact miss him. If only she could have skipped the rest of this dance to go back to the billet to write to him!

No such luck – the band was beginning again, and already Pauline was waltzing with Curly-top, Josie with a lean, freckle-faced corporal, and a nervous-looking engineer had come to ask Jinny to take the floor with him. At least he wasn't Sergeant Randall – quite the reverse, in fact, seeming too worried about his dancing to make conversation.

'I'm not much of a dancer,' he muttered in a soft West Country accent. 'Expect you can tell that already?'

'Don't worry, you're doing very well.'

'Quickstep is bad enough,' he went on, finding his voice, 'but the waltz – I can't get the hang of the timing! Never thought when I volunteered for the artillery that I'd have to dance.'

'It's supposed to be fun!' Jinny said, laughing.

'Things are only fun if you're good at them,' he told her bleakly, and she had to agree that there was something in that.

The rest of the dance passed off without problems, except for one sticky moment when Jinny saw Bart Randall moving by with a blonde girl who was not from the pay office, and at his scornful blue stare Jinny flinched and began to talk animatedly to her partner, who seemed amazed that she had so much to say.

'Wasn't too bad, was it?' asked Josie later, when they were back in their dormitory. 'Apart from your little run-in with that sergeant, of course.'

'As I said before, I just hope I don't see him again.'

'I can set your mind at rest there. That dance was the battalion's farewell – I heard it on the QT from one of the chaps. They don't like broadcasting their movements until they actually go, so I don't know the date, but it'll be soon.'

'That's a relief. Can't think why he asked me out then.' Jinny looked suddenly anxious. 'You don't suppose he'll be left here, do you?'

'Not he! I bet he's the kingpin of the whole thing. You've only got to look at him to see he'll know everything.'

'Well, if you hear any more on the grapevine, let me know.'

'Such a shame you had to meet him,' commented Paulie, back from the bathroom and draped in a towel. 'But what did you think of my chap, then? Chris Fielding, he's called. Didn't you think he was sweet? Did I tell you he's asked me out?'

'I'm sure everybody around heard that!' Josie exclaimed. 'Wednesday night at the flicks, eh?'

'I'm so glad he's in the Pay Corps and not an engineer,' Pauline said with satisfaction. 'He's got bad asthma, you know, and I'm sorry about that, but it does mean he's staying here.' She put a hand to her lips. 'Oh, dear. Do I sound selfish? Sorry, girls. I know you have fellows who'll be fighting somewhere.'

'No need to apologise,' said Josie. 'There isn't one of us who wouldn't feel like you.'

Later, when the dormitory lights were out and Jinny was lying awake, she thought of Ross and of her renewed wish to be with him again, to feel safe, protected from the likes of Sergeant Randall. And then she felt ashamed about playing the 'little woman', as though she needed protection, when she was perfectly capable of looking after herself. Except that to think of being with Ross was just so comforting, she couldn't blame herself too much for wanting to have his shelter.

When would they, in fact, meet again? On Christmas leave, perhaps? That's if they could get Christmas leave, which was doubtful. Deciding to hope for the best, she fell asleep.

# Sixty

In the event, neither Ross nor Jinny managed to get Christmas leave, and though Jinny succeeded in being given New Year leave instead, Ross wrote that he didn't expect to be home before Easter. His present to her was a pretty silk scarf he'd found locally, while hers to him was a pair of silver cufflinks from an antique shop in Chester. Lovely gifts, but they had had to be exchanged by post instead of in person, and there was the disappointment, but it couldn't be helped. So many folk were so much worse off, Jinny felt she couldn't complain, and in fact she knew she was lucky, being able to go home for Hogmanay. Not only would she see her father and May, there was the added bonus of seeing Vi, who had leave from the driving course she was taking following her basic training.

'Oh, I'm so excited about it!' she told the family when she arrived the day after Jinny. 'You know I had a few lessons before the war – didn't get round to taking the test – but when they asked me after basic training if I'd like to drive for the army and that I'd be trained for it, you bet I said yes!'

'And you're on the driving course now?' asked May. 'I'm sure you're looking very well on it!'

'Aye, you look grand,' Josh agreed, 'And so does Jinny – it's only your poor old dad who looks his age these days, eh? Going downhill fast without my girls around me.'

'Oh, Dad, what a thing to say!' Serene May was actually frowning. 'Especially when I'm always coming round!'

'Och, that's true, and I don't know what I'd do without you, pet.' Josh grasped her hand. 'But I used to have you all, eh? All my girls together. Didn't know how lucky I was.'

'It's only for the duration,' Vi said easily. 'Then we'll be home again.'

'And how long is the duration going to be?' Josh demanded. 'I think we're in for years of war before we finish off Hitler, if we ever do. He's won everything he's taken on – except the Battle of Britain. I don't see him giving in very easily.'

'You're not supposed to talk like that, Dad,' Jinny told him, shaking her head. 'Think victory, that's the word. And he didn't win the Battle of Britain, so that shows he can be defeated.'

'That's right,' Vi agreed. 'And in the meantime, we have to do what we can for the war effort, though I'm glad I'm not expected to do any fighting. In fact, I told the ATS selection folk that I wasn't interested in doing anti-aircraft stuff – "Ack-Ack" as they call it – as shooting down planes was not for me, but when they offered me driving, like I say, I was thrilled. So, that'll be me – army driver.'

'Driving what?' asked Josh. 'Thae great army lorries you see thundering through Edinburgh?'

'Oh, no, it'll be ambulances. I'll probably be attached to a military hospital, no idea where, but I'm delighted. It's just what I wanted.'

'That's wonderful, Vi,' Jinny told her, with May agreeing and Josh nodding his head.

'Sounds grand, Vi, think I needn't worry about you, then. But what do all the fellows think, having you women driving around the place, then?'

'What fellows? They're needed for active service. Nearly all the drivers I've met lately have been women, and damn good they are!'

'So, you're not meeting many men,' May said thoughtfully, catching Jinny's eye.

But Vi only snorted her disapproval of the idea. 'No men,' she declared. 'Or, at least, very few.'

And May and Jinny, still exchanging glances, didn't need to put their thoughts into words. Vi was the same dear old Vi. She hadn't changed a bit.

Of course, wartime Hogmanay was not the Hogmanay they all knew. In a city where you couldn't show a light in the blackout without being in trouble with the air-raid wardens, there didn't seem to be much point in trying to meet outside to see the New Year in, and the numbers of revellers were down, anyway, with so many men in the forces.

People did still go out – some to pubs, some to take in the night, some to do their first-footing, arriving at doors with bits of coal and Christmas cake if there happened to be any left. The Hendries, however, decided to spend New Year's Eve at home, where May joined them, with the plan of staying the night so that she needn't go home in the dark, and Josh opened a bottle of port he'd been keeping for some time for their toasts.

'Absent friends' was first, and Jinny thought of Ross, though at the same time wondered, as ever, where Viktor might be, and May, of course, raised her glass to Allan.

'Any news of leave for him?' Jinny whispered. 'I don't really like to ask.'

'Well, I daren't even talk about it,' May answered, her blue eyes very bright, 'but in his last letter he said there was a chance that he might get back in the spring some time. Nothing's sure, but it's just so grand, being able to hope.'

'Poor lad,' Josh muttered. 'Here, let's have a top up and toast the New Year.'

1941. They thought about it. After the long months they'd already endured, it was a temptation to hope that the year to come would bring an ending to the hostilities, but Josh had already made it plain how little faith he had in that, and the girls, in their hearts, had to agree with him.

Still, there were their glasses ready and the toast to be made, so they made it.

'To the New Year!' they cried. May added, 'May it bring peace, and everyone back home!'

'Aye, bring us peace,' Josh echoed, and they sipped their port, set down their glasses and hugged one another, smiling and kissing. But as the last stroke of Big Ben's midnight chimes on the wireless died away, somehow they couldn't bring themselves to say, as they'd always said in the past. 'Happy New Year!'

# Sixty-One

Although she had not been able to see Ross, Jinny felt better from having her leave. She was so very glad to have seen her family again – Josh, May and Vi, who was so soon to be embarking on her new life as a qualified ATS driver. There'd been friends to meet up with too and, of course, the staff at Crombie's, where she'd visited everyone she knew – Mrs Arrow, still moaning about their present difficulties and her girls, so worked off their feet; Norah, still helping out as a baker; Mabel, still typing for Accounts and getting on rather better with Mr Lennox, but always nostalgic and sighing for the 'old days'.

'Oh, it's not the same," she told Jinny, who had asked her out for a sandwich lunch in the West End. 'Not the same at all. Mr Lennox is all right, but Ross he is not, and Mr Crombie's so depressed these days, not knowing what's happened to his family.'

'You mean his sister and her husband in Vienna?' Jinny asked carefully.

'Yes, Viktor's parents.' Mabel's eyes slid away from Jinny's. 'He hasn't heard from them at all, but I told him it wasn't likely he would, seeing as they're in an enemy country. How would they be able to get letters out to him? I mean, there'll be no diplomatic help there now.'

'I was thinking of asking him about them.' Jinny looked down at her dry cheese roll. 'But I didn't want to upset him.'

'Best not to say anything,' Mabel agreed. 'And I suppose you've no news of Viktor, either?'

'No, no news at all. He couldn't write to me and he could be anywhere with the German army – they're in so many countries.'

'Such a shame for you, dear.' Mabel's tone was sympathetic, her eyes sharp with curiosity. 'At least you've got your work in the Pay Corps, though. I'm sure you're a natural for that!'

'Oh, yes, I might get a stripe one day,' Jinny told her with a laugh. 'Though Ross, of course, is an officer.'

'You keep in touch with him, dear?'

'Just a letter now and again,' Jinny said smoothly. 'How about another of those drinks they call coffee?'

It was on her last day of leave, when she'd been trying without success to buy some tobacco for her father in Princes Street, that, of all people, she met Senga Brown pushing a pram in which a large baby was sleeping.

'Senga, fancy meeting you!' she cried, at which Senga stopped and gave a pleasant enough smile.

'It's me should be saying that to you, Jinny. I thought you were in the ATS, and here you are in Princes Street. So, where's your uniform?'

'I am in the ATS, but I'm on leave, going back tomorrow, so I'll be wearing my uniform then, all right. I've just been looking for some tobacco for my dad, but there doesn't seem to be any.'

'Tell us something new – there's never anything you want in the shops these days.'

The two young women studied each other, privately deciding that the other looked well, and then Jinny looked in at the baby, a boy named Gordon, and the image, Jinny said, of his father, Terry Brown.

'Look, he's got the same ginger hair!' she exclaimed, but Senga put her finger to her lips.

'Ssh, he's teething and only just gone off – I don't want him to wake up before I see what Mrs Arrow's got for me at Crombie's today. Want to walk along?'

'Mrs Arrow?' repeated Jinny, walking beside the pram. 'I saw her the other day. What does she find for you, then?'

Again, Senga put her finger to her lips. 'Just one or two rolls, you ken, and a few buns. Saves me queuing.'

'That's grand. But are you managing all right, Senga, with Terry away? Do you know where he is?'

'No details, but he's in the Middle East somewhere. His letters are always being censored – great bits blocked out. But I'm doing OK. No worse than any other lassie with a husband in the forces. How about you?' Senga's voice was casual. 'D'you ever hear from Viktor?'

Sighing inwardly, Jinny shook her head. Did these people who asked after Viktor not realize it might be painful for her to admit she knew nothing of him? But perhaps she shouldn't judge them; it was only natural they should be interested in a man who had once been a colleague. And, of course, her attachment to him was widely known and had, in Senga's case, been upsetting. At least she was happily married now, even if her worries over Terry must be acute. It should come as no surprise that she might ask Jinny for news of Viktor.

'I don't know what's happened to him,' she admitted. 'We've rather lost touch.'

'Just as well, Jinny,' Senga said with some satisfaction. 'I mean, he is the enemy now, eh? It never would've worked out, would it? Once the war came?'

'Perhaps not.'

'And you've no' found someone else?'

Preferring not to answer, Jinny shook her head again. 'Here's Crombie's,' she said brightly. 'Hope you have some luck with the rolls and buns, Senga. It's been nice seeing you.'

Remembering the custom of giving babies money, she opened her bag and took out two half-crowns, which she laid on the baby's pram cover.

'For his money box, Senga. Sorry I didn't get it to him earlier.'

'Ah, that's nice of you,' Senga said, smiling. 'It was very nice to meet you, too, Jinny. Take care, then, and good luck!'

'Remember me to Terry!' Jinny cried and, after watching Senga push her pram into the shop, to the annoyance of the queue that had formed some time ago, she turned to make her way back home.

All the talk of Viktor had been unsettling. She didn't want to dwell on her past love for him and her lack of knowing whether he was alive or dead. Best think about her family and how she must soon say goodbye to them again, and then, maybe, to wonder if there might be a letter from Ross waiting for her when she returned from leave. Yes, that was something cheerful to think about – a ray of sunshine on this dark January day.

# Sixty-Two

She was in luck – there was indeed a letter from Ross waiting when Jinny returned to the pay office, and it contained hope of news to come of his own leave. Couldn't go into details, he wrote, but it looked promising for April.

April? Jinny's rising spirits fell. As it was now only January, April seemed an age away, but after a little thought she decided it was just as well he wasn't coming any earlier, for there would be no way she could get any more leave herself before some time had elapsed. Even April would be difficult, but she'd try for it anyway. All she could do now was write back to Ross as soon as she could, giving him news of her time back in Edinburgh, and then get on with her daily routine. It was what most people were doing, anyway, though Pauline had seemed particularly starry-eyed since Christmas.

'Things going well with Chris?' Jinny asked during one coffee break, and Pauline's smile was wide.

'Oh, yes! We really do hit it off well. It's just so lovely being with him. I didn't really want to go home for Christmas, though of course I enjoyed it, and Mum and Dad are always so keen to see me, anyway.'

'And you were better off than me,' Josie said, lighting a cigarette. 'I never even got Christmas leave, did I? Roll on my week away in February.'

'No hope of seeing your chap?' the others asked.

'Not a snowball's.' Josie shrugged. 'All you can do is put up with it.'

As they left the canteen, she moved closer to Jinny, letting Pauline go ahead.

'Listen, have you heard that Enid and Shirley are being posted?'

'No, where?'

'Salisbury, but the point is they're lance corporals, right? And they're being made up to corporal and leaving, which means there'll be vacancies for us.'

'For a stripe?' Jinny's eyes shone. 'I wouldn't mind getting promotion, but Sarge hasn't said a word . . . Why should it be us?'

'Oh, she's always saying we work well and should be going up the ladder – things like that.' Josie tapped Jinny's shoulder. 'We can but wait and see, but I reckon things look hopeful. Might cheer you up a bit, eh?'

'Who says I need cheering up?'

'You've looked a bit down since you came back. I wondered if it might be something to do with your ex-boss. OK, I'm being nosey again, but it might help to talk about it. I mean, is he important, or isn't he?'

'Honestly, Josie!' Jinny hesitated. 'All right, he's important, but there's nothing settled. It's all a bit up in the air.'

'He's probably worrying about the war. Some guys think it's not fair to ask girls to make commitments when . . . well, you know what might happen.'

'He's only in the Isle of Wight,' Jinny said, paling a little. 'And I don't even know exactly how I feel myself.'

'Oh, I think you do,' said Josie, nodding her head. 'And remember, he won't be staying in the Isle of Wight.'

Which was what Ross had once said himself, Jinny reflected, returning to her desk to pay more bills for army requisitions and prepare the invoice copies. It was true that he would not be staying in the Isle of Wight, and where he went next was anybody's guess – except that it would not be anywhere safe. Oh, Josie – why did she have to stir things up?

But of course, she hadn't. Anything she'd made Jinny say was just what she thought, anyway. Yes, Ross was important, and no, Jinny wasn't exactly sure how she felt. Or was that not exactly true? She waited for his letters and wanted to see him . . . Perhaps it was she who was afraid of commitment, then? Was it because of her change of heart over Viktor? As she knew so well, though, Ross wasn't Viktor . . .

Looking up, her eyes a little glazed, she found Sergeant Abbott's gaze fixed on her thoughtfully as she stood in the office doorway, and smiled uncertainly – at which the sergeant moved away.

Oh, dear, had she been found daydreaming at her desk? No hope of her stripe, then. But what on earth did a stripe matter, the way things were? Nothing, really. It would just be nice to have, that was all, as a reassurance that she was doing well, doing her bit, as the saying went. But she decided to put it out of her mind and concentrate on the work in hand, which she wanted to get right, stripe or no stripe.

* * *

Only a few weeks later, when wintry January had melted into dreary February, both she and Josie were awarded their stripes and took satisfaction in telling their families and the men in their lives.

'Of course, my Rickie's already a sergeant,' Josie said with a laugh, 'so you might think he wouldn't be impressed with my one stripe, but he's been really sweet about it. Wrote straight back when he got my letter, and that's not like him.'

'Ross wrote straight back, too,' Jinny told her, 'and guess what – he's got his second pip! He's a lieutenant now, but he was really nice about my stripe.'

'A stripe's a stripe, and anything that makes the men realize we're not playing at soldiers has to be good. Any news of a posting for Ross, by the way?'

'Not any that he's given me, but I have the feeling there's something in the wind that he's not telling me about.'

'Probably knows the censor would black it out, anyway, if there's something you'd really like to know.'

'All I'm really waiting for is news of his leave. Seems so long, Josie, since I last saw him.'

'And you say you're not sure of how you feel,' said Josie with a smile.

February became March and there was still no news of when Jinny and Ross might meet, but at least there was good news from Vi, who had completed her driving course with flying colours and was now settling into a posting with a military hospital in Devonshire.

'I'm really enjoying this,' she wrote to Jinny. 'Driving around narrow little roads, collecting patients and doctors, filling in on any other errands that crop up. Sometimes I have to go quite far afield and it's always a worry about petrol, but up to now everything's been OK. I really feel I've got the job I wanted – not actually killing anybody, but contributing to the war effort. Hope that doesn't sound too weedy?'

'Not weedy at all,' Jinny had written back. 'You're doing a grand, necessary job and I'm proud of you!'

Of course, she knew that Vi would only say, 'Enough of that sort of talk!' But it was true what she'd written – she was proud of her sister, who'd volunteered for a difficult job, which could only get worse if situations arose when casualties were high. In a way, she half-wished she could do something the same herself, for there was no doubt that she was very safe and comfortable where she was.

But she knew she was good at her job and it was certainly one that had to be done; she tried not to do too much soul-searching over it. Just keep going, day after day, and hope the time would come when she and Ross would meet again.

But when she finally received his letter telling her he was coming and would be in Edinburgh by the end of April, she could scarcely believe it. Even when she was told she could only have a weekend pass instead of leave, her spirits remained high, and when the time came to travel up to Edinburgh she felt she was moving there on billowing clouds. They supported her until they were replaced by Ross's passionate hug upon greeting her on Friday evening at Waverley Station.

# Sixty-Three

'I can't believe you're here,' Jinny said breathlessly. 'I can't believe it's really you!'

'I feel the same,' Ross told her, still holding her close. 'Seems an age since we last met.'

'An age,' she agreed, releasing herself to look at him as people from the train surged by. 'But you look just the same. A little thinner, maybe—'

'No, no, I'm no thinner!' He laughed. 'Not on a diet of army stodge! And you look wonderful, Jinny, really lovely. So smart in your uniform!'

'With my one stripe? If anyone looks smart, it's you, Ross. Here, let me see your second pip – oh, very grand!'

'Come on, let's not waste time; let's get out of here. We'll have to take a tram – can't see any taxis at the moment . . .'

'Always looking for taxis,' she said fondly. 'The tram will be fine. But where are we going?'

'I thought we'd have a meal at the club and then – I don't know – I expect you'll want to see your father?'

'He won't be back from the theatre. I'll see him later, and May sometime tomorrow.'

'That's fine. I wasn't expecting you to get a weekend pass just for me.'

Did he really think that? Well, it was true, she did want to see her father and May, but the object of this visit was in fact to see Ross. She hadn't been able to think of anything else since she'd had news of his leave. Which told her something, didn't it? Told her quite a lot.

'All right to come to the club, then?' Ross asked as they climbed the slope from the station. 'I think you enjoyed your visit before.'

'I did. But are you sure no one will make trouble if I'm not commissioned and you are?'

'No one will say a word,' Ross said firmly. 'The club's like a sanctuary, and no one's young enough to be in the services, anyway, so they won't notice anything.'

At the club that seemed so much the same, as though untouched by conflicts outside its walls, they were given a corner table as before, and it was true, as Ross had said: none of the elderly patrons looked as though they would want to take any notice of the rank of army people. In fact, one or two smiled at the attractive young couple dining near them, and Jinny smiled back, thinking what a pity it was that there had to be any different ranks at all, but maybe the army wouldn't function without them? With Ross sitting opposite her, his brown eyes riveted on her face, she soon forgot to worry about it, anyway.

What they had for dinner scarcely registered, and the fact that now there was no wine on offer at all was of no importance. All they wanted was what they had, to be together again, to talk about their different army lives, to study each other, to make the most of the short time they would have.

The only thing that rather distracted Jinny was that she couldn't truly be sure that Ross wasn't keeping something from her. His face seemed at first sight to be as open as ever, yet, every so often, she would have the feeling that there was some shadow crossing his features and that there were words trembling on his lips that were never said.

'Ross,' she said at last, when they were taking coffee in the lounge again, 'is there something wrong?'

'Wrong? No, of course not. Everything's wonderfully right – can't you tell?'

'Yes, but somehow I have the feeling that you want to tell me something yet you never do. So what is it? If there's something I should know, I'd like you to say.'

'I was going to tell you sooner or later,' he answered after a pause. 'But then I thought, why spoil the first time we meet again?'

He gave a wry smile. 'Seems I didn't reckon on your eagle eye, Jinny.'

'You're too honest to keep secrets, Ross.'

'I've always known I wouldn't make a spy.'

Jinny sipped her coffee, then set down the cup. 'Well, what is it, then?' she asked, with a little impatience. 'What is it that I need to know?'

'It's just that . . . this leave I have, well, it's not ordinary leave . . . it's embarkation leave.'

'Embarkation?' Her impatience had died. She knew now why he hadn't wanted to tell her what she needed to know. 'You're being posted from the Isle of Wight?'

'We all are. The battalion is on the move.'

'Where to, Ross? Can you tell me?'

Again, he hesitated. 'India.'

'India? Oh, no, Ross, no! Why should you go there? You won't be fighting Germans; it's not involved in the war . . . why should you go to India?'

'Certain tribesmen are attacking British stations on the north-west frontier. We've been given the job of sorting them out.' Ross moved his coffee cup to and fro. 'That's the situation, Jinny. I agree, we won't be fighting the Germans, perhaps for some time—'

'Some time . . .' Jinny's voice was very low. 'How long will you be going for, then?'

'We don't know.' He raised his eyes to hers. 'Depends on the situation, but it might be . . . hell, I don't know. You can see why I didn't want to tell you.'

'I suppose wherever you went' – her voice was trembling – 'it would have been as bad. I mean,' she tried to laugh, 'I don't want you fighting Germans, either.'

He caught at her hand and pressed it. 'One day, you have to believe it, the war will be at an end and we'll be free of anxiety, free to live our own lives again. That's what you have to hang on to, Jinny, and in the meantime . . .' His eyes on her were tender. 'We have our weekend.'

'Our weekend,' she repeated. 'Yes, at least we have that.'

# Sixty-Four

In spite of all their efforts, however, they could not take real pleasure in their weekend. They had looked forward to it for so long, wondered if it would ever happen, but now that it had, the news from Ross of his embarkation had cast a shadow they could not lift.

Of course, they still carried out what they'd planned, meeting early the next day to climb Calton Hill again and look out at the views over the city that Ross said he'd carry with him to India, have lunch at the place they'd found in Thistle Street, then walk for a while below the castle in Princes Street gardens.

'I suppose I should look in at Comrie's,' Ross said as they found a bench and sat together. 'I won't be seeing them for a while.'

'You could,' Jinny answered. 'I'm sure they'd appreciate it, but I don't think I'll come with you.'

'I'll leave it till Monday, then.' Ross looked bleakly toward the castle, Jinny's hand firmly locked in his. 'I have a couple of days left after you've gone tomorrow.'

Tomorrow. The word sent an arrow piercing their hearts. Tomorrow they must say goodbye.

'Come on,' said Ross, leaping up, 'there's time to go to the Botanic Gardens. I'd like to see them before I leave, then have a cup of tea. If they're still doing teas.'

'Where shall we go this evening?' Jinny asked as they went for yet another tram. 'Were you thinking of the club again?'

'No. Someone told me of a place in George Street where they still have quite decent food. I thought we might try that.'

'I've got a better idea. Why not come back to Fingal Street? If you don't mind having something light? I got some salad stuff in this morning and there's ham and cheese. No coffee, I'm afraid, only tea.'

'Jinny, that's a marvellous idea! Just to be alone, the two of us . . .' Ross's eyes were shining. 'Who cares about coffee?'

The thought of being by themselves raised their spirits for the first time that day, and by the time they arrived at the flat in Fingal Street they were so keyed up for this first time alone, they'd managed to put tomorrow's goodbyes from their minds.

'It's not going to be much of a meal,' Jinny said nervously as she laid out the things for their supper. 'I wish I'd been able to boil eggs, but of course, Dad's got no eggs.'

'Jinny, come here,' Ross said gently. 'Stop worrying about what we eat. I don't give a damn.'

As soon as she'd moved into his arms, she sensed his transformation from special friend to man in love, and knew she felt the same herself. Knew she'd crossed from not being sure of her feelings to being so sure she was glad to kiss him as passionately as he kissed her, and to lie close to him on the old sofa. If only – if only – they stared at each other wildly, longing to put what they wanted to say into words, until Ross stood up and gave a long shuddering sigh.

'It's no good, Jinny. We can't risk it.'

'Can't? Folk do this all the time, Ross.'

'And regret it.'

'Not always.'

'Maybe not, but I'm not talking about the usual worry, though it is a worry when we're parting tomorrow. I'm thinking that I might be away for years, you won't see me, and as the time goes on, you might . . .'

He halted, looking down at her with those brown eyes that had always been so kind, so concerned, and now were more troubled than she'd ever seen them.

'Might what?' she whispered.

'Not feel the same.'

'You think because my feelings changed for Viktor they'd be likely to change about you? This is different, Ross. I promise you I'm not going to change.'

'There's time involved, Jinny. It can do strange things. And I don't feel I can ask you to wait. When, apart from anything else, I might – well, you know what might happen—'

'Don't, Ross,' she said quietly. 'Don't talk about that.'

'But you see why I'm not going to ask you to be committed to me? It just wouldn't be fair.'

'Do you think you will stay committed to me?'

'Yes. Yes, I do. I'm sure.

'Then why shouldn't I be sure, too?'

'You're younger, you're beautiful, you could meet someone – anybody—'

'No,' she said steadfastly. I won't meet anybody, because I don't want to. Look, let's not talk about this any more. Let's not think about the future, just today.'

'Today,' Ross agreed, and their mouths met in long, long kisses, until Jinny drew away, sighing, and suggested they have something to eat.

'As though we were hungry,' she added, with a laugh.

'It looks very good,' Ross remarked, taking a plate. 'This was such a wonderful idea of yours, Jinny, having time alone.'

Especially for their last evening, both were thinking, but neither put that into words.

# Sixty-Five

After they'd eaten what they could, they sat close together on the sofa, Jinny resting her head on Ross's shoulder, while he put his arm around her. They felt so completely as one there seemed no need to talk, but Jinny at last sat up and asked Ross what she knew was an impossible question: how long did he think the war might last?

'Oh, Jinny, what a thing to ask!' he answered with a groan. 'Years, I should say. We're nowhere near defeating Hitler, and we've now got Mussolini to worry about in North Africa. There's talk that Rommel and the German Afrika Korps will soon be arriving, and that's bad news too. Rommel's a very talented general – no one fancies being up against him.'

At the dismayed look on Jinny's face, Ross shook his head and held her close for a moment. 'Look, I don't want to upset you,' he murmured, smoothing back her hair. 'We shouldn't just be looking on the dark side. "Look for the silver lining" – isn't that what people say?'

'Trust you to be optimistic!' Jinny said, sighing. 'Not everyone can see it.'

'OK, there is a bit of good news I've just remembered.'

'I wish you'd tell me, then.'

'Well, there's another rumour going about that Hitler's planning to attack Russia. If he does – and they say he's already got German troops massing on the borders – he might well be shooting himself in the foot. Russia's so vast, has such a terrible climate, as well as the Red Army, that it's unlikely he'll succeed there, and if he loses a huge amount of men, he'll be weakened.' Ross, looking hopeful that he had cheered her, turned Jinny's face towards his. 'Does that sound encouraging?'

'I don't know.' The words 'German troops' seemed to be echoing through her mind, coupled with 'huge amount of men', and just for a moment the question arose: would Viktor be among them? If only she knew what had happened to him . . . It seemed right that she should, they'd been so close once . . . But now the man she loved was gazing at her, and she leaped to her feet, saying she would make some tea, her father would soon be home from the theatre and would be delighted to see Ross.

How quickly their weekend was running away from them, she thought with a pang as she put on the kettle and set out cups. Already, Saturday, their main day, was almost over. To come, there would be their passionate yet melancholy parting, followed by the night to lie alone, and tomorrow, after their last meeting, Ross would see her to the station, for he'd changed his mind about railway farewells, and that would be it. No more contact except for letters – for how long? Years, perhaps, Ross had said.

Years? At the thought, her heart was as heavy as stone, but she stoically made the tea, hearing her father's step on the stairs, and resolved to be as totally committed to Ross as he'd said he would be to her. And when the years were past and the war was over, then, maybe, they could think about their happiness. Maybe.

'Why, Ross, hello!' Josh was crying. 'My, isn't it grand to see you, then? Let me shake your hand.'

Everything worked out just as Jinny had thought it would. After the long goodnight in the street and she had watched Ross move reluctantly away, she lay awake most of the night, wishing she had not had to spend it alone, and in the morning, after a sweet visit from May, she and Ross went out together, just walking in the city, before having lunch, for which they had no appetite, at a George Street hotel. Then it was back to Fingal Street for Jinny to change into her uniform, pack her kitbag, kiss Josh goodbye and hurry with Ross to the station for the train to Chester.

'You really shouldn't be seeing me off,' she told him. 'You did say you hated station farewells.'

'I did, but this time I don't want to waste any time I could spend with you. Every minute is precious.'

'I know, I know. I'm glad you came.'

They were standing close on the platform, surrounded by other couples and families saying goodbye. Already some were crying, and Jinny was close to tears herself, yet trying to keep them back, at least until she was on the train.

'This is where we promise to write,' Ross said softly. 'But we will write, won't we?'

'We will. I don't need to promise.'

'Nor do I. But if there's a delay in our letters, you'll understand, Jinny? We're going to have to travel a hell of a long way, and I've no idea how things will be in India. There may be times when I just can't write, but it won't mean I haven't been wanting to—'

'Ross, don't worry about it. I'll be grateful for anything that comes.'

Jinny's words were brave, but her face was pale, for her train was arriving, and it was time for the last embrace, the last long kiss. In spite of herself, a sob escaped her as she wrenched herself from Ross's arms and saw the misery on his face. Reaching up, she kissed him one more time, then turned to board the train, but he was with her still, trying to make a path for her between the soldiers already waiting, who called out, 'Watch it, darling!' until they saw the look on Ross's face and said no more.

Finally she was aboard, staying close to the open window, and as the train began to move she waved and waved, as Ross waved too, until he was a speck on the platform and she was alone, even though surrounded by others. Then she let the tears fall.

'Oh, you poor thing!' Pauline exclaimed when she and Josie first saw her on her return. 'Must've been awful, saying goodbye.'

'He'll come back,' said Josie. 'Don't worry.'

'And I've got some news,' Pauline told her. 'Though I don't want to make a big thing of it—'

'Go on, Jinny'll be pleased for you,' Josie said shortly. 'We all are.'

'Fact is,' Pauline whispered, 'I'm engaged.'

'Why, that's wonderful!' cried Jinny. 'Yes, I am pleased for you, Pauline. Of course I am!'

'Show her the ring,' ordered Josie, and Pauline duly showed off the pretty ring on her left hand, which Jinny praised with quite genuine feeling.

'What are the plans, then?'

'Oh, no plans yet. Maybe a wedding next year.'

Pauline's face was so wreathed in smiles, Jinny gave her a quick hug, and tried not to compare her own lot with her friend's. It was good that someone was happy, eh? But as she turned away she caught the sympathy of a fellow sufferer in Josie's eyes, and had to go into the bathroom before she began to cry again.

# Sixty-Six

Now began the long years without Ross that Jinny had braced herself to face. Sometimes she wondered what she would have done without his letters, that gave her not only the joy of knowing she was loved, but the courage to keep going, and supposed that she would have had to survive, just as people without such support had to survive. But, oh, she was so glad she had them, and when it happened that he was unable to write, even though he had warned her that there would be such breaks, she felt quite bereft until she saw the familiar handwriting on an envelope again.

Like everyone else, she followed the war news with avid interest, noting not long after Ross had left that he'd been right about Hitler's invasion of Russia, which happened in June. Not right, maybe, that Hitler had made a mistake, for when three million German troops poured into the attack, with three thousand tanks, it seemed at first that Russia was not retaliating well.

'Oh, dear, bad news,' said Pauline. 'Chris says the critics of Hitler have got it all wrong. He's winning again in Russia, just like everywhere else.'

'Except over here,' Jinny reminded her, but she too felt troubled in case Hitler was proving invincible, before she again found herself wondering if Viktor was one of those millions of German army troops involved. He had become so shadowy, however, that her thoughts didn't linger on him, especially when the news came later in the year that the Russians had suddenly begun to fight back, with all the strength people had always expected of them. Even when Leningrad was put under siege by the Germans, the people there did not give in, which showed, everyone said, how difficult they would be to beat as a nation.

Still, there seemed no real hope of victory over Hitler until, in December 1941, the Japanese without warning attacked the American Pearl Harbor, which brought America into the war. True, the Japanese had joined the German Axis, but now that America, with all its huge resources, was one of Britain's allies, at long last there was something to be cheerful about. That was on a national scale, but also, for Jinny and May, there was something personal, for though it still seemed unbelievable, Vi, it appeared, had acquired a young man. As Christmas approached, she wrote to Josh and her sisters, saying she would be coming home on leave and bringing 'a friend'. The friend's name was Barry Graham, a sergeant stationed near the hospital where she was based.

'All right if he has the little bedroom, now that you've got May's room?' she asked Josh. 'Barry's parents are dead and he has nowhere to spend his leave, so I invited him home. I'm sure you'll like him – I do, anyway.'

'Vi's bringing a fellow home?' Josh cried to May. 'I don't believe it – she's never taken the slightest interest—'

'She says she likes him,' May pointed out. 'And he is an army sergeant, Dad. He's doing his bit, so you'll probably like him too.'

'I did think I could rely on Vi not to start bringing fellows home,' Josh retorted. 'Och, seems I've lost the lot o' you!'

'Hang on, no one says Vi is going to marry this Barry,' May said reasonably. 'Let's wait and see what happens, eh?'

But May lost no time in writing to Jinny, asking her to do her best to get leave, so that they could both see what Vi's young man was like, and Jinny, marvelling over that phrase – 'Vi's young man' – wrote back to say she'd move heaven and earth to get home to meet this amazing fellow. Her luck was in – she was given her leave – and on Christmas Eve she arrived home to find May and her father, who'd finished early at the theatre, ready and waiting for Vi and the unknown sergeant.

'It all looks lovely,' she told May. 'The fire burning and the little tree with the dear old fairy on the top, just as always.'

'Remember how Vi once said she should be retiring? We weren't having that!'

'Ssh!' cried Josh. 'I hear the door. They're here.'

Silence fell as Vi, in uniform, appeared in the doorway, ushering in a tall man, also in uniform, who took off his cap and stood smiling, looking from one expectant face to another.

'Dad, May, Jinny – this is Barry,' Vi announced. 'Barry, may I introduce my father and my sisters? You've heard all about them. Here they are.'

He stepped forward to shake Josh's hand, a strong-faced man in his thirties, with short, clipped brown hair and light blue eyes – not handsome, yet pleasant to look at, and with the army way of holding himself: very erect, very straight-backed. Jinny could imagine him being good on the parade ground, yet his manner now was easy and relaxed, although his eyes on Josh were perhaps just a little anxious.

'Mr Hendrie, I'm very glad to meet you,' he said in a northern English accent. 'It's so kind of you to have me for Christmas – I do appreciate it.'

'That's all right,' Josh muttered, clearly impressed. 'Glad you could come. May, Jinny, shake hands with Mr Graham.'

'Barry, you mean!' cried Vi. 'We don't stand on ceremony. Any chance of a cup of tea? We're parched and had to stand all the way to Waverley.'

'Tea's coming up,' said May, when she and Jinny had greeted Barry. 'Vi, show Barry his room while I get the cups.'

'I'd just like to put a few things under that Christmas tree, if I may,' Barry said, taking up his bag. 'Only a few odds and ends, but I did get a bottle of whisky for you, Mr Hendrie – I hope it's OK.'

'A bottle of what?' Josh shouted. 'I've no' seen any whisky since the start of the war!'

'He'll be your friend for life now,' May told Barry with a laugh. He replied seriously, 'I hope so.'

In this way began a truly pleasant Christmas, with all the difficulties and shortages disregarded, as May and Jinny did their utmost for Vi's sake to make Barry feel at home. Even though their own loved ones were far away, the sisters took genuine pleasure in Vi's radiant acceptance that she could fall in love, just like anyone else, and were happy to see how beautiful she looked, and how she and Barry seemed right for each other. Of course, they couldn't know him in the short time since he'd arrived, but Vi knew him, and the way things were going they were prepared to trust her judgement.

'Oh, he is right for me!' she exclaimed when Josh had taken Barry to a Boxing Day football match and the girls were alone in the flat. 'He's perfect for me, shares all my ideas about equality and human rights – that's how we came to go out together, after we'd met at a hospital dance. We danced a bit, and then he told me he'd worked in a factory before the war and been the trade union representative and, of course, that got me started. By the end of the evening we were already fixing up to meet again.'

Vi gave a wide smile and sighed. 'All I've got to worry about now is how soon he'll be posted away, but so far there's no sign of it, so, fingers crossed, eh?'

'Fingers permanently crossed,' said Jinny. 'I've heard that Ross's regiment is leaving India, but only for North Africa, so there's still no chance of seeing him.'

'And Allan's in Tobruk,' put in May. 'No chance of seeing him, either.'

'Now I really understand what you're going through,' Vi said quietly.

Christmas leave was over, but before she left, while Barry was doing a last check round in his room, Vi caught her father's arm.

'Dad, do you like him?' she asked fiercely.

'Barry?' He looked down at her, his dark eyes serious. 'Vi, I do. If my girls have to go, I want 'em to be with a fellow who'll be right, and Barry's right. A grand lad, och, yes. If he's the one for you—'

'He is!'

'Then I'm happy for you.' He gave her a quick hug. 'And I hope all goes well for you both. Goes without saying, eh?'

'Thanks, Dad,' Vi answered, sniffing a little, as Barry came out, ready to go, and then there were handshakes, brief kisses and more hugs with May and Jinny, and final waves as the couple left for their tram to the station.

'That's it, then,' murmured May. 'Christmas is over.'

'Still got Hogmanay,' Josh said.

'I'll be away before then,' said Jinny. 'Anyway, I don't feel like celebrating. Who knows what the New Year will bring?'

'But have you ever seen Vi looking better?' asked May.

'Never,' they agreed, and then were silent, thinking of what might happen, for Vi and Barry, for all of them, in the time to come.

# Sixty-Seven

What happened to Jinny was that, after being awarded a second stripe, she got posted. To Salisbury! Oh, no! She didn't in the least want to go and leave everyone she knew to start afresh in Southern Command. Oh, why couldn't they leave her where she was?

'You must suffer for promotion,' Josie told her. 'What about me? I'm getting a second stripe, too, but I have to go to Aberdeen.'

'Well, I haven't got any stripes,' Pauline said cheerfully, 'but I'm on my way as well. Might as well tell you now.'

'On your way where?' asked Jinny.

'Home. To my mum and dad. Can you believe it? But I've got no choice.'

'Just because you'll be married?'

'No, because I'll be getting the green ration book. Now, do I have to spell out what that means?'

Green ration book. Jinny and Josie exchanged looks. They knew that green ration books were only for expectant mothers, to make sure they had the food they needed.

'Yes, it's true,' Pauline said, laughing. 'I'm in the club. Jumped the gun, I'm afraid, and Mum's furious. Has to be only a register office wedding now, you see, with just her and Dad, and Chris and me, of course. Sorry, girls, I can't invite you, but if Mum can get the stuff, I'll send you a bit of wedding cake.'

'Congratulations, anyway!' cried Jinny, embracing her. 'What's it matter if the baby wasn't planned? I think it's wonderful, anyway.'

'And for you the war is over,' Josie added, smiling. 'If I could knit I'd make some bootees; as it is, I'll be sending a christening mug. Oh, but we're going to miss you, Pauline!'

'We're all going to miss one another,' Jinny said bleakly. 'Just think of Josie and me having to start all over again.'

'As corporals, though,' Pauline reminded her. 'You'll do fine, both of you, and I'm going to wish you all the best. You and your fellows, too. We'll keep in touch, eh?'

Of course they would. For a time, anyway. But Jinny was worrying how she would get on in a new place, and of how she must let Ross know as quickly as possible, hoping that her letter would get through, for of late their letters to each other had been slow to arrive, with some, Jinny feared, not arriving at all. The only good news, really, was that she'd been awarded that second stripe. Corporal Hendrie. It sounded good.

Only two weeks later, she left for Salisbury, butterflies fluttering inside her, but once she arrived it wasn't so bad. It was all right, in fact. Her new billet was in another large house, not unlike the one she'd been used to, the pay office was just what she'd expected and the people she met were friendly and helpful. Another captain, another sergeant, more ATS faces to get used to, and new recruits she'd been told she'd be training, but all looked promising.

I think I could settle here, she thought, and was surprised at how easy her move had been.

'First, a short course,' announced Captain Horton, erect, very military in bearing but missing fingers from one hand, his reason for no longer being on active service. 'Just to familiarize you with a corporal's duties and the techniques of training others. Sergeant Teller will fill you in and I know from your records that you're a quick learner so you'll have no problems. Nice to have you with us, Corporal Hendrie!'

'Nice to be here, sir,' she replied.

# Sixty-Eight

It was here in Southern Command that she was to stay for the rest of the war, observing – at the safe distance she felt rather guilty about – the long progression of events that was finally to bring about the end, though she wasn't to know, of course, when that would be until it happened.

So many battles, so many 'theatres of war', to use a phrase liked by the BBC. She found it depressing to read and hear of so many, and all involving people hoping to kill other people. But that was what war meant, and you just had to keep on remembering that this war, against fascism, was a just one.

All the same, it was terrible to think of the suffering involved. In Russia, for example, where the continuing fighting with the German attackers was causing thousands of deaths and casualties. In the Far East, where Japan had taken Singapore, Hong Kong and Burma in ruthless fashion and had so far held off British advances. In North Africa, where the British were fighting the Italians and Rommel, the most feared of German generals, and where there were immense numbers of casualties after cat-and-mouse warfare.

Naturally, Jinny's anxieties were very much centred on that particular 'theatre', for it was there that Ross and Allan were both involved. Every day she dreaded receiving a telegram, heaving sighs of relief when none came – until, following the great battle between Rommel and the British General Montgomery at El Alamein, the news came from May that Allan was to be invalided home. A shell had exploded close to him during the battle and his hearing had been badly affected.

He was alive, that was the main thing, but poor chap, how terrible that he should not be able to hear properly! Jinny resolved to see him as soon as possible, but along with her sorrow for his troubles was her anxiety over Ross. She'd heard nothing, which might be thought of as good news, but then again, might not. If only she could see him again . . .

When she did manage to visit Allan, by then at home, it was to hear that the doctors had found he had some residual hearing and had fitted him with two powerful hearing aids. Even with these he would not be able to serve again in the forces, and might be advised to study lip reading, or signing, in case his hearing deteriorated even further.

'Not such good news,' he told Jinny, his voice sounding odd – rather distorted, in fact – 'but it could have been worse. That's what I keep telling myself.'

'You're alive,' May said softly. 'You're here. And that's all that matters.'

'I should say so!' Jinny cried, noting with distress Allan's haggard looks and the lines of strain around his eyes. Also, he seemed constantly to be holding his head forward, as though it would help him to hear, and when it didn't, he would fiddle with his hearing aids to try to make them work better. Which did very little good.

'What are you planning to do?' Jinny asked, speaking as clearly as she could. 'Will you open your shop again?'

'He's thinking of it,' said May, as Allan did not reply. 'But he's worried how he'd manage with the customers. I've told him I'll help, but he could always get them to write down what they want done if he can't hear them.'

'The hearing aids must surely do some good?' Jinny asked.

'Oh, they do, they do. It's just a question of getting used to them.' May was doing her best to appear as calm as usual, but the lines of strain were appearing round her eyes too. 'I'm sure we'll work something out.'

'Of course you will!' cried Jinny.

Before she left, she asked if Allan had any news of Ross, but he managed to tell her that the two had not met. He was sure she would have heard if he'd been hurt, however, and no doubt he was now involved in further activity in North Africa. There was a lot to do, even though the battle of El Alamein had been won.

'But you won't be doing it, thank God,' said May, then glanced at Jinny and bit her lip. Quickly, she touched her sister's hand. 'Ross will be all right, Jinny, I'm sure of it. As Allan says, you'd have heard if he wasn't.'

In fact, only a day or two later, she received a letter from him that had miraculously filtered through. He was fine, had come through without trouble, with only a slight shoulder wound that was already healing, and she was not to worry. One of these days they would meet again, no question!

And in May 1944, though she could scarcely believe it, his words came true. Thin and worn, though bronzed and smiling, he arrived in Edinburgh for his first leave in years, which was, even then, only to be a couple of days, and Jinny was there at Waverley to meet him, on only a short leave herself. It wasn't long, but it was enough, it was everything – yet as he came towards her, seeming at first a stranger, she hesitated, so anxious to greet him but not sure how she should. Until, that is, she saw his brown eyes searching her face, those same brown eyes she had always found so comforting, and in a moment she was in his arms, the years rolling away, and they were strangers no longer.

'I never thought this day would come,' she whispered, tears unshed, ready to fall. 'And you look so well, you've not changed at all—'

'Come on, that's not what I see in my shaving mirror,' he laughed. 'But it is true of you, Jinny. You're as lovely as ever, just as you've always been in my dreams these years away. Now, are there any taxis, do you think?'

'You and your taxis! There might be, if we're lucky. But I want to ask you, Ross, will you stay with us instead of going to the club? There's a small room you could have.'

'That would be wonderful, just what I want. But still, let's hunt down a taxi!'

# Sixty-Nine

The brief leave passed like a dream. Sometimes, when they were alone, with moments of rapture that stopped just short of 'going all the way', as some described it; sometimes with long catching-up talks of how the world had been for them in the years that had passed, when Ross said all there had ever been for him had been warfare and thoughts of Jinny.

'I used to worry about you,' he told her. 'Of how you were not meeting other people because of me, and then, of course, I'd worry in case you were!' He lowered his eyes for a moment as he spoke and held her close. 'Was I wrong to do that? You wouldn't blame me?'

'Of course I wouldn't! It'd be natural to worry. But you never had any need, Ross.' Jinny moved back his copper-coloured hair and smoothed his brow. 'I used to go to the pictures, or to dances, but always in a crowd. Soldiers did sometimes try to make dates but I always put them off, and, you see, I'm here now. Isn't that so?'

'It is!' he cried. 'And I'm a damned lucky fellow, is all I can say.'

'Let's just hope your luck holds, then,' she said quietly. 'And I don't mean with me.'

'It will, it will, I promise you.'

Their talk shifted to the future of the war, with Ross being so optimistic that Jinny's heart lifted a little.

'You really think we can beat Hitler now? That would be wonderful!'

'I do think that. He's not exactly a spent force, but ever since he was defeated in Russia – and you remember the Germans surrendered back in 1943 – there's been a question mark over his powers to survive. And now you know what's coming, don't you? Why my regiment's back home?'

'You mean, D-Day?'

Now her heart was plummeting again. D-Day – the date when the Allies were to enter Europe that everyone talked about and no one outside the top brass knew when it would be – would for her be the biggest nightmare yet if Ross were to be part of it. Vi had said, in confidence, that Barry, at present at some unknown place abroad, would almost certainly be included in the D-Day assault, and Jinny had shivered to think about it. Now it looked as if—

'Oh, Ross, you're not going to be involved, are you? Do you mean that's why you're back?'

'I'm afraid so,' he replied seriously. 'We're home for preparation and training. It's what we've been working towards for some time; it's something we have to do.'

'It will mean killing, terrible killing.'

'And victory, Jinny. If we want to overcome evil we have to have victory over Hitler. Lives will be lost – on both sides – but it's the only way.'

She knew he was right, that victory was essential and must be paid for, but the price – it was so high she couldn't bear to think about it, and leaped up to begin making preparations for their meal. May and Allan were to join them, and Josh, too, for he was taking time off from the theatre for Ross's last night.

'What did you think about Vi finding a lovely young man?' May asked Ross over the wonderful gigot lamb chops she'd given Jinny, having been thrilled to be offered them by her butcher. When he'd heard about Allan he had been even more helpful to May, though Vi would probably still have put his helpfulness down to May's beautiful blue eyes.

'I'm very pleased for her,' Ross said now. 'Barry sounds like a damn good soldier, and from what I've heard he and Vi are really suited.'

'Aye, she's happy,' Josh put in. 'And Barry's such a grand lad, you have to be happy for her, eh? Just hope he comes through what's ahead, along with all you young men.'

There was a short silence after that, with Allan heaving a deep sigh and Ross finding Jinny's face and saying, 'Don't worry, we'll be fine!'

If only he's right, she prayed. If only they all come through, Ross, Barry and all the young men who meant so much.

But when D-Day arrived on 6 June, and the first Allied assaults were made on Normandy, though Ross survived, many of the other young men with him did not. And one of these was Barry.

# Seventy

All those who knew Vi expected her to be stoical over the death of Barry, and so she was. Though it must have been hard to endure the euphoria of other people seeing an end to the war at last, she showed no emotion, driving her ambulance when she returned from a short time at home with the same dedication she'd always displayed. Only her face, so lacking in light, in any expression, revealed her feelings.

'Oh, to see her not crying, not giving way, makes me want to weep,' May told Jinny, and Jinny, trying to imagine how she would have managed had it been Ross who'd been killed, could only agree. There was something so poignant about Barry's death, coming when there was real hope of victory after all the years of fear, that it made the grief of the Hendries very real, and because they could not share it with Vi herself, all the more difficult to accept.

Josh, in particular, was very affected. Such a fine young man, he would say, such a wonderful soldier. What good times they might have shared in the future, liking the same things such as football and going out for a pint! He might have been the son Josh had never had, mightn't he? And talk of a son was something his girls had never heard from their father before.

All they could do was let Vi come to terms with her grief in her own way while they did the same, always thinking of her. In the world outside, the fighting went on that would eventually see the death of Hitler in his bunker. Nothing was easy – everything had to be taken after a struggle, but gradually the Allies reached their objectives, taking Rome, Florence and Athens, liberating Paris and finally crossing into Germany and reaching Berlin in April 1945. With the writing on the wall for Hitler, he ordered the destruction of everything that might be of use to his enemies, but his people were unwilling to put up resistance, being more concerned with escaping the Russians who would not have forgotten Germany's attempt to overpower their country. It was the Russians, however, who, along with the Americans, encircled Berlin, and whose iron grip would cause trouble in the future. But when Germany had officially surrendered, all the Allies and their people at home could think of was celebrating victory, which they did on 8 May 1945, with immense joy and relief.

Of course, there was still the war against the Japanese in the Far East to be won, which the families of those involved bitterly pointed out, but after all they'd been through no one could deny the survivors of the war in Europe their chance to celebrate. Whatever happened tomorrow, today they would dance and sing, light bonfires, have street parties and, if they could find anything to drink, make toasts to everyone in sight.

As for the Hendries, they had their own private celebration of a different nature, which was the birth of May and Allan's daughter on the day after the German surrender.

'No street party for me!' May had declared, laughing, when Josh came in to see her and his new granddaughter, who was to be named Victoria, and he'd shed a tear or two before hurrying to a phone box with all the money he could find to ring first Vi, who said she was delighted, and did sound so, and then Jinny at her billet.

'And she's to be called Victoria?' asked Jinny, experiencing a little twist of feeling at the name, which was so close to Viktor's. 'Oh, but that's wonderful, Dad, thanks for telling me. Oh, I'm so happy for them – now all I want is to be demobbed and to be at home!'

And with Ross, she added to herself. But when would that be? Please God, let it be soon, she prayed. Like everyone she knew, she'd had enough of her temporary wartime life and longed to get back to her own. It was true, she'd made some good friends – Josie, for instance, and Pauline, now the mother of a fine son, and young Sukie, and hoped they'd keep in touch, but there was a real life waiting for her somewhere and a real love. How soon before she could find them?

# Seventy-One

With the process of demobilisation not beginning until June 1945, it was not to be expected that she'd be home very soon, but she was pleasantly surprised when her turn came six months later and the following January she was once again returning to Accounts. Not yet with Ross, though he was due to take up his old post soon, then Mr Lennox would depart and everything would be as it had always been.

Not quite, for Comrie's Bakery was not the same. Shortages, difficulties of every sort, made the atmosphere after the first euphoria of victory strained and tense, as it was in so much of post-war Britain, and it didn't help to see the newsreels at the cinema that showed the horrors of the German concentration camps, or the photographs of the atomic bomb explosions that had certainly brought the war in the Far East to an end, but had also destroyed two Japanese cities in the most terrifying manner. And then there were the endless problems of refugees everywhere, the misery of devastated cities, and the realization that everywhere there was so much to be done.

It was no wonder that Mrs Arrow took comfort in her usual complaints about supplies, and her new ones about the girls back from munitions being so discontented they'd already had enough of the queues and critical customers. Who'd won the war was the question. Nothing seemed different now there was peace.

* * *

All of this, Jinny might have expected to hear on her first day back, but what she had not expected was the news Mabel rushed to tell her, even before Mr Lennox had arrived.

'Mr Comrie's not in this morning,' she told Jinny, drawing her urgently into his office. 'He only manages the afternoons these days, poor man. He's not at all well. But he wouldn't be, would he? After the news he got not long ago.'

'What news?' asked Jinny, beginning to worry.

'Well, it was terrible. Someone in Vienna – a friend of the family – wrote that they'd been trying to trace him, you see. They knew Mrs Linden had a brother and they wanted to tell him—'

'What? Tell him what, Mabel?'

'Why, that she'd been killed in the bombing of Vienna, dear, and her husband too. Their bakery was completely destroyed. A direct hit, it seems.' Mabel's eyes were bright and intense. 'Viktor's parents, eh? But no one knows, the friend of the family said, where Viktor is. And you don't, do you, dear?'

'No, I don't know.' Jinny, her face white, turned away. 'I think I'd better get back to my desk, Mabel. Thank you for giving me that news.'

'Well, I knew you'd want to know. But you're looking awful pale, Jinny. Are you all right?'

'Fine. It's just – been a bit of a shock.'

Mr Lennox had just arrived when she returned to the accounts office, and held out his hand to her. 'Welcome back, Miss Hendrie! It's good to see you here.'

'Thank you. It feels a bit strange.' She sat down, putting her hand to her brow. 'I've just been hearing about Mr Comrie's sister and her husband in Vienna.'

'Oh, my word, yes, that was terrible news. He's been very badly hit by it. Not himself at all.'

'I'm not surprised.' Jinny tried to rally. 'Suppose I should try to get on with some work—'

'Don't worry about that this morning, Miss Hendrie. You look as though you're feeling shocked yourself. Why not go and have a cup of tea?'

'You're very kind, Mr Lennox. And you've been wonderful, taking over, the way you did.'

He smiled. 'Had to do my bit. But we'll be having Mr MacBain back soon, I expect. Then I'll be on my way. But you go and have your tea. Work can wait.'

* * *

Later, when she was at her desk again, she stared unseeingly at a pile of bills she was meant to pay, her thoughts dwelling on Viktor's parents and Viktor himself – whether he were alive or dead, and whether he would ever know what had happened to his parents.

And poor Mr Comrie, losing his sister and her husband, and possibly his nephew, too, the talented young man he had so much admired. She must try to see him when he came in and give him her sympathy. And in her lunch hour, she would write to Ross, whose support she had never needed more.

As soon as Mr Comrie arrived after lunch, Jinny leaped up from her desk and asked very politely if she could have a word.

'Of course, Jinny, of course! I was going to welcome you back, anyway. Come into my office.'

He had lost weight, his jacket hanging loosely on his once plump frame and his face gaunt, marked by new lines of strain, but he tried to smile as Mabel withdrew and Jinny accepted the chair he pushed forward.

'How was the ATS, then? You glad to be back?'

'It wasn't too bad at all, being away, but yes, I'm glad to be back.' Jinny hesitated. 'Mr Comrie, I hope I'm not speaking out of turn, but I'd just like to say how sorry I am about your sister and her husband. It's terrible news.'

'Yes.' He looked down at his blotter and played with a pen. 'It's been hard to take – the two of them, Clara and Bruno. I couldn't believe it at first.'

'I didn't even know Vienna was bombed so much.'

'Oh, yes, there were oil refineries, depots, that sort of thing. The city's been ruined, I've been told – bomb craters everywhere, buildings just shells. It'll take years to rebuild.'

'I'm so sorry.'

'I wanted to go over there but it's not possible. Travel is very difficult, and I'm not fit, Jinny. I'm not able.' Mr Comrie ran his hand over his brow, his breathing suddenly rasping, filled with effort. 'And then there's Viktor to think about. You don't know anything?'

'I haven't heard anything from him, Mr Comrie. I have no news at all.'

For some moments he sat very still, his breath becoming even more laboured, one hand at his chest, but then he began to fiddle with a desk drawer as drops of sweat gathered on his brow.

'Oh, God!' he whispered. 'My chest – the pain – Jinny, call . . . call Mabel. My tablets . . . I need them—'

For a second she sat, frozen, then leaped to her feet. 'Yes, Mr Comrie!' she cried, and ran like the wind to find Mabel, who rushed in with Mr Lennox at her heels. 'The tablets!' Jinny cried. 'Where are they?'

'In his drawer! Quickly, Jinny, some water!'

But Mr Lennox was already on his way, and as Mabel found the tablets and shook out two, he returned with a glass of water which he managed to make Mr Comrie drink as Mabel gave him the tablets.

'He's bad,' Mr Lennox whispered. 'Look at his colour! I'm going to ring for an ambulance. Wait here with him, Miss Hyslop.'

'He's collapsing!' she cried. 'He's losing consciousness!'

'Just stay with him – the ambulance won't take long; we should be in time—'

But it appeared that time had run out for Mr Comrie. By the time he reached hospital he had gone too far down his last path, and the following morning the staff at Comrie's were informed that he had died the previous evening, in spite of all efforts to save him.

# Seventy-Two

The unexpected death of its owner threw Comrie's into confusion. For who was now the owner? What would the will say? Now that Mr Comrie's sister and her husband were dead, there were no relatives to inherit the business, except for his nephew, Viktor, whose whereabouts were unknown, and who might even be dead, too. Was he even a beneficiary, anyway? If it turned out that he was and had to be found, would the business have to be closed for probate, and would everyone lose their jobs, even if only temporarily?

These were genuine worries that Ross, who had arrived back early, his demob having been unexpectedly brought forward, was able to put to the lawyers. They agreed to a meeting with the staff, at which they announced that Mr Viktor Linden was indeed the sole beneficiary of his uncle's will, and that the business would not go into probate but be allowed to function until the results of a search already underway for him were known. In the meantime

Ross, as the senior accountant, would be required to keep track of all finances, and wages would be paid.

'Thank God they let you home early,' Mr Whyte told Ross fervently. 'I don't know what we'd have done without you. I'm no good at talking to these legal fellows.'

And with everyone agreeing with Mr Whyte's words and thankful to know where they stood, Jinny, back with Ross in Accounts, sneaked a kiss and told him he was their saviour.

'What did I do? I only asked John Dixon to talk to the staff and he should have done that earlier, anyway.'

'Well, it's wonderful that it's sorted out, at least for the time being.'

'I suppose so, but I'm pretty upset to have lost Mr Comrie. And what's going to happen if Viktor turns up and begins changing everything, as he'd be entitled to do?'

'I don't think he's going to turn up, Ross.' Jinny's tone was quiet, yet definite. 'I believe he's dead. If he were alive he'd have found a way to get in touch with me when the war ended.'

'You think that?' Ross asked uneasily. 'Is that what you want?'

'No! Well, only to know what had happened to him. I would like to know that.'

And she was to know, rather sooner than she'd ever imagined.

Some days later, while Ross was dictating letters to Mabel in Mr Comrie's office, Jinny sat working alone at her desk. A wind was rattling round outside, there was the promise of sleet, or even snow, and the accounts office was by no means warm, but Jinny, absorbed in her calculations, scarcely noticed. Nor did she notice when the door behind her opened. Only when a voice said her name did she turn round, and then her heart gave a lurch and the blood left her face.

A spectre was standing in the doorway. Or so for a moment it seemed. But he was not a spectre, he was a man, one she hadn't seen for all the years of the war but instantly recognized.

'Viktor?' she whispered. 'Viktor?'

Wearing a long, black overcoat marked with sleet, he was still tall, still handsome even, his bristling short hair still fair, but the etched lines around his eyes and his mouth told their tale. He had known suffering.

Oh, God, what had happened to him? Jinny's heart was thudding as her gaze rested on him – so much the same yet so different, so marked by what he'd known and she could not imagine. Even his erect military carriage had left him, and if Ross had once called him *Der Leutnant*, he would not do so now.

'Yes, I'm Viktor.' He gave a faint smile. 'Clever of you to recognize me.'

'I – I thought you were dead,' she stammered. 'Where have you been?'

'To hell and back. Or, if you prefer, a Russian prisoner of war camp.'

'You . . . were in Russia?' Jinny, now trembling so hard she could scarcely speak, felt as though she were in some sort of dream, talking to someone she'd believed lost or dead, as one might in dreams. But this was no dream, this was real. This was Viktor . . . real . . .

'How – how come you're here?' she asked, holding her cold hands together. 'How did you leave Russia?'

'God knows. Suddenly, after the German surrender, they let us go, though how we weren't shot in the first place I have no idea. Not many prisoners were taken – on either side. Jinny, may I come in?'

'Oh, I'm sorry, please do! And let me take your coat – it's quite damp.'

She hurried to hang up his coat with her trembling hands, noting that the suit he was wearing was too big for him and of cheap material, and he smiled again as he caught her glance.

'A charity purchase after I'd burned my prison uniform, or what was left of it.'

She hesitated, still trying to accept that he was there, standing before her, amazed that she could speak at all. 'Viktor, I was so sorry to hear about your parents. It must have been terrible for you, to come back . . . to find . . .'

Instantly his face appeared to shut down and he looked away, and Jinny, now feeling almost faint, said he must see Ross, he was just next door.

'Ross? He's here? He was in the army?'

'Oh, yes, went right through the war. I was in the ATS myself – the women's army. But please sit down, Viktor, while I tell Ross you're here.'

As soon as he saw her face, Ross leaped towards her, his hands outstretched, while Mabel stared, her mouth slightly open and her eyes wide.

'Jinny, what is it?' cried Ross. 'What's happened?'

'He's back, Ross. He's in our office . . .'

'Who? Who's back?'

'Viktor.'

There was a brief, trembling silence. 'Oh, God,' said Ross.

After a moment they all went into Accounts, Jinny and Mabel following Ross, who had managed to recover his poise as he shook Viktor's hand.

'This is amazing, Viktor! To see you back here, when we thought – well, we didn't know what to think.'

'I've been in a Russian prisoner of war camp since 1942.' Viktor's voice faltered. 'I only just got back to Vienna a few weeks ago.'

'They let you out? That was lucky.'

'Luckier that they took me in the first place.'

'I'm sure that's right. We heard a lot about what happened in Russia. You . . . know about your uncle?'

'I do now. When I first came back, I didn't. Didn't even think of him, when I found—' Viktor stopped, couldn't speak.

Ross said gently, 'I can't even imagine how it was for you.'

'Yes, well, when I could, I thought of him and was planning to get in touch, of course. It was only when I saw the lawyers' notice that I discovered he was dead.'

'Notice?'

'They put a German notice in all the main papers, asking Viktor Linden to get in touch regarding his late uncle's estate and then gave their details.' Viktor put his hand to his head for a moment. 'I couldn't believe it at first, but then I knew I should come over. I borrowed the money for the air fare and managed to get a flight. I saw Mr Dixon this morning and he told me about my uncle.'

'And the will?'

Viktor's face was impassive. 'And the will.'

'Let us welcome you as the new owner, then.'

'Oh, yes,' said Jinny, as Mabel nodded with enthusiasm. 'We wish you all the best, Viktor.'

He turned his shadowed, reddened eyes upon her. 'There are some things I'd like to discuss with you, Jinny. Would it be convenient for you to come for lunch with me – at Logie's, say?'

She glanced immediately at Ross, whose anxious eyes had instantly found hers. 'I expect that'd be all right, wouldn't it, Ross?'

'Perfectly all right,' he said hoarsely.

'We'll get our coats, then.'

* * *

Trying not to show how strange she found it to be with Viktor again, how fiercely gripped she felt by memories of the past, Jinny walked beside him from the shop, not looking at Mrs Arrow or her assistants, just keeping on through the falling sleet to Logie's.

'A table for two, please,' Viktor said to a waitress, and when she had escorted them to window seats and taken their coats, they looked at each other but did not smile.

'Like old times?' asked Viktor. 'Or perhaps not?'

Jinny did not reply.

# Seventy-Three

They ordered the vegetarian cottage pie, as the waitress said it was better than the beef version, with just coffee to follow.

'I shan't eat much of whatever we have,' Viktor remarked. 'I eat only very little.'

'Why is that? We eat anything we can get.'

He shrugged. 'After years of cabbage soup they say it will take time to get back to ordinary food.'

'Oh, Viktor, how awful! You're so very thin.'

'Never mind about me.' His eyes were steady on her face. 'I wanted to speak to you to tell you I am sorry that, once the war came, I was never able to write to you. I knew you would be hurt, wondering where I was, but there was no way of letting you know.'

'I did realize that.'

'That's good, then. But once the years began to stretch out, I never expected you to wait for me, you know. That would have been unreasonable.'

She flushed a little. 'I did wait – I mean, for a long time—'

'Quite. But then you forgot me.'

'Viktor—'

'It's all right, I understand. I became unreal. It happens.'

'Wasn't it the same for you with me?'

'Perhaps. Where I was, everything outside became unreal.'

The waitress came with their order, and while Jinny began to eat, Viktor took a mouthful, then played with his fork. 'That's the way it was, you see,' he went on. 'Only my life in the army seemed real to me. And it was the same in the camp. Life centred on what happened there – there was nothing beyond.'

'Try to eat something,' she urged, but he shook his head.

'Even my parents went from my mind,' he said in a low voice. 'They only returned to me when I got home. But by then, they were dead.' His fingers clenched around his fork. 'Both dead. Like Vienna. It's in ruins, Jinny. A dead city. All is gone.'

She put down her knife and fork, her eyes filling with tears for him. 'I'm so sorry, Viktor, so sorry. If only there was something I could do—'

'For me?' His mouth twisted. 'There's nothing anyone can do for me. I must accept what's happened to my parents and think of Vienna, the people of Vienna.'

He shook his head, suddenly touching Jinny's hand. 'But I didn't ask you to see me to talk of my troubles.'

'Viktor, it's all right, you can talk to me. I want to hear—'

'No, there are other things I want to say.' His gaze on her was deeply intense. 'The first is that I'm happy for you, now I've seen you with Ross.' He lifted his hand as she tried to speak. 'No, he's right for you, and it's plain from just seeing you together that you love each other.'

She was silent, wanting to say it was true, but not finding the words.

'The second thing,' he went on, 'is that I'm not going to keep the bakery or my uncle's house. I'm going to sell them both and return to Vienna.'

'Vienna.'

'Yes. I'm going to help in the rebuilding of the city, but first it will be necessary to help those who are struggling now as though they are refugees. No homes, no money, no jobs. All they had, taken. That charity I mentioned to you does excellent work for all who need it and I'm going to work for them. It has been arranged.'

'That's wonderful, Viktor, but what about your career? Your cake-making?'

'My cake-making.' His smile was bitter. 'I can't imagine anything less needed than *Sachertorte* at the moment. I have found other things to do, now that my life has been spared.'

She could say no more.

When they'd had coffee, she asked diffidently if she might pay for the lunch, Viktor having no money, but he was dismissive.

'That will not be necessary. I've been given something in advance from the estate by the kind Mr Dixon. And to give you lunch again, just this once, has given me great pleasure.'

'Thank you, then. I appreciate it.'

When they had put on their coats and left the restaurant for the ground floor, Viktor put his hand on Jinny's arm. 'Before we go back, Jinny, may I tell you something?'

His eyes were suddenly as blue as she remembered them and, for a moment, gazing up at him, she saw beyond the gaunt façade of the returned soldier to the man she had once loved. It was true, that love was over and she had a new love that would always be hers, but she would not forget Viktor, just as, it seemed, he would not forget her. For, in those last moments they had together, he put a promise into words.

'I want you to know, Jinny, that I will always remember you, my Scottish love. The war drove us apart and now you have a new future with someone else, but I'll remember what we had – and maybe you will, too, I hope, with some affection?'

'I will,' she said quietly. 'I still have my Edelweiss brooch, but I won't need it to remember you.'

He was silent, studying her face, then bent and kissed her cheek. 'Good luck, Jinny, and also to Ross.'

'And to you, Viktor. You'll let us know how things go for you?'

He smiled. 'Perhaps.'

When they returned to Accounts, it was to find Ross waiting with every appearance of anxiety, but as soon as Jinny went to him and pressed his hand, he relaxed and smiled.

'Had a good lunch? Logie's seem to do better than most places for food.'

'Never mind the lunch, Ross, Viktor has some news,' Jinny said quickly. 'He's going to sell Comrie's and his uncle's house and go back to Vienna.'

Ross for a moment said nothing, his gaze resting on Viktor. 'Sell Comrie's?' he repeated. 'Is that definite?'

'Quite decided, Ross. I have other plans than running a bakery. I have been telling Jinny I want to do something for the people of my city. They've been affected badly by the war and now that I'm all right – or will be, soon – my plan is to help them rebuild their lives.' Viktor sighed. 'Then perhaps we can rebuild Vienna.'

'I see. That sounds admirable.' Ross appeared thoughtful. 'I don't suppose you've any idea yet of an asking price? I mean, for the bakery, not your uncle's house.'

'Nothing is arranged yet. I have to see Mr Dixon again soon to discuss the matter.'

'You will, of course, be hoping for a good offer. Money is always useful.'

'I am not looking for too much,' Viktor answered cautiously. 'I shall need money for what I want to do; otherwise, I don't any longer consider it important.'

Ross folded his arms and fixed Viktor with a long, serious gaze. 'May I ask you, then, if you would consider me as a purchaser?'

'Ross!' cried Jinny, her dark eyes enormous, 'what are you saying? You can't afford to buy Comrie's!'

'Perhaps not by myself, but I know that Arthur Whyte would be interested in joining with me. He has money that came to him recently and we sort of discussed a purchase before we knew that you'd inherited, Viktor. As I have what my father left me, depending on the price, I think we might just manage it.'

'I can't believe it!' Jinny cried. 'It seems impossible.'

'Not at all,' Viktor declared. 'I think Ross's suggestion is just what my uncle would have wanted. He'd believe that Ross and Arthur would be the right people to run Comrie's, as I do also.'

'You mean that?' asked Ross.

'I do. In fact, it would relieve my mind if I thought someone like you would take on my uncle's business, Ross. It meant so much to him.'

'It would mean a lot to me, too, and to Arthur Whyte.'

'Shall we see Mr Dixon, then, and see what can be arranged?'

'If you're sure.'

'I am sure,' Viktor said steadily.

And the two shook hands.

'I'm in another dream,' Jinny whispered when Viktor had taken his leave, promising to meet Ross at Mr Dixon's the next day. 'I never knew you had any money, Ross!'

'You'd have found out one day, wouldn't you? When I stood up at the altar and said something about 'with all my worldly goods I thee endow'?

She stared at him, a light taking over her face as her lips parted and her eyes shone. 'This isn't a proposal, is it?'

'What else?' He drew her to him. 'We've never spelled it out, what we'd do, but we always knew, didn't we? Now I think I should buy the ring before all my money goes on Comrie's. Shall we go shopping on Saturday?'

When Mabel came in and found them kissing, she blushed deeply. 'Oh, dear, I'm sorry, I'm sure . . . just had your letters to sign, Ross. Has Viktor gone, then?'

'Yes, but I'll be seeing him tomorrow,' Ross told her. 'We have something to discuss.'

'Do you think it will really happen?' Jinny whispered.

'I've every hope that it will.'

And so it proved. Ross and Arthur Whyte's offer was accepted by Viktor to much celebration at Comrie's, while Viktor returned home to regain his health and to work, as he'd promised, for those in need in Vienna.

'Take care,' he'd told Jinny and Ross on his last morning. 'Be happy. Keep in touch.'

'We will,' said Ross, 'but mind you do the same.'

When the final embraces had been made and the taxi bearing Viktor had driven away, Ross turned to Jinny and stood with her in silence for a little while. Then they moved into each other's arms, content.

# Seventy-Four

It was some weeks later that the Hendries gathered, together with Ross, Allan and three godparents, for the christening of baby Victoria at the local kirk, and afterwards for tea at a small café, which had even managed to provide an iced cake. The meal was over, the cake sliced and served, and now Josh was on his feet, ready to say a few words and call for a toast.

'First, I want to say a few words about myself,' he began as Victoria slept peacefully in her carrycot. 'There was a time when I was all for my girls staying at home with me. I couldn't imagine a time without them, but after what we've all been through, I managed to learn a valuable lesson. What's important is that whatever happens we come through the bad times, we still love each other, and if there are new people in the family it just expands, that's all, and there's still room for everybody.

'So, I want to give my blessing to Jinny and Ross, who are going to be married, as I've already given it to May and Allan, who's doing so well with his shop again, and to Vi and her Barry, who is no longer with us. She'll forgive me for saying that I've been worrying about her, but she says she has plans to make people's lives better and will be happy in her own way. Maybe she'll try for the council, and – who knows – parliament. Isn't that right, Vi?'

'That's right,' Vi agreed and managed a smile as people tapped their approval. 'But get on with the toasts, Dad, eh?'

'Aye, I've talked long enough. I'm proud of you, my family and friends, and the new little lassie as well – may she grow up in a better world. Shall we drink to that?'

They drank to that and then to Barry, to all those who had gone before, and finally to the future.

'May there be peace in the world,' said May, speaking distinctly as she turned to look at Allan, who smiled and bent to pick up Victoria, as Jinny and Ross led the kisses and hugs and joined with everyone's hope: that one day May's wish might be realized.